Dread
on Arrival

Claudia Bishop

BERKLEY PRIME CRIME, NEW YORK

THE BERKLEY PUBLISHING GROUP
Published by the Penguin Group
Penguin Group (USA) Inc.
375 Hudson Street, New York, New York 10014, USA
Penguin Group (Canada), 90 Eglinton Avenue East, Suite 700, Toronto, Ontario M4P 2Y3, Canada
(a division of Pearson Penguin Canada Inc.) • Penguin Books Ltd., 80 Strand, London WC2R 0RL,
England • Penguin Group Ireland, 25 St. Stephen's Green, Dublin 2, Ireland (a division of Penguin
Books Ltd.) • Penguin Group (Australia), 250 Camberwell Road, Camberwell, Victoria 3124, Australia
(a division of Pearson Australia Group Pty. Ltd.) • Penguin Books India Pvt. Ltd., 11 Community
Centre, Panchsheel Park, New Delhi—110 017, India • Penguin Group (NZ), 67 Apollo Drive,
Rosedale, Auckland 0632, New Zealand (a division of Pearson New Zealand Ltd.) • Penguin Books
(South Africa) (Pty.) Ltd., 24 Sturdee Avenue, Rosebank, Johannesburg 2196, South Africa

Penguin Books Ltd., Registered Offices: 80 Strand, London WC2R 0RL, England

This is a work of fiction. Names, characters, places, and incidents either are the product of the author's
imagination or are used fictitiously, and any resemblance to actual persons, living or dead, business
establishments, events, or locales is entirely coincidental. The publisher does not have any control over
and does not assume any responsibility for author or third-party websites or their content.

PUBLISHER'S NOTE: The recipes contained in this book are to be followed exactly
as written. The publisher is not responsible for your specific health or allergy needs that may
require medical supervision. The publisher is not responsible for any adverse reactions
to the recipes contained in this book.

DREAD ON ARRIVAL

A Berkley Prime Crime Book / published by arrangement with the author

PUBLISHING HISTORY
Berkley Prime Crime mass-market edition / April 2012

Copyright © 2012 by Mary Stanton.
Excerpt of *A Taste for Murder* by Claudia Bishop copyright © 1994 by Mary Stanton.
Cover illustration by Karen Strelecki.
Cover design by Diana Kolsky.
Interior text design by Laura K. Corless.

ISBN: 978-0-425-24707-5

BERKLEY® PRIME CRIME
Berkley Prime Crime Books are published by The Berkley Publishing Group,
a division of Penguin Group (USA) Inc.,
375 Hudson Street, New York, New York 10014.
BERKLEY® PRIME CRIME and the PRIME CRIME logo are trademarks of
Penguin Group (USA) Inc.

PRINTED IN THE UNITED STATES OF AMERICA

10 9 8 7 6 5 4 3 2 1

ALWAYS LEARNING   **PEARSON**

For Nate

Cast of Characters

The Inn at Hemlock Falls

Sarah "Quill" Quilliam-McHale . . . . *owner, manager*

Margaret "Meg" Quilliam . . . .
. . . . *master chef, owner, Quill's sister*

Jackson McHale . . . . *Quill's three-year-old son*

Doreen Muxworthy . . . . *housekeeper, Jack's nanny*

Dina Muir . . . . *grad student, receptionist*

Kathleen Kiddermeister . . . . *head waitress*

Bjarne Bjarnsen . . . . *head chef*

Elizabeth Chou . . . . *sous chef*

Mike . . . . *groundskeeper*

Phillip "Skipper" Bryant . . . . *guest, antiques collector*

Andrea Bryant . . . . *guest, Skipper's wife*

Jukka Angstrom . . . . *guest, antiques collector*

Edmund Tree . . . .
. . . . *a guest, producer and host of* Your Ancestor's Attic

Cast of Characters

Melanie Myers . . . .
. . . . *guest, Edmund's assistant producer and director*

Marco . . . . *bodyguard*

Bruce . . . . *bodyguard*

Joseph "Belter" Barcini . . . .
. . . . *guest, producer and host of* Pawn-o-Rama

Josepha "Mamma" Barcini . . . .
. . . . *guest, producer, Belter's mother*

Josephine Barcini . . . . *guest, producer, Belter's sister*

Max . . . . *a dog*

And others

Citizens of Hemlock Falls

Rose Ellen Whitman . . . . *owner of Elegant Antiques*

Marge Peterson-Schmidt . . . .
. . *businesswoman, the wealthiest citizen in Tompkins County*

Harland Peterson . . . . *dairy farmer, Marge's husband*

Elmer Henry . . . . *mayor of Hemlock Falls*

Adela Henry . . . . *Elmer's wife*

Davy Kiddermeister . . . . *sheriff of Hemlock Falls*

Howie Murchison . . . . *town justice, practicing lawyer*

Miriam Doncaster . . . . *town librarian*

And others

Cast of Characters

STAFF OF LA BONNE GOUTÈ CULINARY ACADEMY

Madame LeVasque . . . . *owner, CFO*

Clarissa Sparrow . . . *newly named director, expert in pastry*

Raleigh Brewster . . . . *chef, soups and stews*

Jim Chen . . . . *chef, fish and seafood*

Pietro Giancava . . . . *chef, sauces and sommelier*

Bernard LeVasque (deceased, but very much a presence)

Bismarck . . . . *a cat*

Prologue

Edmund Tree stood in front of the painting displayed on the shoulder-high easel and smiled toothily at Ida Mae Clarkson. He was tall and thin. His scanty blond hair fringed his pink scalp like a hairy doily. He was dressed in an elegant three-piece suit; navy blue, with pale pinstripes. Ida Mae Clarkson thought he looked a lot smaller in person than he appeared on TV.

"And what have you got for us here at *Your Ancestor's Attic* today, Mrs. Clarkson?"

The grip on the number three camera panned from Edmund to the painting. Ida Mae knew the guy was called a grip. She'd gotten familiar with the TV talk right off the bat. It didn't do to let these highfalutin types think they could push a person around.

The painting was in oil, about twenty inches across and at least seventy-two inches high. It was very old and a bit flaky around the edges. At least as old as Ida Mae's great-aunt Cecilia, who had bequeathed the thing to the Clarksons, instead of any of her money, which had annoyed Ida Mae to no end and still did. A three-tiered marble fountain sat in the middle of the canvas. Three sparrows perched on the grass at the fountain's base. A platter of lemons, oranges, and grapes sat to the left of the fountain. Ida Mae, who had dressed with care for this, her first TV appearance, nervously re-buttoned the jacket of her best black pantsuit. She hoped like heck her stomach wasn't sticking out. That British accent of Mr. Tree's was a lot easier to understand when she and the coffee club sat and watched the show at home in Delray Beach. Here under the bright lights he seemed to talk too darn fast. She was confused and a little uncertain and not generally used to being either.

"Those grapes look so realistic that one could almost find one's self plucking the fruit and eating it, doesn't one, Mrs. Clarkson?"

Well, that was pretty stupid. That painting had been in her guest room for twenty-two years and nobody had tried to eat it yet. "Be a darn fool if you did," Ida Mae said brusquely. "All's you get would be a mouthful of paint." She smiled nervously and wondered if her deodorant was working the way it should. "And call me Ida Mae, Mr. Tree. Most folks do."

Ida Mae was short and round. In addition to her best black pantsuit, she wore a new pair of black strappy sandals with silk roses pinned to the ankle straps and a bright pink cotton blouse. She wiggled her fingers at the camera, so that the family at home in Delray Beach would know she was thinking of them despite the glamour of her being on the TV show like she was.

"That perfect illusion is precisely the point," Edmund said with a show of well-bred, if snooty, excitement. "This painting is of an extremely special type that goes back all the way to the ancient Greeks."

That sounded pretty good. Better yet, it sounded pretty

valuable. Ida Mae sent a brief, silent prayer skyward and said hopefully, "It came down to us from my great-aunt Cecilia. On my husband's side, she was. Auntie had the best taste of all the Clarksons, which isn't saying much, now that I think on it, especially if you—"

"The style is called trompe l'oeil," Edmund Tree interrupted smoothly. "There are many valuable trompe l'oeil works in the great cathedrals of the world. I refer of course to Antonio da Correggio's *Assumption of the Virgin* in the Duomo of Parma, to Pietro da Cortona's *Allegory of Divine Providence* in the Palazzo Barberini, and of course to the works of that great, whimsical Carpaccio himself."

Ida Mae shifted her black faux-leather purse from her left arm to her right. The word "Carpaccio" was the only halfway familiar word in this flood of foreign nonsense. She and the coffee club girls ate out at least twice a week. "Tuna?" she said. "You've lost me there, sonny. What's tuna got to do with this trump loy stuff?"

"Trompe l'oeil," Edmund said, with an air of disdain Ida Mae was quick to spot. "A rough translation would be 'fool the eye.'"

"Didn't fool me any," Ida Mae said. "Those aren't real grapes. You're saying it fooled you? And you on TV and all? Who's going to pay me a bunch of money to get fooled?"

"Oh, many, many patrons of the arts are ardent supporters of trompe l'oeil. The phrase refers to a special way of painting images. The artist renders them as real as possible. This creates an optical illusion. The illusion that the subject matter is in three dimensions. You feel as if you can pick the object up, but you can't, of course. Hence the meaning: fool the eye."

"So what's it worth?" TV audience or no TV audience,

Ida Mae had always favored the blunt approach. It saved time and blather.

"This painting is interesting because it also presents an architectural illusion. The viewer feels as if the space beyond the fountain has opened up. It is in the *quadratura* style. A work in the *quadratura* style, such as your great-aunt's painting here, would be worth many, many thousands of dollars."

Ida Mae heaved a sigh of content. That fifty-inch HD Frank wanted for the den was getting closer by the minute. "How many thousands of dollars?"

Edward kept on talking. "A painting such as this would be placed in the *giardino*—the garden—with the expectation that guests would be amused at the verismo . . ."

"Ver-what?" Ida Mae scowled.

"The truth. The reality. Or I should say, the seeming reality of a painting of grapes so realistic that the hand stretches out to grasp the succulent globe without conscious thought."

Ida Mae blinked at him. "What I want to know is how much the darn thing is worth."

Edward laughed tolerantly. "Of course you do. That's what our enormously popular show is all about. Humble folk like you, Mrs. Clarkson, digging into the treasures in their ancestor's attic, and bringing their cherished antiques in for professional evaluation."

Her lower lip jutted out at a bewildered angle. With a certain degree of sensitivity to her feelings, the grip refocused camera three on the grapes, then, in response to an impatient gesture from the host, back on Tree himself.

Edmund purred, "Now, a painting like this, Mrs. Clarkson, dating from the 1650s, painted by a major artist, would fetch anywhere from one hundred to two hundred thousand dollars at auction."

Ida Mae's eyes bulged. Her cheeks turned pink. "Glory!" she breathed. "Glory, glory, glory."

"But!" Edmund thrust his right forefinger into the air. "I am afraid you are doomed to disappointment, Mrs. Clarkson."

"Two hundred thousand dollars!" Ida Mae shrieked. "Oh my goodness. Oh my goodness." She fanned herself with both hands.

"This painting fooled everyone's eye but mine, I'm afraid." Edmund's smile was smug. "This painting is a poor imitation of its noble progenitors."

"It's a what?"

"It's a fake, Mrs. Clarkson, with an approximate value, I should say . . ." Edmund stroked his chin and swept his gaze over the piece from top to bottom. ". . . of perhaps forty dollars."

Ida Mae's jaw dropped. "Forty dollars?"

"I'm afraid so, madam."

"Forty dollars?"

"Perhaps less," Edmund admitted. "Trompe l'oeil is coming back in fashion, so if you wait a year so it might be worth as much as . . . eighty dollars." He snickered. "Your great-aunt Cecilia certainly didn't know how to pick them."

Ida Mae set her jaw. "They don't treat folks like this on the *Antiques Roadshow*, I can tell you that."

"I'm sorry to disappoint you, Mrs. Clarkson," Edmund said with an intolerably smug quirk of his eyebrow at the number three camera. "Let's move on. And now, viewers, as our show here in South Florida draws to a close, I would like to remind you all that *Your Ancestor's Attic* will soon visit the bucolic paradise of Hemlock Falls in upstate New York." The camera zoomed in on Edmund's face. "I am, as you all may know, about to be married to the love of my life, and I have chosen the beauties of this singular Eden as the perfect venue. We will also be offering the good citizens of that picturesque village an opportunity to discover just what treasures lie . . . in their ancestor's attic!"

The tech at the TV monitor gestured for the theme music to come up.

"What the hell do you mean, insulting my great-aunt?" Ida Mae demanded off camera.

Edmund held his gaze steady and looked directly into the lens. "Hemlock Falls, home to some of the most stunning waterfalls and natural gorges in the world, is located in the heart of the Finger Lakes wine region . . . ooof!" Abruptly, he bent over, as if somebody had whacked him in the stomach, which indeed Ida Mae had.

Ida Mae's outthrust chin and determined lower lip mashed up against the lens of camera number three. "All you viewers out there?" Ida Mae scowled. "You turn this third-rate show off and go straight to PBS. Let's hear it for the real deal instead of this cruddy guy: the *Antiques Roadshow*!"

"Cut," Edmund wheezed.

The camera panned back, to reveal Ida Mae with her purse dangling from her right hand.

"Dammit! I said *cut*!" Edmund lunged at the grip running camera three. Ida Mae swung her purse wide, clipped Edmund over the head, and thrust her pink-cheeked face close to the lens. "Phony!"

~

Belter Barcini hit the off button on the remote, just as *Your Ancestor's Attic* cut to black. He reconsidered and clicked the TV back on. It wasn't every day he got the chance to see that skinny nose-wipe Eddie Tree get his butt kicked by a little old lady, but nope, a dog-food commercial danced across the screen and if good old Fast Eddie was getting his clock cleaned, the TV audience wasn't about to see it.

Belter hit the off button again and scratched meditatively under one armpit. His office was in the rear of his pawn shop, and it was littered with a couple of days' take that he hadn't gotten around to cataloguing yet. He swept one meaty arm across his desk, dislodging a Colt .45 which had (probably) been Buffalo Bill Cody's favorite shooter. He kicked aside a samurai sword that had (almost definitely) been owned by the late Japanese emperor Hirohito. He mounded his hands over his substantial belly and thought hard.

The clip of Ida Mae's assault with a non-deadly weapon was going to be all over the Internet faster than Belter could down a Molson Golden, which was pretty damn quick. Which would bump *Ancestor's* ratings. Which—if you counted the highest-ranking used goods reality shows, *Antiques Roadshow* and *Pawn Stars*—would make Barcini's own *Pawn-o-Rama* number four in a four-horse race.

Barcini scratched the other armpit. He hated the odds. He hated being last. Most of all, he hated Ed Fancypants Tree, or whatever the hell his mamma named him. He'd like to knock that man's block off his skinny little neck.

It might just be the time to take a little trip to Hemlock Falls, New York.

1

~Clarissa Sparrow's~
Tartes Sucre

1 lb all-purpose flour
8 ounces chilled unsalted butter
3 ounces chilled white vegetable shortening
1 large egg plus iced water to make a total of 2 cups
2 teaspoons salt
¼ teaspoons sugar

Using a large fork, combine flour, butter, and shortening into an oatmeal consistency. Add salt, sugar, and liquid. Work lightly with hands into a ball. Roll out. Cut into a circle sufficient to cover a nine-inch tart pan. Sprinkle with one-half cup coarse unprocessed sugar. Bake in a preheated 425-degree oven until evenly browned.

"Of course, both Edmund and I have been married before, Quill," Rose Ellen Whitman said in her soft, whispery voice, "so we don't want a really *white* sort of wedding, if you understand me."

"I think so," Sarah Quilliam said.

Somebody must have told Rose Ellen Whitman she looked like Audrey Hepburn. Quill thought she did, sort of. She had very dark hair, drawn into a simple bun. Her eyes were dark, doe-like and long-lashed. The illusion was enhanced by Rose Ellen's preference for elegant sheath dresses, high heels, and a string of very good pearls. Rose Ellen's boutique Elegant Antiques was the newest addition to the Hemlock Falls shops on Main Street. The prices had astonished the village. The fact that her first shipment flew out of the store purchased by hordes of eager tourists had astonished the village even more.

Quill, her sister Meg, and Clarissa Sparrow, the newly appointed director of the Bonne Goutè Culinary Academy were in a meeting to help Rose Ellen with her wedding to Edmund Tree. The wedding would be held two days after Edmund taped an episode of *Your Ancestor's Attic,* which was going to be produced in the Hemlock Falls High School auditorium, for the first time ever.

The wedding itself was to be at Quill and Meg's twenty-seven-room hotel, the Inn at Hemlock Falls. The Inn didn't have enough room to handle the reception for the Tree-Whitman wedding, so the partry had to be held elsewhere. The beautiful old stone Inn sat across the Hemlock Gorge from Clarissa's Bonne Goutè Culinary Academy. Rose Ellen had hired Clarissa Sparrow, and the academy's vast dining room, to cater a reception for three hundred guests.

The four women sat at a round table made of aged oak, in the lavishly appointed wine cellar that housed the academy's collection of New York State wines. After the death of her husband, in that same wine cellar some weeks before, Madame LeVasque had decided the best way to keep the ghoulishly curious hordes out of the wine cellar and back in the gift shop spending money was to assign another function to the space. So it became the conference room.

Quill, who was sensitive to atmosphere, had been a little unnerved throughout the planning of the wedding, and not just because the wine cellar had briefly housed a corpse. Meg was her much-loved sister. Clarissa was her best friend. And no matter how you looked at it, two young, ambitious gourmet chefs in the same small town were bound to be competitive.

So far, the discussion between her volatile sister and Clarissa had been edgy, yet polite, but Quill wasn't about to relax just yet. Rose Ellen was a natural born nitpicker and the meeting was running on way too long. The monthly meeting of the Hemlock Falls Chamber of Commerce would start in less than an hour. She'd been Chamber secretary for more years than she wanted to count, and she hadn't been on time to a Chamber meeting yet. It wasn't a record she was particularly proud of.

"Nothing truly formal, but elegant, if you see what I mean," Rose Ellen continued, "which is why I've arranged for the wedding itself to be at Quill and Meg's Inn, Clarissa."

Clare's nostrils flared, but she didn't rise to the inference that the Bonne Goutè Culinary Academy was short on elegance.

"The Inn's kitchen is far too underequipped, of course, which is why I'm having the reception here."

Meg scowled. Quill dropped her pencil on the floor so she would have an excuse to duck under the table and take a look at Meg's socks. The socks were a fair indicator of her sister's temper. Today's pair was black, with a four-color Mickey Mouse pattern, which might be a reflection of Meg's opinion of Rose Ellen Whitman. But maybe not.

"I think you've made very smart decisions," Clarissa said, with a set smile. She hadn't been Bonne Goutè's director very long—only a few weeks—but the job clearly suited her. Clare wasn't a pretty woman, but her high cheekbones and aquiline nose made her striking. She had a natural, easy air of command and even Meg agreed that Clare was the best pastry chef in the Northeast, if not the whole country.

"Not hiring us for the reception was the only sensible decision you could have made," Meg pointed out. "As much as I'd like to, there's no way the Inn's kitchen could do a sit-down dinner for three hundred." She rather spoiled the graciousness of her comment by adding, "We keep the kitchen small in order to be as selective as possible. Just so you know."

Quill glanced at her sister but didn't say anything. Clare flushed, but kept a smile on her face. The Inn at Hemlock Falls and the Bonne Goutè Culinary Academy had been rivals in the not so distant past, and its late (unlamented) director Bernard LeVasque had been a master at fomenting ill will, bad feelings, and downright hostility. When Madame LeVasque appointed Clarissa director in place of her late husband Bernard, Quill had crossed both fingers for luck. Clare was a good friend. Meg was a good sister. Both women were fiercely proud chefs. Both were trained in the classical French tradition. Neither one of them could take refuge in being resident experts on exotica like Asian fusion or Guatemalan charcuterie. The potential for tantrums was awesome.

"Besides," Meg added airily, "we'll be pretty busy with the media crowd from New York."

"What media crowd?" Clare asked suspiciously.

"I warned Meg that the juxtaposition of the *Attic* episode so close to the wedding is bound to attract attention," Rose Ellen said. "As you all know, any kind of publicity is abhorrent to me, but one must be prepared."

"One must," Meg agreed solemnly.

Clare put her hand to her mouth and coughed. Quill realized both chefs were suppressing giggles, which made her grateful to Rose Ellen for providing a bonding moment. "Well," she said rather vaguely, "it's all very exciting, I think. There's such a lot to get through. Perhaps we should move on."

"Let's take a second to recap," Clarissa said. "I want to make sure my menus don't conflict with the items Meg plans to serve at the rehearsal dinner and the engagement party." She smiled, suddenly, a genuine smile this time. "Can you just hear the sneers if I tried to palm off our pâtés on guests who'd already tasted Meg's?"

"It's why I'm staying away from pastry," Meg admitted. "Just in case Clare decides to do *tartes sucre*. As a matter of fact, Rose Ellen, you should insist that Clare give you her *tartes sucre*. She's internationally known for her pastry. And your *petit choux* pastry, Clare, is to die for."

Clarissa's thin cheeks turned attractively pink. "Meg's even better known for her pâté."

"It all sounds lovely," Rose Ellen said, her voice just this side of boredom.

When the conversation turned to food, Quill knew to leave it to the experts. She sat back as the discussion flowed around her. She looked at her small, dark-haired sister with affection. Clare, who was almost as tall as Quill, was dark-haired, too, but she wasn't nearly as decided and determined a character as Meg. Rose Ellen Whitman, who was not only the most beautiful woman in the room, but probably the most beautiful woman between Hemlock Falls and New York City, didn't draw the eye the way Clare and her sister did. The three women made an interesting study.

Quill flipped to a fresh page in the sketch pad she used to take meeting notes and reached for the charcoal pencils she always kept in her skirt pocket.

"Are you sketching us?" Rose Ellen asked. "Now that would be a fine wedding present. A genuine Quilliam."

Quill blushed. She always did, when somebody mentioned her work as an artist. She'd had a brief, nerve-wrackingly successful career in the arts community before she and Meg had purchased the Inn twelve years ago.

Rose Ellen smiled faintly and got to her feet. "Let's leave these two and take a walk."

"You don't want menu approval?"

Rose Ellen shrugged. She was slim and tall, taller than Quill, who was five foot eight in her bare feet—but she also wore the highest heels Quill had ever seen. Her calves twinged just looking at Rose Ellen's shoes. "I'll fax the menu to Edmund tonight. He'll have opinions of his own. He always does. It doesn't matter all that much to me." She made a face and glanced over her shoulder at the two chefs, who were huddled over the menus. "Not what those two want to hear, certainly. The look of the wedding is very important, of course. What with Edmund's position in the world of antiques, and my own high profile, it's essential that it look just right. That it conveys the right message to the people who matter. So I wanted a word with you about the décor."

Quill glanced at her watch. "Actually, I have a Chamber of Commerce meeting in about twenty minutes. So I won't be able to stay with you too long."

Rose Ellen drew her beautifully plucked eyebrows together. "The Chamber of Commerce? Isn't that the village organization run by that funny little man? The one with the dreadful wife?"

"Mayor Henry," Quill said. "And his wife, Adela." Quill's first rule as an innkeeper was "don't belt the guests." Sometimes it was a hard rule to keep. "We're very fond of them in Hemlock Falls."

"Well, the funny little man can wait, for the moment. I do want your opinion on my color scheme for the ceremony. I've made some sketches of my own I'd like you to see." She held an oxblood Hermès portfolio in one hand and raised it slightly.

"A few minutes, then." Quill led the way out of the wine cellar and into the academy's large atrium.

Bernard LeVasque hadn't spared a penny of borrowed money to build the academy. The atrium was the center of the vast building. The floors were wide-planked cedar. The tasting room, directly across from the wine cellar, had ceilings that soared to twenty feet and the antique wine racks that covered the walls had come from LeVasque's own vineyards in France. And the kitchens . . . Quill paused, thinking of the kitchens. Clare and her staff could handle eighty students at a time. There were twenty dual-fuel Viking ranges, arranged in blocks of four each. Each four-range station was equipped with a prep sink and all the bowls, graters, knives, spatulas, spoons, pots, and pans any cook could dream of. The academy's splendor certainly overwhelmed the two-hundred-year-old Inn at Hemlock Falls. But, Quill reflected, Meg had had her chance to run the academy and had turned it down to remain the master chef at the Inn's small kitchen. Old, well-loved things were definitely the best.

"I certainly agree with that," Rose Ellen said.

Quill's eyebrows rose.

"About old things definitely being the best. I've made a lot of money out of old things." She tapped her foot. "Are we headed somewhere? Or are you just going to stand there looking at nothing in particular?"

"I didn't realize I'd spoken aloud." Quill rubbed her cheeks briskly. "Sorry. My little boy Jackson just turned three and both his grandmother and his father are away from home right now. Well, actually, Doreen isn't really his grandmother and she got back from visiting her sister in Omaha this morning, because my husband Myles and I had been away for a month, and Jack is just delighted . . ." She stopped. She was babbling. "Anyhow. Between managing the Inn and him, I'm a little short on sleep." She gave herself a mental shake. The *Attic* taping was in a week's time, the wedding was in ten days, and everybody in both parties was staying at the Inn. She had a lot to do.

The first, and most important, was to get this annoying woman out of her hair. She said, too heartily, "And of course you'd know that old, well-loved things are to be treasured. How is the antiques business these days? You've settled into the village so well, Rose Ellen. I hope you're happy with the new shop." She touched Rose Ellen's shoulder to guide her toward Clare's office.

"I really prefer not to call it a shop." Rose Ellen's tone was brusque. "It's a high-end boutique catering to the select customer and it's going beautifully." She shrugged off Quill's hand. "Where are we going?"

"Just in here. This is Clarissa's office." Quill opened the door and stepped aside. Bernard hadn't spared a penny in here, either. Area rugs the color of café au lait covered the cherrywood floors. Tall filing cabinets out of the same wood flanked a counter with a bronze bowl sink, an undercounter refrigerator, and a slate countertop. A long cherrywood conference table sat in front of tall windows overlooking shaved green lawns.

Rose Ellen looked around and slung her portfolio onto the conference table without regard for the finish. "It's too corporate," she said. "Not an ounce of charm. Very nouveau riche. Clarissa could use some advice about her taste, I think, but I'll have to put that off until after the wedding. Now, Quill. I've a photograph of my dress, and drawings of the flowers to be shipped in, but I'd really appreciate it if we could do a little bit of a floor plan, so that everything shows to the best advantage."

~

"So you made the sketch of the floor plan, I suppose," Meg said almost an hour later. They were in Quill's Honda, headed back to the Inn. "I'll bet she asked you to sign it, too."

"The sketch?" Quill smiled. "She did ask me to sign it, as a matter of fact."

"What do you want to bet you find the thing matted, framed, and for sale in that shop of hers two seconds after the wedding?" Meg stretched out in the passenger's seat and ran her hands through her short hair. "That woman doesn't miss a trick, and a signed Quilliam, even of a wedding that's bound to bore everyone out of their skulls, is worth a couple hundred bucks, easily."

Quill made a noncommittal noise and slowed down as they passed the entrance to Peterson Park. She took the curve into the village at a sedate thirty miles an hour and drove down Main Street into the heart of Hemlock Falls. She, Jack, and Myles had spent the last four weeks in a cabin in the Adirondacks, and she hadn't had time to look at any changes in the village since they'd been back.

The old cobblestone buildings glowed in the warm September light. The flower boxes under the lampposts overflowed with Oriental lilies, English ivy, and pale green hydrangea. Nickerson's Hardware had substituted topiary for their usual display of wheelbarrows, rakes, and fall flowers on the sidewalk in front of the store. The trim on the building that housed Marge Schmidt's Realty and Casualty had been freshly painted, and a brand-new hunter green awning hung over the plate-glass window. Quill blinked. Somebody had put a bucket on top of the parking meter directly in front of Marge's office. She rolled down the car window to get a better look.

"Marge," Meg said, following Quill's glance. "She's still mad about those new parking meters Elmer Henry put in."

"They're a good source of revenue for the town," Quill said absently. "I haven't had time to pay attention to things lately. But isn't the village looking—sort of spiffy? What happened to the usual geraniums in the flower boxes? What's with all the topiary? We're starting to look like a high-end tourist trap."

"The Ladies' Auxiliary is all excited about the *Attic*'s road show being taped here," Meg said. "Somebody told them geraniums looked cheap."

That same somebody had convinced Esther West to put the "Cs" back in her sign, so it read COUNTRY CRAFTS and not KOUNTRY KRAFTS. Esther had put topiary next to her front door, too.

She slowed even more as she passed Rose Ellen's shop . . . boutique business, Quill corrected herself. The place looked exceptionally attractive. An evergreen topiary in a bronze pot stood to the right of the mahogany front door. The window display this week was an oil—a trompe l'oeil depiction of a fountain with a bunch of grapes at the foot. Right next to Elegant Antiques was the Balzac Café, a coffee/specialty cupcake shop that had opened up the week before. The coffee shop occupied the space where Meg and Quill had briefly run a white linen restaurant, and Quill had always thought the space unlucky. But a line of tourists stretched out the door and onto the sidewalk, and it looked like a hit.

The scent of fresh coffee floated through the air.

Meg sniffed appreciatively. "Jamaican Blue Mountain blend."

Quill sighed aloud.

"What?" Meg demanded.

"We're getting so . . . 'sophisticated' is the wrong word. So . . . tarted up. I miss the way it used to be. I like geraniums. I don't care if they look cheap." She stopped on the red at the one traffic light in town. "I was wondering why somebody like Rose Ellen thought Hemlock Falls would be a good place for stratospherically priced antiques—and I realized I haven't been paying much attention to what's been happening in town lately. The village has gone upscale, Meg."

"Change is good," Meg said, with a depressing lack of sentiment. "And the tourist traffic is even better. We're booked through New Year's and Labor Day last weekend was the best we've ever had. Clare said she's running eighty-percent full for her cooking classes until Thanksgiving. We're not a backwater anymore, Quill, and that's a good thing. Why would you want to go back to the old days, when we were starving to death?"

The not being a backwater anymore part was true. The past three years in Hemlock Falls had been prosperous ones. The Finger Lakes district in upstate New York was one of the most beautiful spots in the world. The freshwater lakes formed the heart of the area. The glaciers that had moved through the land ten thousand years before had left waterfalls, gorges, and sparkling streams in their wake. The Hemlock River and the gorge that divided the village from Meg and Quill's Inn was only one of many such beauties in the surrounding countryside.

Surrounded by lush, fertile ground, the five counties of the Finger Lakes held a hundred or more boutique wineries, apple and peach orchards, cheese makers, dairies, and even a handful of upscale distilleries and breweries. The new, large resort hotel that fronted the Hemlock River just on the outskirts of town catered to the thousands of tourists. The tourists came through the village in spring, summer, and autumn looking for hikes through the gorges that ran through the drumlins and wine tastings at the family-held vineyards. The Inn at Hemlock Falls benefited from this surge of outlanders just like everyone else.

Quill waited until she parked in the lot behind the Inn before she answered her sister. "We were never even close to starving to death."

"Well, no. That's true."

"That's not to say that we weren't exactly successful for a bit, either. And I don't miss the scary parts of almost being broke. I miss . . . I don't know what I miss. Maybe it's that I don't like Rose Ellen Whitman and all she stands for. Conspicuous consumption. A sort of arrogant greediness. Phrases like 'people who matter.' I mean, most people love and appreciate good food, good company, and that's how we make our living these days, but we aren't snobs about it and that's what's hit the village." Quill tugged at her hair, which was red and wildly springy. "Snobbism," she repeated glumly.

"Pooh." Meg opened the car door and jumped out. "You sit there and wallow in nostalgia if you want. I've got to put in a food order." She halted halfway across the lot and shouted, "What about Jack? I haven't seen the kid today."

"Doreen took him to a playdate with Harland Peterson's grandson." Quill looked at her watch. "Although they should be back. She must have put him down for his nap, by now."

"Then don't you have a Chamber meeting to go to? Get with it, Sis. Get a move on!"

"Yikes," Quill muttered. "So I should." She tossed her keys in the ashtray. Nobody ever locked their cars in the village. She got out of the car, stretched, and took a moment to check out the vegetable gardens just off the back door to the kitchen. Mike the groundskeeper must have picked the last of the tomatoes and the last of the yellow squash. The nasturtiums were cheery spots of bright red, yellow, and orange among the last of the dill and the oregano. The roses that grew against the stone walls of the building were in full flower. Before long, the beds would be spaded up and the roses covered for the winter, but for now, the air was alive with the mingled odors of Quill's favorites: Apricot Nectar, Peace, and Malmaison.

The creamy pink blossoms of the Peace rose quivered, and Max the dog emerged with a yawn. Quill bent down and rubbed his ears, which were large, floppy, and a mixture of colors as odd as the rest of his coat: black, white, gray, and a sort of muddy ochre that made him look in perpetual need of a bath.

"So where's Jackson Quilliam-McHale, Max? Your young master. My best boy? How come you're not with him? Is he still at his playdate? Is that how come you're skulking in the bushes?"

Max wagged his tail and cocked his head intelligently. The screen door to the kitchen banged open. "Jack's back from his playdate," Doreen said. "and takin' his nap, just on schedule. Which is more than I can say for you. Bein' on schedule that is." Doreen stood with her hands on her hips. Quill looked at her with affection. Doreen had been the Inn's first hire, and she had terrorized the staff for years. She was lean and wiry, and with bright beady black eyes. Jack loved her to distraction, and so did Quill.

"I know, I know." Quill dropped a quick kiss on her housekeeper's mop of wiry gray hair, and moved lightly past her to the kitchen. A quick glance assured her all was well; Bjarne, the head chef, loomed over Meg, eyebrows raised, as they looked through the menu notes she'd brought from the meeting with Clare. Elizabeth Chou chopped tomatoes, humming happily.

Quill sniffed; roast lamb for the special, it seemed, and it smelled absolutely delicious.

She passed through the swinging doors to the dining room. There was always a nice, expectant air about the dining room just before they opened for dinner. The wineglasses gleamed in the sunshine streaming in from the floor-to-ceiling windows. The cutlery sparkled. The flowers in the vases on the table were the last of the dahlias. Outside, the rush of water over the falls reached her ears in a faint, reassuring susurration.

Quill passed from the dining room into the front hall. It was small for a reception area, no more than twenty by thirty. A cobblestone fireplace occupied one wall. A soft cream leather sofa piled with needlepoint pillows sat in front of it. The curved staircase to the second and third floors was opposite the massive oak front door. The pine floors were covered with an Oriental rug in cream, celadon, peach, and sage green. The two giant Chinese vases that flanked the reception desk were filled with late lilies. Dina Muir, her receptionist, sat behind the mahogany front desk, her nose in a textbook. She looked up as Quill whizzed by on her way down the short hall to the Chamber meeting and shouted, "Whoa!"

Quill skidded to a halt. "What is it? I don't have time for my messages right now. I'm late for the Chamber meeting."

Dina's expression said: so what else is new? But she pushed her red-rimmed glasses up on her nose with one slim forefinger and dropped her voice. "I'm thinking maybe you don't want to go in there."

"I don't?" Quill took a couple of steps forward and looked down the short hall to the conference room. It wasn't really a conference room, just as the wine cellar at Bonne Goutè wasn't a conference room, but there wasn't any need for a keeping room, which had been a salient feature of the two-hundred-year-old Inn, so they had converted it.

Quill lowered her voice, too. "What's going on?"

"It's a lynching."

"A what!?"

"Well, okay. Not a real, actual, physical lynching." Dina marked her place in her textbook with a pink While You Were Out slip. She was a graduate student in freshwater pond ecology at nearby Cornell University. While rigorous in the pursuit of accuracy of the life cycle of her copepods, she tended to the imaginative in her approach to human beings. "But there's been a ton of screaming and yelling going on down there, and Marge stomped out here twice, wanting to know where the heck you were."

Quill relaxed. "Chamber meetings are always a little volatile, Dina. It's the *Attic*'s road show taping that's got everyone in a flap, I expect."

Dina shook her head dubiously. "You think? How much hoorah can there be over a bunch of old furniture?"

"A lot, I should think," Quill said. "*Antiques Roadshow* sometimes features tons of valuable stuff. Paintings, porcelain, jewelry."

"*Your Ancestor's Attic* doesn't," Dina said cynically. "If you ask me, they just follow along in the *Roadshow*'s wake, picking up all the junk the *Roadshow* didn't want to feature. Did you see that episode where Edmund Tree announced he was coming to Hemlock Falls? Did you see that pissed off little old lady whack him over the . . ."

A crash from the vicinity of the conference room made them both jump.

"I don't watch it."

"Even if it is a riot over old junk, you still don't want to go in there. I mean, Mrs. Henry stomped right in after Marge Schmidt came out here the second time looking for you and called Marge an old boot."

"Adela called Marge an old boot?" Quill discovered most of her hair had fallen out of her topknot. She swept it up again and pinned it firmly in place. Adela, Elmer Henry's imperious wife, was the real power behind the mayor's throne and a stickler for what she called ladylike manners and grace under pressure. "No! You must have misheard her."

"She did. And you know Mrs. Henry. She's about the most unflapped person in Hemlock Falls. But there she was, hollering away and red in the face."

"My goodness," Quill said, equably.

"If you ask me," Dina said unhappily, "we're on the verge of revolution, right here in the village. Who would have thought something like that could happen here, of all places?"

Quill smiled at her. Years of happy attention to the pond life of upstate New York clearly hadn't prepared Dina for the messiness of human behavior. "You remember the second rule of innkeeping."

"'Keep your shirt on'?" Dina shook her head. "You go on in there. You'll see."

2

~Hemlock Falls Ladies'~
Auxiliary Coffee Cake

2 large eggs
1 cup salted butter
1¼ cups sugar
2 cups flour
½ teaspoon baking soda
1½ teaspoons baking powder
1 cup sour cream
1 teaspoon vanilla
¾ cup ground pecans combined with 3 tablespoons
  brown sugar

Combine eggs, butter, and sugar. Add flour, baking soda, and baking powder. Mix well. Fold in sour cream and vanilla. Put half of batter into a Bundt pan. Sprinkle one half of the pecan sugar mixture over it. Add second half of batter and sprinkle remainder of sugar over the top. Bake in a cold oven set to 350 degrees for about an hour.

The conference room was at the end of a short flagstone hall. Quill paused before going in and put her ear to the door. It was ominously quiet.

She rapped twice, out of habit, and turned the knob and went in.

The room was long and narrow, with a low ceiling. Two hundred years before, it had been a keeping room, storing fruits, vegetables, cured hams, and barrels of flour and sugar. Quill had taken a utilitarian approach to the space. A credenza set up for coffee service was on the long wall facing the door. The floor was brick, impossible to keep warm in the winter, and it was with real reluctance that she'd installed Berber carpeting. She'd placed a series of whiteboards on the walls, and installed a conference table that seated twenty-four.

Twenty of the twenty-four spaces were filled with members of the Hemlock Falls Chamber of Commerce. They were all silent, with the kind of uncomfortable body posture that nice, middle-class Americans adopt when embarrassed. Elmer Henry sat at the head of the table, a mulish expression on his face. His majestic wife Adela, sat next to him, dressed in a bright orange pant suit and a ruffled navy blouse. Her face was red. Howie Murchison, the town justice and senior partner in Hemlock Falls's only law firm, sat next to Adela. Howie was in his early sixties, with a fringe of graying hair and a comfortable paunch. He raised both eyebrows in greeting as Quill walked in.

"There you are, Quill. We've had a motion to form a new political party sponsored by the Chamber of Commerce. We need your vote to break the tie."

This was so completely unexpected that Quill turned

around to make sure she had come in the right door. Then, "A what?"

"You heard Howie," Marge Schmidt said. "Siddown and vote."

Twenty faces swiveled and looked at her. Quill knew all of them and liked most of them a lot. Harvey Bozzel, Hemlock Falls's best (and only) advertising man. Nadine Peterson, owner-operator of the Hemlock Hall of Beauty. Dookie Shuttleworth, the mild-mannered pastor of the Church of the Word of God. Harland Peterson, president of the local Agway and Marge Schmidt's husband.

Marge herself, the richest woman in Tompkins County, sat right next to Harland, dressed in her usual chinos, a navy blue Peterson Dairy Farms windbreaker, and red-checked shirt. Her ginger hair capped her round skull in newly tight curls, which meant she had just made her biannual visit to Nadine's beauty shop.

Marge narrowed her machine-gun gaze and growled, "'Bout time you got here. All right, Mayor. We got twenty-one here now, and we gotta break this tie." She smacked her meaty fist on the table. "I call for another vote. And this time, it'd better go my way. You vote yes, Quill. Got it?"

"She'll vote no," Adela said. "Or else."

Everybody looked at Quill.

She smiled cheerfully. The third rule of innkeeping was to retreat in the face of certain disaster. She looked at her watch. "Sorry. I just dropped in to tell you that I have a small emergency. I was going to ask Miriam if she'd mind taking the minutes for me. I have to be off right now."

Miriam Doncaster, the town librarian, was a particular friend of Quill's. She admitted to being in her mid-fifties, and

Quill had always admired the faint sensual air that clung to her. She wasn't quite sure how Miriam created the effect: it had something to do with her gray blond hair, which was thick and tousled, and her wide blue eyes. She smiled sweetly and patted the empty chair next to her. "Not on your tintype, honey. Sit down and take it on the chin, like the rest of us."

Quill sank into the chair and said with an air of decisiveness everyone knew to be spurious. "What is the motion, exactly?"

Marge sat back in her chair and folded her arms under her considerable bosom. "I'm not saying another word."

"Oh, sure," Carol Ann Spinoza said. "Like you haven't said way too many words already, Marge Schmidt." Carol Ann had been the town's tax assessor for an excruciating three years. She currently held the office of the Hemlock Falls animal control officer. Quill wasn't quite sure why she had abandoned her personally designed animal control officer's outfit, with its belt of lethal weapons, but she had, in favor of a tailored pantsuit.

She drummed her perfectly manicured nails on the table. "And I don't know why we have to stop in our tracks just because Quill's waltzed in hours late like she always does. You don't have to know what's going on, Quill. It's your fault you're late, so you'll just have to go ahead and vote without us going over all this baloney again. All those opposed to sponsoring this party raise your hands." She thrust her right arm up in the air and looked around the table.

"What party?" Quill asked. And then, bewildered, "If I'm opposed to voting, do I vote yes or no?"

"You. Were. Late," Carol Ann said, as if speaking to a disagreeable deaf person. "Now, vote!" Carol Ann's cheerleader good looks, perky smile, and gleaming white teeth concealed the soul of a piranha. She wasn't the town's meanest tax assessor any longer, so her power to intimidate was considerably lessened. But old habits die hard and a few hands went hesitantly in the air, Harvey Bozzel's among them. Marge frowned at him and he hastily patted his hair, which was blond and gelled to perfection.

"Hang on a bit," Howie said easily. "Due process is due process, Carol Ann. We have to at least describe the motion before calling for a new vote."

"If the secretary had been here," Carol Ann said viciously, "we could have had her read the motion back from the minutes. But she wasn't and she can't."

Esther West sat forward timidly. "I jotted a few notes. Pastor Shuttleworth asked me to, just in case." She held up a scrapbook covered with glitter hearts and rainbow decals. "I ordered these for the shop and I can't tell you how handy they are. It's a three-ring binder, as you see, so I can just take these Chamber notes right out and ta-da! I have my scrapbook back again, ready for photos or anything. They're only ten ninety-nine, while they last. Useful for anything, these scrapbooks are."

"Mayor," Carol Ann said, her voice stickier and sweeter than usual. "I have a question. Are these Chamber meetings supposed to be places where some people think they can sell overpriced stuff from their shop or not? I say not. I move to have that blatant advertisement for Esther's Country Crafts stricken from the record."

"There isn't any record," Howie said. He looked as if he would like to tear his hair, if he'd had any. "That's part of what this discussion's about. Esther, if you would, please read the motion, just to clarify matters."

Esther patted her curls, adjusted one faux pearl earring and cleared her throat. "A motion was made by member Marge Schmidt Peterson that a new political party dedicated to the welfare of the citizens of Hemlock Falls be officially sponsored by Chamber members. The party is named . . ." She squinted at the scrapbook page, then said, "Pfft?"

"Not pfft!" Marge said. "People for Free Parking. PFFP."

"PFFP," Quill said, scribbling her own notes. "Got it."

"And what it will do," Marge said between her teeth, "is get those damn parking meters off Main Street."

"Oh," said Quill. "I see."

"That's not what it says here, actually . . ." Esther said.

"No, you don't see." Marge was furious. "I got people coming to the Croh Bar for breakfast, lunch, and dinner and they gotta cough up fifty cents? And all those cruddy meters give you is two hours before my customers have to haul their behinds off of the barstools and go feed the meters? And when they come back in, do they want another beer? You have any idea how much beer sales are down since those darn meters poked up all over town?"

"Now, Margie," Harland patted Marge's shoulder with a couple of comforting thumps.

"All voting against this stupid motion," Carol Ann began.

Quill hadn't been secretary of the Chamber of Commerce for twelve years without learning a few tricks. She raised her hand. "Point of order, Mr. Mayor."

"Huh?" Elmer's gaze was a little glassy. Adela poked him sharply in the side. "Yeah. Okay. The chair recognizes Quill. Ms. Quilliam. Ms. Quilliam-McHale, I mean."

"I move that the motion be tabled for further discussion," Quill said promptly.

The silence was short but powerful.

Howie smiled. "I second that very smart motion."

"All in favor?" Quill said.

"Aye!" came a chorus of relieved voices.

"Against?" Elmer said.

"Nay!" Marge and Carol Ann roared. This was the first time in Quill's excellent memory that the two women had voted the same way on any issue at all. She put a big star next to the record she'd made of the vote.

"So moved and passed," Elmer said rapidly. "This vote is tabled for . . . whenever. Now if we can just get down to some real bidness . . ."

"Now just a darn minute," Marge said. "Are you going to represent the people of Hemlock Falls or not, Elmer Henry?"

"Perhaps a study would be in order," Quill said. When crossed, Marge had the temper of a tank gunner sitting on a wasp and a taste for revenge. "I move that a committee be formed to look into the advisability of the Chamber sponsoring a political party. I mean, the Chamber's supposed to be independent of political bias, isn't it? Maybe we should form a committee to look into the town's support for the parking meters. A whole party formed just to get rid of parking meters? It doesn't make sense." Then, apologetically, since Marge's little gray eyes had narrowed to glittering slits, as if taking aim with an Uzi, "It seems a rather narrow platform, is all."

"What it says here in my meeting notes," Esther said loudly, "doesn't only have to do with parking meters. What it says here is that the party platform is to assure free and righteous elections."

"Elections?" Quill said.

"That's right." Marge settled back into her chair with the air of a woman who had her target firmly in her sights and was happy to pull the trigger. "I'm running for mayor."

Quill came to attention. So this was what all the animosity was about. Elmer was reelected like clockwork every four years, and he usually ran unopposed.

"No! Like I said before. You've never done a thing for this town, Marge Schmidt," Carol Ann said furiously. "Who's the only person to have adjudicated fair taxes for this town? Me. Who's the only person to have kept the streets of this town free of dangerous animals? Me. Anybody notice how many burglaries have been committed in this town the past four weeks?"

There was an apprehensive murmur.

"Exactly. Crime is up. And it's not just burglars. Many people are in violation of important codes in this town." Carol Anne's big blue eyes narrowed into icy points. *"And you know who you are."*

Dead silence greeted this alarming statement.

"So. Who can run this town better than Mr. Chubby over there? Me." Carol Ann's perfectly glossed lips firmed into a thin, determined line. "If there's going to be any political party endorsed by the Chamber of Commerce, it'll be mine. This town should be headed places, moving on up. Not down. I'm running for mayor, too. And you can bet your bottom dollar when I get in, this town's going to be run right."

The room erupted into argument.

Early in the summer, Quill had counted up how many Chamber meetings she'd been to over the years. It was more than one hundred. In all that time, the ratio of squabbles to rational discourse was about four to one, in favor of squabble. But this time, the tone was different. Voices were higher. Bodies were tense. Faces were flushed angry-red instead of merely-annoyed-pink.

Quill leaned sideways and whispered at Miriam. "We've got a mayoral election coming up?"

"Where have you *been* for the last month?" Miriam said testily.

"The Adirondacks. With Myles and Jack."

"Oh. That's right. I forgot. How was your trip?"

"I'm beginning to wish I'd never left. What the heck is going on here?"

Miriam sighed. "I wish I knew for sure. Howie and I have talked about it some. Take a look at the table, Quill. Do you know what I see? There's Harland Peterson, biggest dairy farmer for miles around. Farming is a growth industry at the moment. Our farmers are rich, after decades of being poor. Right next to him is Nadine Peterson, whose beauty shop customers are the workers at Walmart, the cashiers at Wegmans, the stock girls at the pharmacy. Those people are victims of the nationwide recession. They aren't going to Nadine's as often as they used to because they don't have the money and she's had to raise her prices anyway. Then there's Harvey Bozzel, Hemlock Falls's only advertising executive, who depends on ad income from the PennySaver and the Hemlock Falls *Gazette*. You and I both know what's happening to newspapers these days."

They both looked at Harvey. He was tall and slender, and paid a lot of attention to his thick blond hair. His attractive, not-very-intelligent face was glum. Quill liked Harvey, even though most of his advertising campaigns bordered on the lunatic. In a weird way, the lunacy added to his appeal.

"Next to Harvey is Frieda Arbuckle, who just opened the Balzac Café, and who is making money hand over fist because of all the tourists. Next to her is Pastor Shuttleworth—who's talking about merging with both the Methodist and Baptist churches from Covert because attendance at the Church of the Word of God is a tenth of what it used to be."

"I get the point," Quill said soberly.

"So there's Marge, our very own Croesus, fussing about the effects of parking meter charges on her restaurant customers because there's nothing she can do about the rest of it. And she cares about this town, Quill. She really does. That's why she's running for mayor.

"Fear. I think that's what we're seeing. Fear. Half the village is getting richer and the other half is looking at living on a street corner with a coffee can full of quarters as their only hope. There doesn't seem to be anything that anyone can do about it. So there's a three-way race for mayor and in my opinion, it's going to get very ugly, very quick."

"It's not that bad, surely?"

"You don't think so? How long have we known about the *Ancestor's Attic* visit?"

"You mean the show? Gosh. It was before Myles and I left for the mountains. A month at least."

"We've had a couple of TV shows come here over the years. How has the village handled it in the past?"

Quill chuckled. "The Chamber forms a committee. Harvey starts an advertising campaign. Elmer tries to find an angle that will benefit the town. The usual self-interest balanced by civic pride."

"You heard Carol Ann about the number of break-ins?"

"You mean that's not just a Carol Ann statistic?"

"Nope. And do you know what's being burgled?"

Quill shook her head.

"Attics. Basements. The Volunteers of America charity shop. Even the Historical Society. Me!"

"Oh my goodness, Miriam. I am so sorry! I had no idea! Was anything valuable taken?"

Miriam shrugged. "Who knows? It's stuff I haven't looked at for years. Old files were riffled through, old boxes were turned over, a trunk I've lugged around for years was pried open. I don't know if anything important is missing or not." She rapped her knuckles on the table, like a first-grade teacher calling the class to order. "Here's the thing. Our good citizens are sneaking around ripping off forgotten items in the hope that Edmund Tree will tell them they've found a treasure. So there's no nutty ad campaign from Harvey and no Ladies' Auxiliary committee to set up a fancy reception for Edmund Tree and his TV cameras. Just petty theft. Or," Miriam added with a conscientious air, "grand theft, depending. Who knows?" She shook her head. "I'm telling you, Quill. It's a sorry state of affairs. It looks to me like greed's got the upper hand."

3

~Roast Leg of Lamb Quilliam~

Bone a leg of lamb. Flatten meat onto the prep table.
Sprinkle a small handful of coarse sea salt, rosemary,
and freshly ground black pepper on both sides. Roll up
lengthwise, secure with kitchen twine. Bake at 450 degrees eight to ten minutes a pound.

"You're kidding. Marge is running for mayor? And Carol
Ann, too? Against Elmer?" Meg paused in the middle of
making a roux, egg whisk in midair.

Quill, more unsettled than she wanted to admit by the conversation she'd had with Miriam, had decided to reveal the
most immediately sensational news from the Chamber meeting to Meg. "Wow. How long has Elmer been mayor?"

"Ever since we've been here. Carol Ann's platform is
Progress for the People. Whatever the heck that means. More
Ten Most Wanted Animals posters in the post office, I guess."

Quill had been wandering around the kitchen. Mindful
of being in the way, she settled into the rocking chair by the
stone fireplace. The activity around her was purposeful but

peaceful. The dining room would open in an hour. The special tonight was roasted lamb, and the air was redolent with rosemary, garlic, and butter. Dried herbs hung from the old wooden beams that crossed the ceiling. Late afternoon sunlight flooded in from the large back window. Meg's collection of copper pans glowed against the wall. So what if the prep table was battered from years of being whacked by butcher's knives? So what if the twelve-burner stove was dulled and scratched? Who needed spiffy new Viking stoves in a multi-million dollar building like the academy? It was shabby, but it was home.

"There've been some burglaries, too, while I was away?"

"Oh, yeah. I forgot to tell you about that." Meg ran her hands through her short dark hair, leaving a trail of goo. "No big deal, from what I hear."

"They may not be a big deal to you, but it sure looks like Carol Ann is trying to work up a law-and-order platform."

"Phooey on Carol Ann." Meg finished the roux, edged past Elizabeth Chou to put the pan at the back of the twelve-burner stove, then disappeared into the pantry. She reappeared with a pound of bitter chocolate and handed it over to Bjarne. "She'll never get elected. Everybody hates her."

"Everybody's *scared* of her," Elizabeth Chou said. "And I don't even have a dog, like Max, that she can arrest now that she's animal control officer. When she was tax assessor, I didn't have a house she could tax, either. I'm still scared of her."

"Well, don't be," Meg said. "Forget about Carol Ann. She's a nitwit. Any time we spend talking about Carol Ann Spinoza is time lost forever. None of this has anything to do with us. How's that tapenade coming along?"

Elizabeth looked at the pile of tomatoes on the cutting board. "I forgot about the tapenade."

"See? You were way too caught up in gossiping about Carol Ann. Move, move, move!"

Kathleen Kiddermeister, the Inn's head waitress, bustled in with her notepad held aloft. "Both dinner sittings are fully reserved," she said. "I don't know if we're going to have a problem with walk-ins or not." She bustled out again, the double doors to the dining rooms swinging in her wake.

"Jeez," Meg said. "I hate to turn people away. Maybe we ought to think about full service in the lounge for real, Quill." She grinned, suddenly. "Nice to have this kind of problem, isn't it? But with the *Ancestor's Attic* people doing the show here, we're bound to get some major word of mouth going, and we've got to look to the future." She grabbed a fistful of leeks from the sieve in the prep sink and began to peel them with manic energy. "If we go ahead with the expansion I can turn twice the number of tables we're turning now."

Quill set the rocker going, resisting the impulse to run upstairs. Jack was still asleep, and she'd learned to her cost not to wake him up. She'd give herself ten minutes of downtime here in the kitchen, and then she'd get back to work. And she wouldn't think about how nice it would be to go upstairs, cuddle his warm and sleepy little body next to hers and drift off herself. "You're already working six days a week, and half the time you don't even take your Monday off. You're not serious about expansion."

"Why not?"

There was a challenging set to her sister's shoulders.

"I mean it's certainly a possibility," Quill said cautiously.

"Ha. I know you too well, sister. That's the classic Quilliam brush-off. You got it from Dad. Listen." Meg waved a leek at her. "We give Bjarne a raise . . ."

"That is a very good idea," Bjarne said from his post at the stove. "Even if we do not expand, it is a good idea to give me a raise."

"Me, too," Elizabeth said. "My rent's going up next month."

"And we hire a couple of really good people . . ."

Quill threw up her hands. "Where are we going to find these really good people?"

Meg glanced from side to side, then said in a whisper, "I think a couple of people at Bonne Goutè are ready to jump ship."

Quill stopped the rocker. "You're kidding me."

"Nope. I know it for a fact. Rather," she added with a conscientious air, "I'm pretty sure they're ready to, if the offer's right."

"I didn't mean you're kidding me about that. I mean you have to be kidding me about wanting to *do* that. Steal Clare's staff? Clare's a good friend of ours! What the heck is all this?"

"Hey. We're in business aren't we? And it's the business of a business to make a profit. I'm telling you, it's time we took a few chances here."

"I knew it."

"Knew what?"

"That Hemlock Falls is infected. All these changes in the village. All this . . ." Quill waved her arms in the air. *"Development. Competition. Greed."*

"You're calling me greedy?" Meg said, a dangerous glitter in her eye. "And a traitor?"

"I didn't say a word about being a traitor."

"Oh! Oh! But I'm a pig, is that right?"

She jumped to her feet. "Listen, Meg. Now's not the time to go into this, but I'm here to tell you right now that we are not expanding, we are not stealing Clare's staff, and we are not, not, *not* going to turn into crazy people."

"Jeez," Dina said as she came through the dining room doors into the kitchen. "I can hear you two all the way out in reception."

Quill realized that everyone else in the kitchen was quiet. Meg was pink with rage. Elizabeth Chou looked scared. Bjarne didn't have much of an expression at all, although he stirred the chocolate he was melting in a pan over the stove a little faster than was good for it.

"I think you need to leave this kitchen right now," Meg said. "You are obviously coming down with something."

"I'm feeling just fine."

"I hope so," Dina said. "Because if you're in a snit now, you're going to be in an even bigger snit in a few minutes. And all I have to say is, it wasn't me, and if you've got a stack of Bibles around, I'll swear on as many as you like."

Quill took a couple of deep breaths. It helped. Sort of. She'd known it; she'd known it all along. Despite their friendship with Clarissa Sparrow, Meg was in full competitive mode. She shoved the thought aside, counted backward from ten, and turned her attention to Dina. "It wasn't you that did what?"

"Didn't book this guy's reservations. I've been telling everyone who calls up for the past week that we're full up starting in three days, and he claims that he reserved the Provencal suite last Monday for a whole week beginning today and he didn't. Rose Ellen Whitman has, for the wedding, which I've known perfectly well for weeks, since I did make that reservation myself."

Quill took a moment to sort through the participles. Dina could be aggravating in a number of different ways, but she was good at her job. "All right. He says he made a reservation. He didn't. Let's go talk to him."

She followed Dina back through the dining room. As she approached the foyer, she caught sight of a portly guy in wrinkled shorts, a faded red T-shirt, and flip-flops stamping back and forth. His toenails were dirty. He had his hand cupped to his ear and was chuckling into his cell phone. Dina stopped short, caught her arm, and whispered, "That's the guy. He looks familiar somehow. He says his name is . . ."

Quill's visual memory was excellent. "Barcini. It's the man who stars in *Pawn-o-Rama*."

Dina snapped her fingers. "Sure it is. Belter Barcini. That's the show that rips off *Pawn Stars*. Just like *Your Ancestor's Attic* rips off *Antiques Roadshow*. Why is it when something kind of cool comes along everybody jumps on the bandwagon and wrecks it?"

"Greed," Quill said darkly. "It's an infection. Competitiveness. That's an infection, too. Progress for the People. Phooey."

Barcini caught sight of Dina. His rubber flip-flops squeaked to a halt. He snapped his fingers. "There you are. That your boss with you? Good. I got a complaint." He hunched his shoulders in a confidential way as Quill walked up to him and said loudly, "Your girlie here screwed up. I made a reservation. Your best suite. For a week. Beginning today. I want my room. Right now."

Quill, mindful of the early diners coming in the front door, smiled pleasantly. "Why don't we talk about this in my office, Mr. Barcini? It's right back here." She stepped behind the reception desk, opened her office door, and waited while he preceded her.

He flung himself back on the couch, legs spraddled, and looked around.

The office was small, but Quill had taken a great deal of care when she'd furnished it. The small overstuffed couch was covered in a chintz woven with bronze chrysanthemums. A small Queen Anne–style table served as an informal conference area. Her desk was cherrywood, with an arrangement of cloisonné bowls next to the landline. She'd restored the tin ceiling overhead.

"Nice," he said. "You know that Queen Anne table's a fake, though."

"It's a reproduction," Quill said. "Not a fake. A fake is when you think you've got the real thing and you don't. Like your reservation."

Barcini grinned and shrugged. "Hey," he said. "Had to give it a try, didn't I? C'mon, Miss . . ."

"McHale," Quill said. "And it's 'missus.'"

"Mrs. McHale. You got a mother, right?"

"I did," Quill said, her smile still pleasant. "She passed away quite some time ago."

"So you understand my problem here."

"I'm afraid . . ."

"Thing is, my mamma and my sister are in the car outside . . ."

The door to Quill's office banged open and a short, round, belligerent lady stumped into the room, an aluminum cane in her right hand and a large black leather purse in her left. Her resemblance to Belter Barcini was marked, except that her hair was dyed an aggressive black.

". . . Or she was," Belter concluded. "Hey, Mamma."

"Don't you say hey to me, you stupid boy. Why are we not checked in? Josephine is waiting in the bus. She has to pee." She tossed a throw pillow from the couch onto the floor and sat down. She set the cane between her feet and leaned on it. She wore crop pants, and a glittery T-shirt that barely contained her considerable bosom. She jerked her chin at Quill. "I am Josepha Barcini, the producer of the famous TV show *Pawn-o-Rama*, which is shot live in New Jersey. This is my son, the famous Joseph Barcini. He is called Belter because of his mighty arm. You are in charge here? Why are we not checked in?"

"Yes, I am Mrs. Barcini. And I'm very sorry indeed, but the Inn is fully booked, or rather, it will be, for the period that you've requested."

"We have a reservation," Mrs. Barcini said. "This stupid boy here, he made it. I hear him myself."

"Let me have our receptionist call the resort across the river. The managers are friends of ours, and we may be able to get you a room there."

"I will tell Josephine to get out of the bus and bring the suitcases in. You hand over the room key and I will settle myself and this stupid boy and his sister. You make sure it is a suite. Joseph will require your best roll-away bed."

"I'm afraid you don't understand, signora. You do not have a reservation. We do not have a room available for an entire week. There is undoubtedly a suite available at the resort

44

across the river." Quill's landline had an intercom system, which she rarely used, since it was easier to call Dina through the open office door, but she decided it would be impressive if she used it now. She punched the intercom button and Dina's startled voice said, "Who's this?"

"Dina, please arrange a suite at the resort for the Barcinis. If they're booked up, try the Marriott on Route Fifteen. And please send for Mike to help with their luggage." Mike Santini, the groundskeeper, was short, phlegmatic, and muscular. His stolid attitude was a lot of help with fractious guests. Quill hoped she wouldn't need his muscles, too.

"I'm on it, Boss."

Quill got up and opened the office door. "I am truly sorry for the disappointment. While Dina's making arrangements, let me take you to our Tavern Lounge. Please feel free to order anything you like."

"You mean drinks?" Belter said. "Wouldn't mind a beer, I'll tell you that right now. That was some long drive from New Jersey."

"You don't charge us, eh?" Mrs. Barcini said. "We have been very much agitated by your screwup." She extended her hand imperiously. Belter hauled her up. Quill, who still couldn't decide whether she wanted to laugh or scream, said, "Absolutely," and stood aside to usher them both into the foyer.

Her relief was short-lived.

Edmund Tree stood at his elegant ease at the reception desk. A pile of Hartmann luggage behind him impeded traffic. He was dressed in his signature three-piece suit, an Armani, if Quill was any judge. It was pale gray, with even paler gray pinstripes. His yellow tie was a masterpiece of silk. Harvey Bozzel, Hemlock Falls's best (and only) advertising executive, would have been pea green with envy.

"You!" Mrs. Barcini said in tones of loathing.

"Yo, Eddie," Belter Barcini said.

"Doughhead!" Mrs. Barcini shouted. She smacked her son in the arm. "What is this person doing here?"

"Beats the hell out of me" Belter said. "Guess he must be here to cheat the good people of Hemlock Falls, New York. What do you think, Ma?"

"I think you are right, *mio filio*. And to steal our ratings."

Edmund raised a meticulously groomed eyebrow. "If it isn't the star of the lowest-rated antiques show on national television. Well, well, well. It's interesting to meet you in the flesh at last. And what a great amount of it there is—the flesh, I mean. What brings you here, Barcini? The cable network finally get around to canceling you? Gotten through all of the town dumps in New Jersey already?"

"Maybe I think this town needs an honest man to take the stink out of your show."

"Indeed." Edmund sneered.

Quill's fingers itched for her sketch pad. It was a grade A, number one deluxe sneer and you just didn't see that many of them in Hemlock Falls. On the other hand, if she didn't do something soon, one of the two might throw a punch, and good innkeepers kept physical altercations to a minimum. "Mr. Barcini was just on his way to the lounge, Mr. Tree, while we find him and his family a comfortable room at the resort. And you, I know, need to get checked in."

Edmund smiled nastily. "No room at the Inn, Barcini? I'm

not surprised. Mrs. Quilliam-McHale has a reputation to maintain, after all."

"I wouldn't stay in a *dump* if you were there, Eddie."

Quill tried to work this out and couldn't. She invoked the fourth rule of innkeeping: calm above all. "I was just about to get you settled in the Lounge, Mrs. Barcini. If you would just come with me?" She tucked her arm under Belter's elbow and led the way down the hall to the rear of the Inn.

Mrs. Barcini turned and shouted over her shoulder: "Doughhead!"

4

~Jack McHale's Favorite~
Tuna Fish Sandwich

1 8-ounce can albacore tuna in water
¼ cup sour cream
¼ cup mayonnaise
2 tablespoons finely chopped sweet onion
2 tablespoons finely chopped celery
1 teaspoon Turkish capers
1 teaspoon finely chopped radish

Mix all ingredients and serve on twelve-grain bread.

"So that," Quill said to her husband several hours later, "was my day. I haven't quite figured out what a doughhead is, precisely, but it can't be anything good."

She lay curled up in the queen-sized bed in her suite on the third floor of the Inn, her phone at her ear. Myles sounded close, but she knew he was across at least one ocean and thousands of miles from her. They had been together a blissful month before he'd had to take off again. She hoped it wasn't Libya.

Myles's voice was amused. "Let's see if I've got it straight. Marge Schmidt is staging a revolution over the parking meters. Carol Ann Spinoza is running for mayor on a law-and-order platform. Belter Barcini and Edmund Tree hated each other on sight and are going to face off with pistols at dawn. Meg's determined to swipe Clare Sparrow's staff and turn the Inn into a megaplex."

"You forgot about the burglaries," Quill said indignantly. "We never had a crime wave when you were in charge."

Myles had been village sheriff until the federal government had coaxed him into his current antiterrorism job.

"That's disturbing, I agree. But not unusual. When times are hard, personal property crime always goes up."

"Miriam seems to think the thefts are related to the taping of the TV show."

"Hm." Myles's tone was doubtful.

"It's possible she's right, you know. None of the new families in town have been burgled. Apparently it's the longtime residents, anybody with an attic or basement full of old stuff. I suppose that somebody could be driven to look for forgotten items that might be of value to take to the auditions."

"And what's the schedule for the show, again?"

"They do elimination rounds to see if there are actually enough antiques to make a show set here worthwhile. The first one is tomorrow, at the high school. If there's enough stuff to make a show, then they do a second round, then they select the people who are going to be on. Rose Ellen told me that you never know if the stuff you have is valuable or not until the live show itself. All you know is that you have something of interest. If stuff is being swiped because of the show, then there shouldn't be any more burglaries after tomorrow, right? At that point, if you haven't been selected, you're out. So no need to steal more stuff." She sighed. "It's all horrible. The changes in the village, the bigger gap between the haves and the have-nots. I don't like it at all, Myles."

"You don't think you're overreacting? Just a bit?"

Quill thought about it. "Maybe," she said. "Although the thought of Carol Ann as mayor is totally sickening. Even you have to agree to that."

"You know, dear heart, if you took a few days off, things would settle into . . ."

"Perspective?" Quill demanded.

"Perspective," Myles said. "The very word."

"You think I'm losing my perspective?"

"I think you might need some time for yourself. Why don't you and Jack go back up to the Adirondacks for a week or two? Or do you think the place will combust without you?"

"I'm sounding a bit witless, aren't I?" Quill settled back into the pillows with a sigh. "It's not like me, having this short a fuse."

"You're settled into your old quarters all right?" His voice was warm and deep, and if she closed her eyes, she could imagine, just barely, that he was across the room, his big shoulders blocking out the moonlight streaming in from the balcony.

"Oh, yes. Everyone's used to it by now. You take off for a month to God knows where, and we settle back in here. And it's just as well we're not in the house, Jack and I. Too lonesome without you. We're doing just fine. And if you say 'that's my brave girl' I'll make a rude noise into the phone."

"Wouldn't dream of it."

"It's not just missing you, which I do, and it's not the spat with Meg, which will resolve itself one way or the other or even the awful Edmund Tree and the equally awful Barcinis. We've had worse guests. Meg and I have had worse fights. It's something fundamental. I guess it's the changes in the village. You know, Myles, the guests and tourists and visitors come and bring their outside universes with them and then they go and things settle back the way they were. Except not this time. They've brought a lot of money with them and it's sticking and things seem to be changing permanently. Progress for the People," she added. "What a lot of hooey."

"You're upset by success?"

"I'm not upset by success. Success is great. It's how people go about being successful that bugs me."

Myles didn't say anything.

"Hello? Myles?"

"Still here."

"You're laughing at me."

"Never."

"You're thinking I should have a glass of wine and go to sleep."

"Not a bad idea."

"I told you that those wretched Barcinis had dinner and refused to pay for it? Mamma Barcini insisted I'd offered them a free meal to make up for messing up their room reservation."

"You did tell me that, yes."

"And did I tell you Edmund Tree had dinner with Rose

Ellen and when Tree wasn't sneering at Belter he was sneering at Rose Ellen's plans for the wedding. He doesn't think the Inn is grand enough for the nuptials. That's what he called his wedding. Nuptials. Ha."

"You mentioned that, too."

"And did I tell you they have *separate rooms*! Rose Ellen's moving in here the night before the wedding. She told me Edmund has old-fashioned ideas about purity." She snorted. "The man's a fruitcake."

"Undoubtedly. Dear heart, I have to go."

Quill sighed. The phone calls were always too short. "Okay. I e-mailed you today's pictures of Jack."

"I downloaded them right away."

"Which is your favorite?"

"I'll look again and let you know when we talk tomorrow. I love you, Quill."

"I know, I know. You're going, going, gone. I love you, Myles. Stay safe."

The cell went dead. Quill tossed the phone onto the coverlet and got out of bed. She cracked open the door that led to Jack's tiny bedroom and checked on her sleeping son. Moonlight streamed in through the open window. He lay on his back, face upturned, mouth slightly open, one hand curled around his stuffed pig. Her angelic boy. She swallowed hard. She was in need of time off if the mere sight of her sleeping son could bring her to tears.

Max snored at his feet. The old dog was getting deaf, and Quill gently smoothed his fur. He was also getting . . . fat?

Puzzled, Quill bent down and peered at his stomach. Max hadn't gained an ounce. There was a large cat curled beneath his perfectly normal-sized belly. The moonlight turned everything in the room silvery gray, but she knew the shape. It was orange, large, and familiar.

"Bismarck," she whispered. "What the heck are you doing here?"

Bismarck mewed. Jack stirred in his sleep. Quill made a small, exasperated sound and hoisted Bismarck onto her hip. He was a Maine coon cat, and weighed upwards of thirty pounds. He belonged to Clare Sparrow and usually watched over the kitchens at Bonne Goutè, but he had a nomad's habit, and a fondness for either Jack or Max or Meg's leftovers. Quill wasn't sure which. Probably all three.

She edged into the light, shut the bedroom door softly, and set the cat on his feet.

"So," she said. "What brings you calling so late?"

Bismarck squeezed his eyes shut and opened them again, in an ingratiating way.

"Clare feeds you. Half the staff at Bonne Goutè feeds you. That's partly why you're such a monster. You think I'm going to feed you, too?"

Bismarck wound himself around her ankles and mewed again.

"You really have to stop sneaking over here at night, Bismarck. What time is it . . . ten? Not too late to call your mistress, then." She picked up her cell phone. Clare was on speed dial and answered almost immediately.

"Don't tell me," Clare said. "I saw it was your number and my cat's missing and I'll bet he's after Meg's pâté again. You want me to come get him?"

"He's perfectly welcome to spend the night, Clare."

"I wouldn't mind getting out of here for a bit. It's Monday and things are a little slow. Jack will be asleep in your rooms, won't he? Maybe we could meet across the hall at Meg's. It's been a while since we've had a girl's night out." She hesitated, and then said in a rush, "I have a bit of a problem. I'd like your advice."

Quill caught the hesitancy in Clare's voice. This rift with Meg had to be affecting her, too. Suddenly, she felt very much like a girl's night out. Maybe the three of them could settle this stupid rivalry and things could get back to normal. "That sounds great. Tell Meg when you come through the kitchen. Our last order's at ten, so she should be free by the time you get here."

Bismarck gave her ankle a determined nudge and gave her a loud "I'm starved" mew. Quill folded and opened a can of tuna fish she'd been saving for Jack's lunch.

She left him to it and wandered out onto her balcony. That Clare was willing to take the first step in mending fences with Meg was great. She knew Meg almost as well as she knew herself; her sister had a generous heart, even when it came to her cherished career. This could all be smoothed over. They'd bonded over Rose Ellen's nit-picking at the menu meeting.

She leaned against the balcony and took a deep breath of the fragrant air. The moon floated on a wispy ocean of clouds. The distinctive scent of autumn was a poignant herald of the winter to come. Her rooms were over the kitchen door two floors below, and she could hear the faint clatter of pans, a murmur of voices, the sounds of the Inn winding down for the night. The kitchen door banged open and a tall, slim figure walked down the short brick path to the parking lot. Bjarne, headed home to his wife in nearby Covert. Then Elizabeth Chou left, always in a hurry, even at the end of a long day.

And then a scrape of heel on iron, quite near.

Startled, Quill bent over the iron balustrade and peered to her left. There were fire escapes on each side of the main building. It sounded very much as if someone had come out the third-floor fire door. The fire door locked automatically on the outside; she hoped whoever it was had figured that out. There was a pause, the rattle of a doorknob, and then the soft thud, thud, thud of feet coming down the iron steps.

"Hello?" Quill said. "If you're locked out, I'll be happy to let you in."

The footsteps paused, and then kept on going down, in a rush.

"Hello?"

No answer. The stairs ended in rosebushes—a flourishing bed of Apricot Nectar, which was exceptionally thorny. There was a solid thump as whoever it was stumbled off the last step, then a muffled, hissed expletive. The footsteps scraped against the gravel and faded away.

In the parking lot, a car door slammed. She heard the low rumble of the motor and whoever it was—she shivered in the chilling air—whatever it was, had gone.

Troubled, she went inside, cracked Jack's bedroom door to assure herself he was still asleep, and then went into the hallway, Bismarck at her heels. She and Meg had re-carpeted all the hallways just last year, in a thick navy blue patterned with pale pink stripes. It suited the old building (to everyone's surprise except her own) and it was excellent soundproofing. Leaving her own door opened, she went to the end of the hallway and to the fire door, which opened directly onto the fire escape. There were carriage lights at each of the three landings and to her surprise, they were out.

Bismarck threaded around her ankles and went out onto the wrought-iron landing. She made a lunge for him and missed. "Darn it, Biz. Come back here."

"Is he being a pain in the neck again?"

Quill jumped.

"Sorry," Clare said. "Didn't mean to startle you." Her hair was a tangle, there was a smudge on her cheek, and she smelled of food. She'd exchanged her chef's whites for jeans and a sweatshirt, but she'd obviously had a long night in the kitchen.

Quill gave her a quick hug. "It's good to see you. I didn't mean to jump. I didn't hear the elevator."

"I walked up the stairs. The elevator didn't come down and didn't come down and I finally gave up waiting."

Bismarck crouched on the iron grill and batted at something. Quill lunged after him.

Clare nudged her gently aside. "Here, let me. It's my lousy cat. Come on, Biz. Come to Mamma. What have you got there? Whatever it is, drop it."

Quill caught it just before whatever it was fell and bounced down the fire escape. "It's the lightbulb from the carriage lamp."

Bismarck jumped up and batted it out of her hands.

"So that's why it's so dark out here." Clare clutched the cat by the scruff of the neck, "Oof, he's heavy. Here, Quill. I've got him. Close the door before he scoots off again." Clare backed into the hallway, Bismarck clutched awkwardly around his middle. His forepaws dangled over her arms and his hindquarters bumped gently against Clare's knees. He regarded Quill placidly. There was tuna fish on his nose.

Clare straightened up with a whoosh of air. "Jeez. He's

either getting fatter or I'm aging faster than I should. I'll put him down and get the lightbulb."

"That's okay. I've got to give Mike a call anyway. We've got to replace the bulbs on the landings or we'll be in violation of some darn code or another. There's this special screwdriver that opens the carriage lamps and . . ." She broke off. "On second thought, maybe I ought to give Davy Kiddermeister a call."

"The sheriff? Why in the world would you want to call the sheriff about a missing lightbulb?"

Quill patted her skirt pocket and found a tissue. "Fingerprints." The lightbulb sat on the top of the stairway. She stepped out and picked it up, careful to avoid touching the surface with her bare hands.

"O-o-o-kay," Clare said dubiously.

Quill wrapped the bulb in the tissue and stowed it in her pocket. "I'll put it in a Baggie, just to be sure." She came back inside and closed the fire door behind her. "Did you park in front or in the back?"

"Just now? I parked in the front and came in the front door. How come?"

"Did you meet a car coming down the driveway?"

"I met a couple of cars coming down the driveway. Your kitchens close at ten on weekdays. It's ten twenty, now. A bunch of people were headed out. Why? What's going on?"

"Somebody just left down the fire escape."

"From here?"

"Well, of course, from here," Quill said.

"You mean, somebody was sneaking around like a burglar?"

"Well. No. He, she, whatever didn't sneak, exactly. But why leave by the fire escape?"

"Umm . . . because I waited and waited for the elevator and it didn't come and whoever it was got tired of waiting for the elevator, too?"

Quill sighed. "That'd be the charming Mr. Edmund Tree. We put him on the second floor, in the Provencal suite."

"That's the one with the blue-and-yellow-print fabric on the bedspread and the drapes. I just love that room, Quill."

"Whatever. I mean, thank you. And yes, it's our most expensive room. Anyhow, Mr. Tree doesn't like having to wait for the elevator, so he wedges it open so it's always available and housekeeping comes along and unwedges it and he wedges it back again."

"Oh, Lord. One of those." Clare wrinkled her nose. It didn't take long for people in the hospitality business to realize a fair number of patrons were hell on wheels to deal with. "How long is he staying?"

"Two weeks. At least he's going to be away from here most of the time. The preliminary auditions for the antiques show begin tomorrow, and then there's the shoot itself, and of course, the wedding. Anyway—that's probably why the elevator didn't come. But how come my burglar didn't use the inside stairs?"

"Why not use the fire escape if the fire door was closer?" Clare asked reasonably. "Really, Quill. A burglar at ten o'clock in the evening? With half the dining room filled with happy eaters? I don't think so."

"But the lightbulbs have been removed from the carriage lamps."

"Was Mike doing building maintenance today?"

"Mike's always doing building maintenance."

"Well, there you are. Honestly, I think you're worried about nothing."

"Maybe you're right."

"Of course, if you want to knock on doors and see if anyone's missing anything I can help you do that." She yawned and hefted Bismarck over her shoulder. "Might annoy the guests. Is the Inn full up?"

"Not right now. There's nobody on this floor except Meg and me. The wedding guests are trickling in over the next few days, and then we're at a hundred percent for almost two weeks. Edmund Tree just arrived today, and three of the other rooms downstairs are filled with leafers." These tourists, in pursuit of the glorious autumn colors that turned upstate New York into living art, were a mainstay of the hotel trade in the fall.

"Bit early for them, isn't it? Although, come to think of it, we've had a couple of busloads in for wine tastings. Anyhow, that's not so many that we can't roust them out in a few minutes. I'm willing if you are."

Quill thought about knocking on Edmund Tree's door and asking him if he'd been burglarized. He was the type to raise a fuss. Or ask for a discount on his bill. Or flounce off to another hotel and get Rose Ellen in a swivet. Miriam had said there had been a rash of burglaries lately. Was there one person behind it? A gang? Gangs in Hemlock Falls? Was anything to be gained by raising a ruckus tonight? "Scarlett O'Hara," she said aloud.

"Huh?"

"That's code for I'll think about this tomorrow. Never mind. You're probably right. It's nothing."

Clare tickled Bismarck under the chin. He closed his eyes and began to purr. "Are you okay? I mean, you've seemed out of sorts lately. Is everything all right?"

"Everything is not all right," Quill said in some surprise. "But it's nothing I can put my finger on. I miss Myles, of course, but I knew what kind of schedule he had when we got married. Jack's wonderful. I'm a little worried about you and M—" She stopped herself. "Forget it. Things are just fine. I don't know what's wrong with me. Anyhow, I have been a little off lately. I apologize. And," she added suddenly remembering her mission to put their friendship back on track, "I am *so* glad that you took the first step and came over tonight."

Clare looked startled. "You are?"

"That delicate matter you mentioned . . ."

"Yes. I'm really hoping you can intercede for me."

"I'll do my best," Quill promised. "She's very reasonable, at heart."

"Do you think so?" Clare asked doubtfully. "That's not what I've heard. You remember that whole kerfuffle over the cat."

"She loves the cat," Quill said.

A faint chime sounded. The elevator doors in the middle of the hall opened up. Meg shoved herself off the elevator and trudged toward them. She looked as weary as Clare.

"Hey, sister," Quill said. "I see you un-wedged the elevator."

"Tree is definitely going to be one of those. You'd better keep Doreen away from the mop closet. She'll whack him a good one if he gets too aggravating." She eyed Clare warily. "I take it you're here to get the big boy back home again. Unless it's a front to get hold of some of my recipes. Ha-ha."

"Yes to the first. No to the second. Ha-ha," Clare said. The two of them eyed each other like a pair of gunslingers sizing each other up in a saloon.

Quill took a deep breath and prepared for battle. "It's been a while since we've had a chance to sit and just talk to each other."

Meg muttered under her breath. Quill ignored it. "Clare. Why don't you come in for a glass of wine before you leave?"

Clare patted the cat a little too hard. "Love to. There's something I'd like to discuss with you."

"Great. You hear that Meg? She came all the way over here just to discuss something with us."

"And to get her cat," Meg said sourly.

"And to get her cat. If you don't mind, could we sit in your place? And could we leave your door open so I can hear Jack if he wakes up?" Meg's rooms were directly across from Quill's.

"No problem."

"Maybe it's a little late," Clare said uncomfortably. "This was probably a bad idea. I should get back to the academy, anyhow. I've got a full day tomorrow."

"No problem," Meg said distantly. She paused with her hand on the doorknob, and then said, "I'm a little tired, though, so let's not prolong things, okay?"

Quill suppressed a sigh. Sometimes her little sister drove her nuts. "You still mad at me about this afternoon?"

Clare raised her eyebrows. "What happened this afternoon?"

"A small sisterly spat," Quill said. "Which shouldn't have happened, right, Meg?"

"No. Yes. Maybe." She grinned, suddenly, looking so much like their Welsh father with her gray eyes and dark hair that Quill's heart jumped a little. "Of course I forgive you."

Quill put her hands on her hips. "Who's forgiving who here?"

"I am forgiving you. Who yelled at me. And I'm sure you are now very, very sorry."

"I'm sorry I lost my temper, sure. But I'm definitely not sorry as to why."

"Whatever. Come on in. Forgive the mess."

Quill followed the two women into Meg's room. She'd lived here ever since they had opened the Inn twelve years before. The one thing made conspicuous by its absence was a kitchen. Meg had a coffeepot, a microwave, and a small kitchen sink. Her comfortable couch was covered in a non-descript khaki. There was a round pine table with four chairs and a shabby recliner sheltered by a reading lamp. The rest of the room was filled with stacks, piles, and baskets of cook-books, brightly colored throw pillows, and pots of healthy plants. Meg's balcony overlooked the front of the Inn, and there was a ghostly view of the waterfall under moonlight through her French doors.

"Have a seat, you guys."

Quill took a corner of the couch, which was where she usually sat. Clare sat down at the pine table and dropped Bismarck on the floor. Meg rummaged under the sink and emerged with a dusty bottle of wine. "A modest little Mouton Cadet I've been saving for a special occasion."

Clare laughed. "Sounds good to me."

"I take it that's not a wine for a special occasion?" Quill said.

Meg took three wineglasses out of the cupboard over the sink, and opened the bottle. "You would be right. But it's drinkable. Highly drinkable." She gave Clare a quick look. "So how was business tonight?"

"Good. And you?"

"Good. Very good."

"I guess you could say our business was very good, too."

There was a short, uncomfortable silence. Meg poured the wine, handed the glasses around, and sank into her recliner. "Very, very good."

Quill, who had restarted her practice of taking management courses at the nearby Cornell School of Hotel Administration, had completed the July session in Advanced Employee Relations: Conflict Resolution. She cleared her throat, pleased to put the hot hours in the classroom to some use. Rule One, she recalled, was to begin with positive feedback. "I thought we had a very effective meeting with Rose Ellen Whitman this morning. I wanted to take this opportunity to tell you both how impressed I was with how well you two got along."

"Rule One," Meg said. "Begin with positive reinforcement." She scowled. "I took that class with you, remember? The one on Conflict Resolution."

"Oh."

"You told me it would help keep things smooth in the kitchen."

"Conflict resolution is a very valuable tool to have on hand. As a matter of fact . . ."

"Phooey. Things are always peaceful in my kitchen," Meg said mendaciously. "In yours, too, Clare, I expect."

"Well, actually . . ."

Meg gulped her wine. "That class, Quill, was a total waste of time. I don't have any conflicts in the kitchen."

"How in the world do you manage that?" Clare said.

"She only hires people who agree with her," Quill said. "They have to pass a flexibility test, too. If they can't duck out of the way of the flying sauté pans, they risk significant head injury."

"Ha-ha," Meg said flatly. "So. Since there's no conflict in my kitchen, there's no problem."

"I think there is a problem," Quill said firmly. "Only it's not in the kitchen."

Clare nodded. "You're right. That's really why I came up here tonight. It wasn't just to get Biz back home."

"That's just wonderful, Clare, that you're willing to talk to Meg about the problem between the two of you. If we all can just sit down together and clear the air . . ."

"What problem?" Meg asked.

Clare rubbed her forehead, which spread the streak of grease across it into a bigger smudge. "I'm with Meg, Quill. You think there's a problem between Meg and me?"

Quill opened her mouth. She shut it. She took a sip of wine (which tasted okay to her, if not to her oenophile sister). "Just what are we talking about?"

"You both know Carol Ann Spinoza, right? I mean, you guys go way back."

"There's the time she put me in jail," Quill said, after a long moment. "And the time she raised the taxes on the Inn by forty percent. And the time she . . ."

"She put you in jail?"

Meg smiled. "Quill stole her purse."

"I did not steal her purse. I . . . appropriated it for a short period of time. It was necessary," Quill said a little stiffly. "We were in the middle of a murder investigation."

"You guys," Clare said with sudden fondness. "Did I ever tell you how grateful I am that you're such good detectives?"

"Yes," Meg said. "And we were happy to prove that you didn't murder Bernard LeVasque, although you probably should have way before the person who did. What about Carol Ann? She's the meanest person in Tompkins County. You don't want to mess with her, even if she isn't the tax inspector anymore. Remember what she tried to do to Bismarck, here." She reached down and petted Bismarck's ears. "She's not after Biz again, is she? I know what you can do. You can put one of those microchips in his ear so if she cat-naps him you can find him before she shoots him, or something."

"You haven't heard then. Carol Ann isn't animal control officer anymore."

"She's not?" Quill said.

"Heck no. She just took the exam for certification for another job. She's applying to become a licensed New York State food inspector. I think she'll get it. And from what I've heard she's bound and determined to close us all down."

Meg stared at her. Then she put both hands over her eyes and howled.

"Hey," Quill said. "You'll wake up Jack."

Meg clenched her fists and shook them at the ceiling. "I am moving to Detroit."

Clare scratched her head. "Why Detroit?"

"Or Burbank. Or Tuscaloosa. Anywhere but here. That woman! A food inspector! What could be worse?"

Clare paled. "She could get elected mayor. Oh my God. What if she wins the race for mayor?!"

"It's a secret ballot," Quill said. "Nobody's going to vote for Carol Ann as long as she can't find out they didn't. Of all the things to worry about, that's the least of it."

Clare brightened. "True. If she does get her inspection license, maybe the inspection people will assign her somewhere else. Like Buffalo. Or Syracuse."

"Maybe pigs will fly," Meg said. "But I don't think so." She drained her wineglass, poured a second glass and drained that, then peered into the depths of the bottle of Mouton Cadet. "One last little drop. Tell you what, Clare. We'll split it."

"You can have mine." Quill shoved her glass across the table. "I haven't touched it."

"Thanks, Sis." Meg straightened up. "You know what, Clare? If the state is nuts enough to certify that woman, we're going to have to stick together, you and me. One for all and all for one."

"It can't be that bad, surely? There have to be laws against abusing that position," Clare said dourly.

Neither woman seemed to realize Clare's comment all but admitted the tension between the two.

The class in conflict resolution had been pretty adamant about getting things out into the open. Quill took the plunge. "Perhaps now would be a good time to have a really honest discussion about how unspoken resentment can destroy a friendship."

Meg shook her head, ignoring Quill completely. "She's that bad. She's worse than bad. Worse than you can even imagine. I'll have to move to the Hundred Acre Wood and live under the name of Saunders." She got up and began to rummage under the sink. "We need a second bottle."

Clare and Meg had finished up the second bottle of wine and settled into a profound—thankfully silent—funk before Quill thought it time to say something. "You're right about one thing."

"I'm right about all of it," Meg said.

"It's important for you and Clare to stick together."

Clare's information had come from a friend in the inspection department. It was Quill's opinion that the threat to close Clare's kitchen down was mere saber-rattling on Carol Ann's part, but there was no denying that the woman knew the two most important things about any restaurant: the chefs were lunatics and given the thousands of regulations in the New York State restaurant code, somebody was always in violation of one obscure code or another. "Not just you two . . . all the restaurants in town should unite."

"All what restaurants?" Meg said in an argumentative way. "There's only four. There's me. There's Clare's Bonne Goutè. There's the resort, but they're owned by this huge conglomerate and they can survive any number of audits so they don't count. There's Marge Schmidt and Betty Hall with their two restaurants and that's it. Four. Against that obsessive-compulsive, neat-freak, squeaky-clean little bi . . ."

"Meg," Quill said.

". . . Nazi," Meg finished. "You know what, Clare? We need a third bottle."

"I agree," Clare said, enunciating her words very carefully. "I totally, totally agree. Totally, totally, totally. But if you want my candid opinion . . ."

"We do," Meg said earnestly.

"We're screwed."

"Screwed," Meg echoed.

"You're forgetting something," Quill said. "There's Marge. And I'd back Marge Schmidt against Carol Ann for mayor any day of the week." She stood up. "I've got a plan. And I'm going to bed."

Meg peered up at her blearily. "Marge? What kind of solution is that? Marge. Marge. That's all you have to say?"

"Just one more thing: I'd think twice about opening that third bottle of wine."

5

~Meg Quilliam's~
Hangover Remedy

8 ounces freshly squeezed tomato juice
1 raw egg, lightly beaten
2 tablespoons each chopped onion, chopped parsley
1 tablespoon kosher salt
1 chopped jalapeño pepper

Whisk together. Drink.

Quill woke to sunshine streaming in the window and the warm breath of her son in her hair. He smelled of peanut butter. The sunlight struck red gold highlights from his curly hair.

"Are you up, Mommy?"

She pulled him close to her, the familiar sense of poignant joy at the miracle of his presence in her life putting every other concern out of her head. "I'm up. Are you up?"

"I've been up forever."

"Is that peanut butter I smell?"

"Max is up, too. He wanted peanut butter. I told him: No,

Max, no. Mommy said peanut butter is not for boys to make all by themselves. But Max didn't listen. He still wanted peanut butter. So he had it."

"How did Max get the jar open?"

Jack tucked his hand into hers, confidingly. "I tested it, in case it was not good for dogs."

"And was it?"

"It was pretty good for dogs. But I tested it a lot before Max ate some."

Quill wiped a smear of peanut butter off his cheek. "I can see that you did."

She let nothing short of a cataclysm interfere with her morning rituals with Jack, which sometimes gave her a late start on the day. He'd been pretty good about the peanut butter; mainly because Max had licked clean both the jar and the bulk of sticky mess on the floor of the kitchen. She was just finishing up Jack's bath when Doreen's familiar rat-a-tat-tat announced her arrival. She stumped in and without any preliminaries said, "Your sister's down in the kitchen looking sick as a dog."

"Gramma Doreen!" Jack shouted. He held both arms up. Doreen swung him onto her hip and gave him a hearty kiss.

"I'm not surprised. Clare Sparrow came over last night and they got into the wine."

"Oh?" Doreen's beady black eyes narrowed. "They fightin' over who's the better cook again?"

"On the contrary. They have united against a common foe. They had their arms around each other and they were singing the chorus to 'Titanic' for the fourth time when I went to bed. There seems to be a temporary truce in place. You want to know how come?"

"You're going to tell me anyways."

Quill did.

Doreen sucked her lower lip and shook her head. "Somebody ought to send that Carol Ann a one-way ticket to the South Pole in nothing but her birthday suit."

"One good thing's come out of it already. Clare and Meg agreed that the restaurants all have to stick together."

Doreen snorted. "Huh! Maybe them two swore off the wine for the rest of their natural lives, too, but I doubt it. Meg was slugging down that tomato juice thing she makes like there was no tomorrow." Doreen jiggled Jack up and down. "How's my big boy this morning?"

"Hungry," Jack said. "Max opened the jar and ate the peanut butter. And there is no peanut butter left for me."

"We'll fix that, young Jack-a-rootie."

Quill looked at the sunlight playing off Jack's curly hair and had a passionate longing to play hooky. "Actually, I don't think I'll need you today, Doreen. I want to take Jack over to Peterson Park and play on the swings and paddle in the river if it's warm enough. Then maybe we'll drive into Syracuse and stop at Gymboree. He could use some new clothes."

Doreen slung Jack over her shoulder. "You just got home from a whole month of R and R with Jack and the sheriff."

"Myles isn't the sheriff anymore, Doreen. Myles hasn't been sheriff since he promoted Davy and left to work for the government."

"Whatever. Thing is, you got too much to do to go haring off with the boy. You got the Chamber in a hoorah over this mayor's race," she continued relentlessly. "You got Meg and Clare drunk as skunks. And now you got Carol Ann sneaking around our kitchens."

"She isn't a food inspector yet."

"She will be," Doreen said ominously. "Plus, you got that prissy little jerk in two-twelve messing with the elevators and that snooty fiancée of his stinking up the place. I'm surprised she don't trip over her own feet, her nose is stuck so high in the air. You got half the town swiping stuff from the other half of the town so they can snoot it over the next one on that durn TV show . . ."

"You've heard about the burglaries in town, then?"

"You bet I heard about 'em. All our old families have been getting ripped off. You ask me, it's those TV people trying to get aholt of the good stuff before everyone else. You just hear about that? You missed a lot on the monthlong vacation of yours."

"The TV people just got into town," Quill said. "They can't be behind the thefts."

Doreen looked lofty. "It's got nothing to do with me."

"Do you have any idea who it is? Because last night I heard someone sneaking down the stairs."

"No kidding? You call Davy?"

"I don't know if anything's missing yet." Quill frowned. Doreen didn't supervise the housekeeping staff anymore now that she was taking care of Jack, but she bullied the woman she'd promoted to the job unmercifully. "Ask around the housekeeping staff, would you? See if any of the guests have made a complaint."

"Will do."

"Have you heard any gossip in the village about who it might be?"

"Maybe I know, and maybe I can guess and maybe I ain't going to do either. You know me. I'm not one to gossip."

Quill snorted.

"Anyways. With all this goin' on, you're sailing off with Jack? That's not good at all. You got to do something about all of this."

"There's not much I can do," Quill said feebly.

"Investigate!"

"I promised Myles I wouldn't anymore."

"If you're not going to investigate, what *are* you going to do about everything?"

"I'm going to the park with Jack."

Doreen fixed her with a beady eye. "Missy. You got a mission, here. And as long as I've known you, you haven't flunked it yet."

"Fine," Quill said loftily. "Okay. I'll fix it all. I am going to do what I do best."

"What in heck would that be?" She brightened. "We got a murder yet? Are we going to be detecting?"

"No murder," Quill said firmly. "I certainly hope there won't be."

"I can think of a few folks I'd like to knock off myself, starting with that Carol Ann."

"I'm going to delegate."

"Delegate? What's that when it's at home? You mean you're planning to tell a lot of other people to do stuff? Long as I've been here you haven't been able to boss anybody yet."

"You just watch me. Keep your cell phone on. I'll be back to pick up the kid by early afternoon, at the latest."

"I'm not holding my breath."

She turned Jack over to Doreen, stuck the tissue-covered lightbulb into a Baggie and back into her pocket, and went downstairs.

It was still just short of eight o'clock. She marched purposefully toward her office. She'd put everyone else to work, and spend time with Jack. And if they resisted? Ha! Like Caesar charming the senate, she'd refuse the job of dictator and decline to rule Rome. Of course, it hadn't worked out all that well for Julius, but that may have been because Julius hadn't stuck to his guns. Or dagger, as the case might be.

Delegation. That was the key.

Quill paused at the foot of the stairs in the foyer. Dina wasn't in yet. She took a quick look into the dining room. Edmund Tree was at breakfast, disdainfully cutting off the top of an egg. Three of the other tables were occupied, but basically, the dining room was quiet. No one paid any attention to her at all.

First? Somehow, she had to contain Carol Ann. Marge Schmidt would run right over that obsessively tidy, revenge-minded bundle of cleanliness quirks. Marge was a fearsome opponent, and she wasn't going to be any happier than Meg and Clarissa at the thought of Carol Ann's latex-gloved little paws poking around their kitchens.

Quill took out her sketch pad and wrote: *Mrg to take down CAS.*

Burglars? She'd turn over the suspicious lightbulb to Davy Kiddermeister and let the burglars fall where they may.

She added *Dvy lghtblb* to the burgeoning list.

The mayor's race? She would stay totally out of it.

Edmund Tree and the impossible Barcinis? She glanced into the dining room again. Edmund had finished decapitating his egg and was spreading marmalade on a piece of toast. If Rose Ellen Whitman and her crummy fiancé gave her a minute's more aggravation, she'd move the entire wedding party to Peterson Park. She'd leave the Barcinis to the tender mercies of the Marriott on Route 15.

She'd have all the time in the world to paddle with Jack in the river.

She walked into her office to find Bismarck sitting on her desk, his large furry rump obscuring her to-do list. He regarded her with a baleful eye.

"You still here?"

Bismarck squeezed his yellow eyes shut and opened them again.

"That does not bode well for the dynamic wine-drinking duo. Is Clare sacked out on Meg's couch?"

Bismarck yawned and began to groom his tail in a relaxed and purposeful way.

Bismarck wasn't worried about the creepy corruption of Hemlock Falls by greedy outsiders. He could give a cat's whisker about Rose Ellen's impossible arrogance. He didn't give a rat's behind for Edmund Tree and the equally awful Barcinis and he remained indifferent to any burglars that might be skulking about the place. There was a lot to be said for a cat's attitude toward life. Meg and Clare seemed united in their opposition to Carol Ann Spinoza, which meant they weren't going to be sparring with each other anytime soon. Whether Marge or Elmer ended up being mayor, Hemlock Falls would still be Hemlock Falls.

The cat lived happily in the moment, and so, by God, would she.

She sat down behind her desk, hoisted him onto her lap, and brushed tufts of yellow fur off her hands.

Her to-do list was nice and short.

She had promised to drop by the high school at ten o'clock. Edmund Tree and his minions were beginning the process of deciding who would actually star on the televised show. She didn't have any objects to offer—antique or otherwise—and her presence was more a matter of support than anything else. So she'd have to do that.

She'd scheduled a meeting with waitstaff and housekeeping at one, to go over the changes to Rose Ellen's plans for the wedding. Kathleen could take care of that.

There were five or six suppliers to call to confirm delivery of stuff for the wedding. Dina was good at that.

Five wedding guests were due to check in today—the group of assessors who staffed the *Ancestor's Attic* show. Rose Ellen—who was proving to be as obsessive as Carol Ann about detail—had attached short bios of each of them when she'd arranged the reservations.

Quill sighed. There was one important job at the Inn she couldn't delegate, and that was knowing enough about the guests to make them feel welcome and comfortable. She rummaged through her in-box to find the notes Rose Ellen had given her on the rest of the wedding party.

The first names on the list were Phillip and Andrea Bryant. Phillip—Skipper, said the note in Rose Ellen's careful handwriting—was an expert in sixteenth-century trompe l'oeil. Quill very much doubted that Hemlockians had any such oils in their attics, but you never knew. He apparently had a working knowledge of European and North American paintings from the sixteenth century on and a sideline in document authentication.

Bryant's wife Andrea was an expert in North American

pottery, with a specialty in Dutch, Amish, and Mennonite crafts. That was more promising. There were several thriving Amish parishes within driving distance of the village.

Jukka Angstrom was a Finn from Sotheby's. He had an "interest," Rose Ellen wrote, in fine china, but his true area of expertise was Victorian and turn-of-the-century jewelry.

Melanie Myers was listed as Edmund Tree's producer-assistant. Rose Ellen had written:

> *Edmund's little dog—seems to think she knows something about early-twentieth-century Americana. She doesn't. Has a new degree from RSI in costume design. Tiresome creature! Edmund's a friend of her family—only way she could get the job.*

Quill would try to be around to greet them as they checked in, but she'd long ago learned this wasn't essential as long as she spent time with them later on. Edmund and Rose Ellen had booked the Tavern Lounge for their engagement party that evening. She could drop in to meet them then. They'd probably be at the auditions at the high school, too.

She wondered, not for the first time, if the *Attic* crew was going to turn up anything of interest. What happened to the show when all they came up with was garage sale stuff? Would they pack up their tents and go home?

The last item to take care of was the de-bulbed carriage lamps on the fire escape stairs. She wrote *Mike!* on the list, and sat back in her chair.

Dina could handle the guests and Mike. She herself would handle the staff meetings. The other two matters—Carol Ann and the suspicious lightbulb—she would hand off to Marge and Davy Kiddermeister first thing this morning. She folded the list and stuck it into her skirt pocket with a feeling of a job well done.

There was a tap at the door and Dina walked in. "You look happy this morning. Hey, Biz, how are you doing?"

Biz jerked to attention and stared past Dina at the open door. He jumped off Quill's lap and marched out. Quill saw Clare stumble past, her hair awry. She raised a hand feebly and headed to the front door.

"Looks like she had a tough night," Dina said. "So what's on the agenda for this morning?"

"I've decided to roll with the punches and let the chips fall where they may," Quill said proudly. "I am taking a catlike attitude toward life. There are no crises. There is only perspective."

"Okay. So that means what?"

"It means I'll be out most of the morning on business, and then I'm taking Jack to the Park."

"You're taking Jack to the Park? With all this going on?"

"I'm delegating. Which means, don't call me unless somebody's on fire or bleeding. It's too gorgeous outside to waste the time with Jack. And there's no major crises anyway."

"No crises? You haven't heard about the mayor's race? That's going to tear this town apart. And the burglaries? You missed a lot on that monthlong vacation you took, Quill."

"Phooey," Quill said. "If you ask me, it'll all blow over. All Marge needs is another project to divert her attention, and I've got an idea how to do that. As far as the mayor's race— who the heck is going to vote for Carol Ann? Marge has too many irons in the fire to waste time being mayor. Nope. Marge is going to drop out of the race and Elmer will get reelected and things are going to be just fine. Change," she added, as she slung her tote over her arm, "can be a very healthy thing. Especially if you ignore it. Oh. I left a couple of things for you to do. The list is right here. But otherwise, we are going to keep ourselves to ourselves, as the Irish say."

Dina held a fistful of pink While You Were Out message slips. She looked at them doubtfully. "So our new management tactic is to ignore stuff?"

"Not stuff related to the Inn, of course. We're running a business. We're just going to ignore things *extraneous* to the Inn."

"An isolationist policy, you mean. Like in World War One."

"Sort of," Quill said cautiously.

"Because it didn't work for Wilson and I don't think it can work for us."

Quill took a deep breath.

"So what do you want me to do with these?" Dina waved the message slips. "Throw 'em out?"

"Let's not call it an isolationist policy. Let's call it a non-busybody policy." Quill hesitated. Old habits were difficult to change. The While You Were Out messages were too insistent. "Are there any of those messages that we can safely ignore?"

"Four of them are from Mayor Henry. Important Chamber business, he said."

Quill made a noise like "phuut!"

"One's from the Hemlock Falls *Gazette*. They want a statement from you about the three-way mayor's race. Who are you going to support? They'd like a comment about the burglaries, too, since you're the best amateur detective in town."

"I'm the only amateur detective in town."

"Huh," Dina said, who had helped on several of the cases. "There's been a lot of gossip about whether or not you're going to take on the case."

"There you go. A perfect example of things we can ignore. We are staying out of the mayor's race. I am retired as a detective, since I became a mother. Forget any statements to the newspaper. What else?"

"Two messages are from Rose Ellen Whitman. Important wedding business, she said."

"Refer her to Kathleen."

"One's from Harvey Bozzel. Important advertising . . ." Quill made a "get on with it" motion with both hands. "Okay. He says you have something for him and what time should he pick it up?"

"I don't have anything for him, do I?" Quill sorted fruitlessly through the piles of paper on her desk until she unearthed the sketchbook that she used for taking Chamber minutes. She flipped to the page recording yesterday's meeting. "I don't. Could you call him and see what it is?"

"I'll bet he wants to get your opinion on the mayor's race."

"I do not have an opinion on the mayor's race. Like Sweden. I'm neutral."

Dina frowned. "Do you think we can get away with that?"

"We *are* going to get away with that."

"If you say so. You're the boss. So that's about it for messages. I really don't think you should ignore any of them."

"Fine." Quill grabbed the message slips, "Out of all those messages, there's only one I need to do myself. I'll call Elmer. The rest I am going to delegate. To you. Tell everybody 'no comment.'" She picked up the landline and punched in Elmer's number.

He picked up on the first ring and responded to her greeting with suspicious heartiness. "Why, Quill. Always delighted to hear from you. How's everything up there at the Inn?"

"Just fine, Elmer. Dina said you had some Chamber business to discuss?"

"Sure do. I'm Chamber president and it's about me. Wanted to know if I could book a party of six for lunch today. Round two o'clock. Know it's a little late, but I got that shindig up to the high school. The auditions. The missus is going to give Mr. Tree an advance peek at a couple of goodies for the show, and we'd like to take him to lunch after. Figure it's the least we can do."

"I'll be happy to let Dina make the reservations for you, Mayor."

Elmer's heartiness increased to a nervous roar. "And now that you've brought it up, that's the other thing I wanted to discuss with you. I know I've got your endorsement for the election, but I was thinking maybe you wouldn't mind doing a little quick sketch for the campaign poster. Adela says there's nobody like you to give it a touch of class. I know it don't take you all that long to whip up a little something, so I asked Harvey to drop by today to pick it up. Anytime you're ready."

"Mayor, I . . ."

"Love to hear you give me that title." He chuckled. "That'll be it then. Thank you for bein' the first to get on board the Keep Hemlock Falls Happy with Henry campaign. Thank you very much. Gotta go! And you go ahead and make room for yourself at our table at two."

He hung up.

Quill dropped the receiver into the cradle.

"Are you going to call him back?" Dina asked. "Tell him that with our new isolationist policy we can't endorse anybody for mayor?"

"Yes," Quill said.

"Are you going to do it right now?"

"No," Quill said.

"Smart," Dina approved. "That's his home phone and Adela's there and Elmer's got caller ID. He'll know it's you and she'll pick up and she'll roll right over you."

"I can handle Adela."

"So call."

Quill didn't move.

"I'm thinking you might not want to call Harvey back, either. He'll want the poster."

"You'd be right." Quill gathered her tote with a sigh.

Dina patted her on the shoulder. "Don't worry about a thing. You just get back here as soon as you can so you can get Jack to Peterson Park."

6

~Betty Hall's Upstate Pancakes~

4 strips maple bacon
2½ cups flour
2 eggs
1 cup milk
1 tablespoon baking powder
2 tablespoons sugar

Fry bacon in cast-iron skillet. Do not drain. Mix all ingredients and pour over bacon. Put skillet in preheated 350-degree oven for thirty-five minutes or until puffed and brown. Ladle seasonal berries over top and serve with whipped cream.

She decided to walk down to the village. At this hour, Marge would be in one of two places: her realty office or having breakfast at her All-American Diner (Fine Food! And Fast!). She checked the diner first and found Marge eating hash browns in the front booth.

"'Lo, Quill."

"Hey, Marge." Quill slid into the booth opposite her. Marge

looked the same as always: chinos, windbreaker, and ginger hair, except that she'd exchanged yesterday's red-checked shirt for a blue.

The All-American Diner wasn't the same at all. Quill had stopped in the restaurant in early August, just before she and Myles had taken Jack to the Adirondacks, and she hadn't been back since. Marge and Betty had remodeled with a vengeance.

The Formica tabletops had been replaced with knotty pine. Muslin panels hung at the windows, replacing the old daisy-print curtains. Ferns in ceramic pots hung from the ceiling. Vivaldi drifted over the speakers. A few of the old farmers from the outskirts of town slouched at the breakfast counter, but the tables were filled with trendy couples from nearby Syracuse and well-dressed retirees. The familiar homey diner was gone. Even the air smelled different.

Quill squelched her dismay with a determined recollection of her new attitude toward change. It was quite nice, really, even if she was up to her eyeballs with endless repetitions of *The Four Seasons*. It was better than endless repetitions of Pachelbel's *Canon*. The diner just wasn't the familiar place she'd loved for so long. She could learn to love this, too.

"When did all this happen? While Myles and I were away?"

"You like it?"

"I guess so." She had a sudden, unwelcome thought. "You didn't make any changes to the Croh Bar, did you?" The bar had been a much-loved, very successful village staple since 1942. When Marge had acquired it several years ago, she'd replaced the tattered furnishings with exact replicas of the orange-flowered indoor-outdoor carpeting and cheap wood venetian blinds, so that the bar looked the same only smelled better. It had been a smart move, but then, Marge hadn't become the richest woman in a five-county area by sheer luck.

"Figured with all the tourists washing in and out, it was time to spruce this place up a bit. Don't know about the Croh, yet. Don't get a lot of the tourist trade in there."

Quill looked around for the sticky plastic menu that advertised Betty Hall's superb diner cooking.

"Looking for the menu?" Marge pointed toward the counter. The red vinyl-topped stools had been replaced with maple captain's chairs. The counter top itself was a handsome butcher block. A blackboard propped on an easel stood at the farthest end. "Menu's on the chalkboard. It's the same thing every day, but the tourists don't know that. Looks fancier to write it down, like the chef has to think about it. Saves on printing menus, too."

Quill squinted, but she couldn't read it. "Does Betty still make those wonderful Upstate Pancakes?"

"Nope." She gestured toward the well-dressed couples. "This lot's fonder of yogurt."

"Meg always said Betty was the best diner cook on the continent. And those pancakes were just sensational."

"Meg would be right. But the customers don't care for the carbs. You'll want the spinach eggs. Lot of carbs in that, too, but the vegetable part makes up for it."

"That sounds just fine."

Marge finished the last forkful of hash browns, shouted, "Betts! Special!" and buttered a piece of toast.

"You're doing well, I take it?"

"Never better." Marge crunched the toast between her strong white teeth. "The time away did you good, I think. Myles is off again?"

"Yes."

"Hope they didn't post him to Libya."

"Me, too."

Marge smiled at her, reminding Quill of the crocodile in the children's poem. "Kinda glad you dropped by. If you hadn't, I was going to come up to see you."

"Oh?"

"Figure you'll give me your endorsement for mayor. Need the whole Chamber on my side for this campaign. Except for Elmer, of course." She shrugged. "Town's going to follow what the Chamber wants to do. Always does. Figure I'd start with you, since the Chamber will probably follow your lead."

Quill blinked. "They will?"

"Funny that they do, isn't it? You keep the worst minutes of anyone I ever met, but you keep getting reelected as Chamber secretary, year after year. And folks seem to listen to you."

Quill was momentarily diverted by a familiar grievance. "I don't even run for secretary. I don't want to be secretary. I mean, every two years I tell you I'm not running and every two years people write me in on the ballot and I go ahead and fold and end up doing it."

"People like you. Even if you are a nitwit about the minutes."

"Oh." She could feel herself blushing. "Um. Well."

"You don't push, see. Anyone can run right over you, and people like that."

"I doubt that," she said indignantly.

"You think? It's a fact. Now me, not many people can run right over me."

Quill thought of several replies to this and rejected all of them. "That's true."

"I'm not all that likeable, though."

"I like you."

"Yeah, but you're a pushover. You like everybody. Except that Carol Ann."

"Speaking of Carol Ann . . ."

Marge was in steamroller mode and rolled right over this. She hunched over confidingly. "There is a direct relationship between success in business and the likeability factor, if you will. The more likeable a person is, the less chance they have of making it big. It's a constant surprise to Betts and me that you've managed to hang onto the Inn all these years."

Quill rubbed her forehead. She was getting a headache.

"You ought to read more of the *Wall Street Journal*. You think anyone loves Rupert Murdoch? One of the richest men in the world and definitely the toughest son of a gun in the valley." She sat back and slapped her hands on the tabletop. "Anyway. I don't give a rat's behind about being liked or not, but when I set out to do something, I do it. I'm fixing to be the next mayor of this town, and you're going to help me do it."

"So this isn't about the parking meters. Not really."

"I need a popular platform, and getting rid of those parking meters is about the hottest political issue in town at the moment."

Betty Hall came up to the table, balancing a plate of eggs in one hand and a coffeepot in the other. She didn't say anything—she never did—but she put the plate down, poured

Quill a cup of coffee, then gripped Quill's shoulder in solidarity.

"We're on it, Bets," Marge said. "She's gonna go for it. She's gonna design the campaign poster, too. I've got Harvey lined up to do the printing on it. We're having a strategy meeting right now."

Betty nodded and stumped away. Quill looked at the special; two perfectly poached eggs on a bed of freshly sautéed spinach. The whole meal was drizzled with hollandaise. A round of golden potato straws nestled in one corner of the plate. She picked up a forkful and put it down.

"I've been thinking about a campaign slogan." Marge shoved her plate to one side and put her elbows on the table. "This People for Free Parking has got a ring to it, there's no doubt about that. But I'm thinking there ought to be something catchy, too. A slogan, like. You know what I mean?"

Quill felt herself nodding yes.

"Tote bags are big. You remember those tote bags up to the academy?"

"The ones with Monsieur LeVasque's face on them? Everybody remembers those. They were gross, Marge. And Madame LeVasque had to recycle every single one of them after he . . . um . . . died."

"Good PR, though. I'm thinking I should order a couple of thousand totes and with the right kind of message my face would be all over Hemlock Falls. Maybe a replica of the ballot with a big red check on my name that says Park It Here. And underneath, one of those little sketches you do at the Chamber meetings."

"Sketches?"

"The doodling you do when you're supposed to be taking

the minutes. I saw that one you did a couple of years ago of me chasing Elmer with a Whac-a-Mole mallet."

"You did? How did . . ."

"You leave the sketch pad laying on the conference table half the time. Everybody knows to look for those cartoons. Anyhow. The Whac-a Mole one was cute. Except I'm not that fat. I was thinking if you did the same kind of doodle, only it's me sitting on Elmer, not whacking him with the mallet, it would make that tote stand out, for sure. You know, you could draw him wriggling and screaming like. It would give a what-do-you-call-it, double meaning to the slogan. 'Park It Here' on the ballot, so it's like 'vote for me,' and 'Park It Here' with me squashing Elmer. Like, 'get rid of this mayor.'"

Quill grabbed her hair with both hands and tugged at it.

"Harland's all for it, of course." Then, her cheeks slightly pink, she said. "Seems to think it's creative. Says he's never heard of anything like it before. You aren't eating your eggs. Something wrong with 'em?"

Quill picked up her fork and began to eat her eggs. "Terrific," she said, through a mouthful of hollandaise.

"Anyway, we need to get started right away."

Quill swallowed. "If we could just set that aside for the moment, I was wondering what you'd think about starting a restaurant owners group."

"Don't have time for it. Don't see a need for it, anyways."

"Well, with all of the growth in town, I was thinking it might be good if we had an association of our own. Those of us in the food business, you see, have a lot of common interests."

Marge grunted.

"And we aren't very well represented in a . . . governmental sort of way. There's a Realtors association, and you're president of that, and Tompkins County insurance group, and you're president of that. I think you'd make a splendid president of a restaurant owners group. We could call it the Village Restaurant Association."

"Doesn't have a lot of zing to it."

"I'm sure you could think of something better. But this organization could act as a go-between with oh, say, the New York State food inspectors, the USDA, that kind of thing."

"I'll think about it." Marge looked at her watch. "It's getting on toward ten. You going down to the high school for the auditions?"

"I told Rose Ellen I'd be there, yes. But if you wanted to talk more about this association idea I have . . ."

"I figure the shoot's as good a place as any to start letting folks know about my campaign. That's what they call it, right? A shoot?"

"It's just the assessors checking out the items to be evaluated. It's quite pleasant here, Marge, and we could sort of sketch out a battle plan for this restaurant thing."

"Everybody in town's bound to be there."

"This association could take a firm stand, a very firm stand, on some of the more unreasonable demands of, say, the food inspectors."

"Bets never has problems with the food inspectors. Keeps the cleanest kitchen in Tompkins County. C'mon. I want to get to the auditions." Marge slid out of the booth and stood up. "Harland went through the old barn and found a whole bunch of stuff his grandpa used to farm back before the war. Some of those tools are pretty interesting. Might be valuable, too. You and Meg dig anything up?"

"Actually, since Myles and I were out of town in August, I forgot all about it. To tell you the truth I can't think of anything that'd be suitable anyway. Honestly, Marge, the real problem behind the . . ."

Marge grabbed her by the elbow and hauled her to her feet. "You drive down from the Inn or did you walk? Walked, I bet. Come on and hop in. You can ride with me. I brought the farm pickup to carry the old tools. You can help me unload 'em."

Quill gave up and followed Marge to her pickup truck.

It was quite a nice one, with the Peterson Dairy Farm logo on the driver's side door. The rear bed was filled with an assortment of scythes, hay forks, a butter churn, and half a dozen old metal milk jugs. Marge paused halfway into the driver's seat. "So what d'ya think that lot's worth?"

"Quite a lot, I should expect," Quill said diplomatically. She hoisted herself into the passenger side, which was partly obscured by Marge's purse and a tattered copy of a price guide to antique farm tools. She picked it up and handed it over. "Actually, you know I haven't a clue. Do you think you have something valuable?"

Marge shoved the catalogue under the seat. "Well, we're going to find out what some people think, anyways."

The high school sat between the southern border of Peterson Park and Maple Avenue, the last residential street within the village limits. It served around seven hundred students, much reduced from the tide of postwar babies in the '60s. The two-story brick school complex always reminded Quill of a movie she had seen with Meg when she was six and Quill was twelve. It was set in a two-story brick insane asylum. Meg had nightmares for a week.

The brick was a grouchy orange red. The roof was an uninspiring asphalt shingle. English ivy straggled around the foundation in a dispirited way. The trim around the double-hung windows was an off-white doing its best to look lively. The whole school was saved by the grounds. Black walnuts, oaks, aspen, mountain ash, and birch surrounded the school on three sides. The lawns were patchy, but the magnificence of the trees gave the school a glad serenity.

The administration offices, gym, and auditorium were in the middle, with the wings containing classrooms stretching out either side. The parking lot in front of the admin building was full, as both women had expected. A couple of kids in orange vests were directing traffic to the athletic field to the rear, which, Marge remarked philosophically, was just fine because the auditorium entrance was around the back, too.

They followed the single lane around the east end of the building

"Good grief," Quill said as they came to a halt behind a line of cars waiting to park. "How can they possibly hold classes with all this commotion?"

"They aren't," Marge said. "The current mayor—who isn't going to be mayor long—talked to the school board and everybody got the day off."

"Looks like they didn't take it."

The athletic field was jammed with cars, vans, pickup trucks, SUVs, and even an old bus. A steady stream of people walked toward the large double doors to the auditorium. The doors were propped wide open. Two large men in sunglasses, sports coats, and chinos stood on either side of the entrance, arms folded. They looked so much like airport security guards that Quill expected them to pat down the people trying to get into the auditorium.

Most of the people in line carried an astonishing variety of stuff: paintings, vases, lamps, old books, small tables, ladder-backed chairs, antique boxes, old clothes, tote bags, wrapped parcels. A smell of mold drifted through the air. The mood of the people streaming in was cheery and hope-filled.

A smaller but equally steady stream of people came out the side door of the auditorium. They were also carrying stuff. Most of them looked huffy. A few were indignant. One or two turned and shouted into the auditorium. All were sour-faced. Quill began to see how Edmund Tree might feel the need for two hefty guys as a matter of defense.

"Rejects," Marge said with interest. "I wondered how they were going to handle this. Must be another guy right inside the door. Takes one look at what you've got and you either get the old heave-ho or the go-ahead."

"Uh-oh." Quill opened the passenger side door and got out. "Look at that bus."

"What bus?" Marge eased herself out of the pickup and squinted at it. "That bus? It's an old school bus painted like the hippie vans in the sixties. What about . . . oh. Well, well, well."

"That's the *Pawn-o-Rama* bus," Quill said, quite unnecessarily, since the side was scrawled with the name of the show in neon orange.

"I watch *Pawn-o-Rama*. Old Belter knows his stuff." She nudged Quill in the ribs. "Look. There he is getting out of the bus. Belter himself. Who's that in the sequin T-shirt? The one carrying the camera?"

"That's a Steadicam," Quill said knowledgeably. "And that's his mother."

"Kind of young to be his mother."

Quill cocked her head and squinted into the sunlight. The woman with the Steadicam was a younger, smoother-faced version of Mrs. Barcini. "You're right. I'll bet it's Josephine, his sister. They're all named alike. His mother's name is Josepha. His name is Joseph. His sister's the camera person on the show from the looks of it. His mother's the producer. They all look amazingly similar, don't they?"

Marge grunted.

"His mother is the one in the tie-dye T-shirt, right behind him." Quill closed her eyes and shook her head to clear it. Then she opened them again. "What do you suppose they're doing here?"

Marge chuckled. "I got a pretty good idea."

"You do?" Quill did, too. She bit her fingernail.

Belter's standard uniform appeared to be shorts, flip-flops, and a succession of T-shirts sized for a thinner man. Today's T-shirt was black. The Pawn-o-rama logo stretched over his belly in electric yellow, orange, and red. He sauntered up to security guy number one, and slapped him on the back. He gave the high sign to security guard number two. Then he waded into the line of hopefuls streaming into the auditorium, grinning, shaking hands, and slapping backs.

"Preemptive strike," Marge said. "Telling people to check with him before they sell anything to Tree."

Belter put one arm around Nadine Peterson in a friendly way. She blushed and opened up the large green garbage bag she carried. He peered into it and shouted "Yahoo!" The security guards exchanged glances and squared their shoulders. The shorter one pulled out his cell phone. The other started after Belter.

Marge began to chuckle. "Good old Belter. You coming with me? I want to get over there."

"Belter wants to talk to them before they sell anything to Tree?" Quill echoed. "But the show just values antiques, they don't buy anything."

Marge rolled her eyes. "Rose Ellen Whitman's got a junk shop, right?"

"A high-end boutique."

"And Belter's got a pawn shop, right? You sell and buy stuff in a pawn shop. You buy and sell stuff in a what-d'ya-call-it? High-end boutique? Old stuff. There's a limited amount of old stuff around. Towns like ours with attics and basements filled with junk are getting harder and harder to find. Belter's out there scoping out the action for himself."

Quill was taken aback. "You know, it never occurred to me that Edmund might be a source for Rose Ellen's stock."

"It should have. Jeez. Does your mother know you're out? Come on. Things are heating up over there."

Josephine Barcini stepped in front of the security guard who had started after Belter and directed the Steadicam into his face. The shorter security guard stuck his cell phone in his belt and shoved the camera away. Mrs. Barcini hit him from behind with her purse. Then Mrs. Barcini screamed: "Doughhead!"

Marge set off at a sturdy trot. Quill hurried after her. By the time they crossed the worn grass to the auditorium doors, the security guards were surrounded by shouting, shoving

Barcinis and a crowd of confused villagers. Nadine Peterson clutched her green garbage bag to her chest. Next to her, Esther West cradled a tissue-wrapped package and looked wildly from side to side. Harvey Bozzel held a majolica vase over his head to avoid the forward and backward sway of the crush. He caught sight of Quill and mouthed: "Help."

Marge grabbed Nadine by the arm and towed her to the sidewalk. Then she took the package from Esther and shoved her in Nadine's direction. She poked Harvey in the ribs to get his attention, gave him Esther's package, and jerked her thumb over her shoulder. Holding both items up as if wading through a waist-deep puddle, Harvey went and stood by Esther and Nadine.

Marge tapped Mrs. Barcini on the back, ducked Mrs. Barcini's roundhouse right, and grabbed her by the neck. Mrs. Barcini's eyes bulged.

"Hey!" Belter shouted. "That's my mamma you've got by the throat!"

Josephine Barcini swung the camera around in an eager circle.

"You're under arrest," Marge said to Mrs. Barcini.

Mrs. Barcini's lips formed the word "Doughhead."

Belter's face reddened. He shoved the security guards out of his way and advanced on Marge. Quill moved forward to stop him.

Marge glared at him. "You're under arrest, too, buster. Disturbing the peace." She released her grip on Mrs. Barcini's throat. "Write 'em up, Quill."

Quill opened her mouth and then shut it.

"I'm making a citizen's arrest," Marge said. She nodded in Quill's direction. "I don't need to tell you, Barcini, that a citizen's arrest is valid when a public offense is committed in the presence of the arresting private citizen. That's me." She looked around the circle of startled faces and said, "You all want to remember that when you walk into that polling booth and vote for me for mayor." She turned back to Barcini. "This is the duly appointed secretary of the Chamber of Commerce. She's going to write up the ticket."

Quill started and fumbled in her skirt pocket for her sketch pad. She found a lightbulb in a Baggie instead. What was she doing with a lightbulb in her pocket?

Marge raised her voice, apparently under the misapprehension that she wasn't loud enough already. "And then I'm taking you down to the sheriff's office where you can explain to Sheriff Kiddermeister where you get off starting a riot in my town and why I had to rescue three of our finest citizens from you and your thugs."

A faint cheer sounded from the three rescued citizens.

"Thugs? What thugs! My mamma and my sister?" Belter said. "There's no riot, either. And if there was a riot, it wasn't me that started anything. You want thugs, you get a load of these two."

The two security guards resettled their sunglasses and looked impassive.

"Are you all perfectly demented?" Edmund Tree stepped out of the shadows of the auditorium and into the sunlight. He adjusted the cuffs of his suit coat, smoothed his tie, and stared icily at Barcini. Rose Ellen drifted behind him, a faint smile on her lips. She settled next to Quill, her perfume an expensive cloud around her.

Belter's little beady eyes lit up and his drawl intensified. "Now looky, looky here. If it isn't the great Mr. Tree hisself."

He stuck his thumb in his belt. Josephine pointed the Steadi-cam at his face and pulled in for a close-up. He grinned widely, revealing the need for some dental whitening strips— or at least a sturdier toothbrush. "What d'ya think, folks? Should I chop him into kindling? Lop off a few of his branches? Trim him down to size?"

"Hoorah!" Mamma Barcini yelled. She began to applaud. "Get the doughhead! Get him!"

In what Quill was sure was a reflex action, a couple of other people began to clap, too.

Belter shoved his face closer to the camera. "Is Mr. Tree ready for . . . the Barcini Slap Down?!"

"Yay!" Mamma Barcini cheered. She put two fingers to her mouth and whistled. "Slap Down. Slap Down!"

"Barcini," Edmund said coldly, "I have no idea what a slap down may be. Nor do I wish to be enlightened. I am asking you to leave. Now."

Belter flexed his right arm, which was surprisingly well muscled. "Well, now, Eddie, I don't think you'd stand a chance against the old Belter here. But I'll challenge you and your stuck-up pals to whatever kind of contest you want. Don't even have to be manly. Belter's man enough to get in touch with his feminine side. Right, folks?"

"You tell 'em, Belter!" Mamma Barcini shouted.

He twirled around on his tiptoes. "Dancing, maybe? Nope? What other kinds of girly things are you up to, Eddie? C'mon. Man up, Eddie. Man up and take the challenge."

Edmund thinned his lips in a grimace of distaste. "I've warned you about harassing me, Barcini." He nodded ele-gantly in Quill's direction. "As Mrs. Quilliam-McHale will attest. Why you persist in trailing after me is anyone's guess, but I'm sick and tired of it. I don't want to warn you again. Get out. Pack up your trashy bus, your trailer-trash hangers-on and go. Get away from my show and leave these good people alone." He snapped his fingers at the security guards. "Get rid of them, Marco," he said. He walked over to Rose Ellen and settled his hands protectively on her shoulders.

The guards grabbed Belter, one on each arm, and hustled him toward the bus. Josephine, still running the Steadicam, walked after him. Mrs. Barcini adjusted her T-shirt around her hips and followed her daughter, head high.

"Edmund." Rose Ellen was barely audible. "The camera? Little sis? We wouldn't want any of this aired, would we? Tell Marco to relieve him of it, can't you?"

"Excellent idea." Edmund raised his voice in a gentlemanly shout. "Marco. The tape?"

The shorter security guard nodded, turned, and wrenched the camera out of Josephine's hands. She shrieked and kicked at him and wrenched the camera back.

Quill cleared her throat. "The camera doesn't belong to you, Mr. Tree. And I don't think Josephine is all that much of a threat to your goons."

Edmund shrugged. "Let it go, Marco."

The guards shoved the Barcinis onto the bus, one by one.

After a long moment, Belter started the engine, put the bus in gear, and pulled onto the lane that led out of the parking lot. He drove slowly. As he passed by, he glared at Edmund through the windshield. Edmund raised his hand in a short, cocky salute and sneered back.

Both of them looked mad enough to kill.

7

~Choux Pastry~

1 cup of water
3 ounces salted butter
1 cup of flour
1 cup of eggs, beaten
(For sweet pastry add 1 teaspoon sugar to flour)

Boil water and butter in a saucepan. Lower heat to low-est setting. Stir in flour and mix with fork until smooth. Put ball of pastry into a glass bowl and beat with spoon. Add egg mixture and beat until smooth. Pinch off dough into balls. Dip balls into beaten egg. Place balls onto greased cookie sheet and bake at 425 degrees for about twenty minutes.

"Marge was amazing. Just amazing. If she hadn't stepped in the way she did, I think we would have had a riot." Quill clasped her hands behind her back and looked over Meg's shoulder as her sister briskly folded raw eggs into a mixture of flour and water with a large fork. "You're making choux pastry?"

"What does it look like? Of course it's choux pastry." Meg nudged her away from the prep table. "You know it makes me crazy when you kibitz. Go sit in your rocker."

"Since when have we specialized in choux pastry?"

"Since I decided on the appetizers for the Tree cocktail party tonight."

"You're not doing country pâté with cheeses?"

"That, too, plus shrimp bites, wild mushrooms in cream, and something with leeks, which I will figure out when I get there."

"Did you get the recipe from Clare?"

"I think I know how to make a choux pastry as well as Clare." Meg whacked the fork against the stainless-steel bowl to dislodge the bits of pastry. "So then what happened?"

"At the high school? Everybody lined back up and took their assembled attic finds into the auditorium."

"What's with the Slap Down business?"

Quill shrugged and sat down in the rocking chair. "I'm not sure. But apparently these kinds of challenges are common enough on reality shows. They stage a challenge and then the audience gets to vote on who wins. That's according to Rose Ellen, who seems to think that Edmund should respond somehow. They both think Belter's going to run the tape on the next *Pawn-o-Rama* program. Rose Ellen says it's a technique to get viewers to participate in the action, which is supposed to keep them loyal supporters."

"Gladiator contests," Meg said dismissively. "It's pretty clear that arm wrestling's out of the picture. I'll tell you one thing that's non–gender specific—cooking."

"True."

"So they could have a cooking contest."

"The mind boggles. Can we forget about the Trees and the Barcinis for a minute? Let's talk about pastry."

"Sure." Meg divided the pastry into two large balls and added a handful of fine sugar to one of them. She began to beat it briskly with a fork.

"I didn't pay a whole lot of attention to the menu planning yesterday morning, but I'm pretty sure Clare's planning something similar for the wedding reception."

"These will be better."

Quill knew that set to Meg's chin. She gave up.

Meg glanced at her and then looked away. "So who made it onto the show? Anybody turn up with a fabulous find?"

"Harvey did, with his collection of majolica. It's beautiful, actually. His mother and grandmother collected it. You'll never guess who else—Dookie brought in a pile of journals and newspaper clippings from the Civil War. Esther had some very nice jewelry from her great-great-whatever-aunts. Those landscapes Adela and Elmer have always had in their living room? I guess they made the cut."

"Those lake and waterfall things? The ones she says came down to her from her many times great-grandpa?"

"Yep. They get to have them evaluated."

Meg pinched off small rounds of dough and placed them on the oversized cookie sheets she used for baking. She did this with incredible speed. "You sound dubious."

"I am dubious. I've seen *Ancestor's Attic*, you know. Tree always has one major disappointment or embarrassment." Quill braced her foot on the floor and set the rocker going.

"He likes making people look foolish, you mean. Not very nice."

"No. He is not very nice."

"I don't remember Adela's paintings all that well. Are they any good?"

"Early American landscapes. Oils. The artist is obscure. Rebecca Winthrop. A woman who painted at a time when women weren't respected at all. And for all I know, she may be experiencing a vogue, now."

"But the paintings themselves?"

Quill shook her head. Musicians wince at flat notes. Writers wince at clunky prose. Painters wince at bad lines.

"So are you going to warn Adela and Elmer? Aren't you meeting them for lunch in, like, ten minutes? You could drop a word then."

"A lot of art criticism is subjective. Not only is it subjective, it's subjective within the context of the prevailing culture."

Meg took a second to work this out. "Hm. So you aren't going to say a thing?"

"I'm not going to say a thing. Not to them, anyway."

"You'll tackle the Great Edmund himself? Phuut! You got hope." She slapped the sheet of pastry into an oven and began prepping a second sheet. "So why do those guys hate each other, anyway? Barcini and Tree. Sounds like a comedy act."

"There wasn't anything funny about this morning, I'll tell you that. Although I don't think they hate each other as much as they like the ratings coming from a widely publicized feud."

Meg stared at her. "My sister the cynic."

"Your sister the realist." She wanted to add, "There'll be further trouble, mark my words," but didn't.

Kathleen Kiddermeister pushed open the swinging door

that led to the kitchen and stuck her head inside. "Quill? Mayor Henry and his wife are here. They said you'd be joining them? I did a setup for five, like you asked."

Quill smoothed her hair, straightened her sleeves, and adjusted her skirt, frowning at the lump in her pocket. She followed Kathleen into the dining room. Suddenly, she remembered why she had the lightbulb in her pocket. "Will you see Davy anytime today, Kathleen?"

"Dina will probably see him before I do. I think they've got a date tonight. Ever since my baby brother was made sheriff, I only see him at a family picnic or a birthday. How come? If it's to fix a ticket, forget it. He won't even fix them for me, and I'm kin."

"I'll give the lightbulb to Dina, then." She smiled at Kathleen's raised eyebrow and turned the smile on Elmer and Adela. "Hi, Mayor. Hi, Adela."

Elmer, who had just taken a large bite out of a rye roll, half rose in his seat and gestured hello. Adela looked stern. Quill sat down, unfolded her napkin, and waited while Kathleen filled the water glasses.

Adela glanced at her watch. "I did think Mr. Tree would have made an effort to be on time."

Quill saw with a pang that the couple had dressed carefully for the lunch; Elmer had abandoned his usual sports coat and chinos for a new blue three-piece suit. Adela wore a deep purple pantsuit with a ruffled navy blouse and her best costume jewelry.

Adela was—Quill searched for the appropriate word—decisive, that'd be it. A decisive woman who tended to decide more for Elmer than he seemed to want, but it was clear the couple was devoted to one another.

Elmer swallowed his roll and grabbed another one. "Mr. Tree's a busy man, Adela. It's okay with me if he's running a little behind. Gives us a chance to talk with Quill about the campaign."

"We appreciate your endorsement, Quill." Adela inclined her head in a rather imperial manner. "Of course, under the circumstances, it's what my grandson would call a no-brainer." Her smile was stiff.

"The circumstances?"

Adela picked up a roll and put it down again. "We didn't get to the high school until things had settled down. But I understand that Marge Schmidt made quite a spectacle of herself. I can't imagine anyone in the village supporting her now. Not that anyone supported her before."

"Would you like to order now?" asked Kathleen, who was hovering.

Adela glanced at her watch again. "I think we'll wait until the rest of our party arrives."

"I'm pretty hungry now," Elmer said. "I'm pretty near starved."

"Why don't you ask Meg for a small starter plate, please, Kathleen," Quill said. "Would either of you like some wine with lunch? A glass each of the Keuka red? Great. I'll join you."

Kathleen bustled off. At two thirty on a Tuesday, the dining room was virtually empty, except for a young couple lingering over coffee in the corner near the wine rack. Adela looked at them and, apparently deciding that they were safely out of earshot, she said, "Marge Schmidt actually threatened Mr. Barcini with arrest, Harvey tells me. I've never heard of such a thing. That woman is the absolute limit. She's no more fit for mayor than Nadine Peterson's poodle."

"Actually," Quill began. "The citizen's arrest was a brilliant tactic. It defused a highly volatile situation."

Adela's cheeks were red, which made her blusher look orange. "Nonsense. A citizen's arrest? Who ever heard of a citizen's arrest?"

"The arrest thing is not a bad idea, campaign-wise," Elmer said. "I called Howie Murchison to get a legal opinion once I got the story from Harvey Bozzel. He says it's okay in New York State, at least the way Marge did it. I asked if I could maybe arrest Marge for impersonating a mayor. That'd show her some."

"Don't be ridiculous, Elmer. And what's all this about her inciting our folk to riot?" Adela folded her arms under her prow-like bosom. "Pushy. That's what the woman is. Pushy."

Quill tried again. "Actually . . ."

Adela's face got redder. "What's more, I heard there's going to be some sort of story on the six o'clock news. A fine thing that would be for this town. I lay all of this terrible publicity at Marge Schmidt's door."

"A story on the six o'clock news?" She knew it. She was right. This whole brouhaha with Barcini and Tree was a publicity stunt.

She saw Kathleen come out of the doors to the kitchen with a large tray and tried to remember when she'd last eaten. She was starving. Kathleen set out the starter plates and a platter of savories. Quill selected one of each—shrimp, tapenade, and what looked like cheese—and served Adela and Elmer before she served herself.

"Quite delicious," Adela said. "Although I think Clare Sparrow may have the edge on the pastry."

"Don't tell my sister. This news story, Adela, about the feud between Barcini and Tree . . . who told you about it?"

Adela's eyes widened in dismay. "They're going to run a story about Mr. Tree and that awful man Barcini, too?"

"Belter's not so bad," Elmer said. "I like these shrimp thingies, Quill."

Quill's head was beginning to hurt. "Too? What news story are you talking about?"

"Harvey called the TV station," Elmer said briefly. "Said Marge was a local hero. Local busybody is more like. Had to fire Harvey as my campaign manager, of course." Suddenly, he looked stricken. "I suppose that means Marge Schmidt will snatch him up. Figures." He heaved a deep, heart-sore sigh. "We might not be mayor after all, Mother. Have to admit it's a possibility."

Adela frowned. "Don't be absurd, Elmer. This town would be nowhere without us, and you know it and everyone else knows it, too." She bit her lip, and for a terrifying moment, Quill thought she was about to cry.

"Well," Quill said brightly. "I wonder what could be keeping Edmund and Rose Ellen."

"They're probably over to Marge Schmidt's having lunch at the All-American Diner," Elmer said.

"Nonsense. Mr. Tree's a gentleman. He wouldn't be rude enough to break a luncheon date." Adela looked at her watch a third time.

Quill shoved her chair back and got to her feet. "Excuse me a moment, will you? I'll just make a quick call and see what could be keeping them."

She kept a cheerful smile in place until she was in front of the reception desk in the foyer.

Dina looked up from her textbook. "You look mad as fire. Anything wrong?"

"Would you get Rose Ellen Whitman on the phone for me?"

Dina reached for the landline. "You don't want to call her on your cell?"

"I don't want her to have my cell number."

"Good thinking. Shall I try the shop or her cell?"

"Cell, first."

Dina dialed, listened a moment, then said, "Hi, Ms. Whitman. This is Dina Muir at the Inn. Mrs. McHale would appreciate a call from you as soon as possible." She hung up and looked at Quill expectantly.

"Voice mail?"

"Voice mail. But you know Rose Ellen. She never picks up. Except maybe for Warren Buffett. She just listens to the messages."

"Warren . . . never mind. Could you try the store? One of the Petersons works there, I can't remember if it's Arlene or Samantha, and if Rose Ellen isn't there, she might know where I can find her."

"It's Arlene. She says Rose Ellen is the biggest witch she's ever worked for in twenty years of retail. What are you going to do when you do find her?"

"Drag her back here by the scruff of the neck. She and Edmund were supposed to have lunch here with the Henrys."

"She's a mean person, Quill. I told you that from the get-go." Dina had the number of Elegant Antiques on her Black-Berry; she looked it up and got the store on the landline. She listened for a moment and looked at Quill: "Voice mail."

"Give me that." Quill took the receiver and heard Rose

Ellen's whispery voice: *". . . Sorry we are not available to take your call. Please leave your name and number."*

Quill pitched her voice a little higher than usual. "This is David Denby's office from the *New Yorker* calling for Ms. Whit—"

"Hello?" Rose Ellen said languidly. "Mr. Denby, is it?"

Quill was generally equable. But she lost her temper. "No, Rose Ellen. It's Sarah McHale. The Henrys are here for lunch. Where are you?"

"You're working for David Denby now?"

"Cut the sarcasm. Why aren't you here? Is Edmund with you?"

"The Henrys. I don't think I know the Hen . . . wait. That chubby little man with the wife with the disastrous fashion sense. We may have mentioned lunch in passing, but something's come up. You'll give them my regrets, won't you?"

"You cannot," Quill said tightly, "insult nice people like this. As a matter of fact, you can't insult anybody like this."

"Oh, my. You are in a bit of a state, aren't you? Well, I'm sure you'll come up with a suitable excuse. Tell them how very, very sorry I am. Oh! You could invite them to the cocktail party tonight. There. That's a nice thing, isn't it? They'll be the only locals there. They'll love it. And if you could drop by the store for just a minute? I've got a great idea to run past you."

Quill dropped the receiver into the cradle with a word that made Dina blink.

"You look pretty mad," she offered, after a moment.

"I am pretty mad. The sooner these . . . people leave Hemlock Falls, the better. Argh. What am I going to tell the Henrys?"

"You'll think of something. But before you go back in there, you might want to comb your hair. If you wouldn't grab at it like you do, it wouldn't fall all over the place."

Quill felt in her skirt pocket for her comb and found the lightbulb. "Are you going out with Davy tonight?"

"Not out, exactly. We're going over to his place for a DVD and a pizza."

Quill offered her the lightbulb.

"That's a Baggie with a lightbulb in it."

"It's evidence. Maybe."

Dina's eyes widened. "We're on a case?"

"Not exactly. Is Davy getting anywhere with the burglaries?"

"Not really. It's hard to value what's been taken since the people who got burgled lost stuff they'd stuck in the attic or the basement because it wasn't worth much. He expects them to stop, now that the *Ancestor's Attic* show has made the selection."

"That doesn't make sense, Dina. It never made any sense. If the burglar was after loot to take onto the show, what's going to happen when the real owner sees it on TV?"

Dina sucked her lower lip thoughtfully. "You've got a point."

"Of course I have a point." She was still cross. She took a deep breath and put the Baggie on the reception desk. "Ask him to check this for prints, would you? Tell him to call me if he wants to know why."

She took another deep breath and went back into the dining room.

Adela and Elmer had finished all the savories. They

sat alone in the dining room like abandoned luggage. Adela turned eagerly as Quill came up to them. "Hey," she said. "I got hold of Rose Ellen."

"They're on their way, then," Adela said.

"I'm afraid they've been held up," Quill said, improvising. "There's been a little accident with one of the crew on the TV show, and poor Edmund had to take care of it."

Adela looked concerned. "Is there anything we can do?"

"Not a thing," Quill said cheerfully. "It's all been taken care of, but I'm afraid Edmund's assistant was supposed to call you and didn't. They are both so, so sorry. They asked if you might care to drop by their private party tonight. Just the two of you and the crew of the show. It's here in the Tavern Lounge at seven."

Elmer expanded a little. "A private party, eh? I think we might be able to do that, Mother?"

Adela's brow furrowed. Quill was pretty sure she was mentally going through her closet. "I assume it's black tie?"

"Yes, indeed. It's their engagement party, as a matter of fact . . ."

"Oh, my. I suppose *Vanity Fair* will send a photographer." Adela turned pink with pleasure. "I'll have to check my appointment book, but I'm fairly sure there is nothing urgent this evening."

"Terrific. If you can't make it, just leave word for Dina. Now, Edmund insisted that the lunch is on him and Rose Ellen, so you order anything you want from Kathleen. Anything. And if you don't mind, I have an errand to run, so I'll leave you now. Try the crème brûlée for dessert. It's one of Meg's triumphs."

Quill marched back into the foyer and into her office. She

retrieved her tote and looked up to find Dina staring at her from the doorway. "What!"

"Nothing. Not a thing. Nada." She pushed her spectacles into place with one forefinger. "Are you headed somewhere?"

"I'm going down to Elegant Antiques and yell at Rose Ellen." She plopped her tote on the desk. "Instead of spending the afternoon with Jack, the way I wanted to." She sat down and put her head in her hands. "I don't think I can do this, Dina. I can't be Jack's mother and run this Inn. I'm going crazy."

"You're missing Myles," Dina said wisely. "I've read about this mommy-stress thing. It's perfectly normal. You just can't let it get to you."

"I have been a little touchy lately."

"Who wouldn't be? Mommy stress is especially hard on older mothers. I mean, if you were like, in your early thirties even, you'd have a lot more energy and . . ."

"Stop right there."

"Um. Sure. I didn't mean to be ageist. Sorry."

Quill cleared her throat.

"Right," Dina said hastily. "Look, it's almost three o'clock so Jack's down for his nap so you wouldn't be spending time with him anyway. That'd he be conscious of, I mean . . . You can go and yell at Ms. Whitman and be back here by four, the way you usually are."

"Unless," Quill said, "I'm in jail for assault."

Dina grinned. "Me or Ms. Whitman?"

"You, I'd like to whack up the side of the head. Ms. Whitman, I'd like to murder."

8

~Pears in Cream~
Serves 6

3 firm seasonal pears, Bosc or Bartlett preferred
3 cups English Cream (see recipe)
3 cups heavy whipping cream, slightly thickened
   after whipping
¾ cup pear liqueur
¾ cup sugar
4 ounces chopped walnuts

Peel and halve pears. Place cut side down on a baking sheet and slice lengthwise into thin strips. Transfer strips to individual gratin dishes, six in all. Combine the English Cream, the whipping cream, and the pear liqueur with a whisk. Divide the mixture into six portions and pour over the pears. Sprinkle sugar on top of each pear. Arrange walnuts to the side of the pears. Broil in broiler for thirty seconds.

ENGLISH CREAM:

1 cup heavy whipping cream
½ vanilla bean, cut lengthwise

3 beaten egg yolks
¼ cup sugar

Bring cream and vanilla to a boil, stirring all the while. Beat egg yolks and sugar together until pale yellow. Carefully combine the two mixtures over medium heat, whisking constantly, until mixture thickens. Cool in the refrigerator.

Elegant Antiques was in a three-story cobblestone building on Main Street. The building had been the Tompkins County Farmer's Bank in the mid-nineteenth century. The bank had been the biggest in the five-county area, and the building was huge. When the bank failed in the crash of '29, the space had been carved into retail shops on the street level, with apartments above. Rose Ellen had rented all three floors of the space on the south corner of the building. The store occupied the first and second. Rose Ellen lived in a small apartment on the third. There were large windows on two sides of the ground floor; the south window faced Elm; the west window faced Main. The Balzac Café coffee shop occupied the space right next door, and there were three more stores after that. It took Quill less than five minutes to get there and another frustrating ten minutes to park.

Until a few years ago, parking on Main Street hadn't been a problem. With the new influx of tourists grabbing all the easy spots, she had to circle the block twice before she found a space for her Honda. In the time that it had taken her to drive down from the Inn and park, she'd calmed down. Dina was right. With luck, she could finish her business with Rose Ellen and be with Jack by four.

The CLOSED sign was displayed on the front door. She hesitated, and then knocked, pushing the door open as she did so. The antique sleigh bell over the jamb jingled, announcing her presence.

"Hello?"

There was no one waiting inside. Quill shut the door behind her. The stairs to the upper stories were at her left. Voices came from above; Rose Ellen's breathy whisper and somebody else. A young woman.

"Hello?" a voice responded from upstairs. "Is that you, Quill?"

Clarissa? "Yes," Quill called. "It's me. Is that you, Clare?"

"Yes," she said tersely. "Come on up. We're having a meeting."

Quill walked past the displays on her way to the staircase. She had to admit Rose Ellen had taste. The square footage was small, but Rose Ellen had made clever use of the space. A very fine nineteenth-century oak dining room table held an attractive collection of Depression glass, a Limoges vase that was not so fine, but was definitely authentic, and a collection of vintage evening bags. There was a genuine Delft teapot and a scattering of heavy silver candlesticks on a carved pine sea chest. The paintings on the walls were grouped very attractively. There was a small Muir, nicely framed, and a collection of tromp l'oeil. Quill stopped at an oil depicting a bowl of fruit. The fly on the pear was so realistic, she almost brushed it away. There was another large oil showing a fountain with a platter of grapes, apples, and chestnuts at its foot.

The perspective behind the fountain was exceptionally well done. It had been in the window the last time Quill had passed the store. Rose Ellen made a habit of rotating the window displays so that potential customers stopped by more often.

"Are you coming up or not?"

Quill looked up. Rose Ellen was halfway down the stairs. She'd changed from the wispy flower print dress she'd worn at the high school that morning into tailored black slacks and a white, long sleeved shirt. An ornate silver medallion hung at her throat. She looked incredibly chic.

"I just stopped to look. I like the tromp l'oeil, Rose Ellen." She pointed to the larger painting of the fountain. "That has a lot of charm."

"It does, doesn't it? I picked it up at one of those giant flea market things. It's not a reproduction—just some unknown having fun with the genre. But the lines are quite nice and the perspective is terrific. You know what? It'd be perfect for the suite Edmund is occupying. The Provencal, you call it?"

"You're right. It would." Quill bent forward to look at the price tag. "You want five hundred dollars for it? I'll have to think about that."

"It's an original, after all. And the genre's about to come back into vogue. When it does, I'll be asking three times the price I've got on it now. Edmund and I are keeping an eye out, so to speak, so let me know if you run across any when you're in New York. As a matter of fact, anytime you come across an amateur oil painted more than a hundred or so years ago, let us know. You'd be amazed at what idiots people can be. There've been a number of cases where some dolt painted over really fine originals in an effort to use up the canvases. We pay a commission."

"I don't get to New York much these days."

Rose Ellen's glance drifted over Quill's challis skirt, her silk T-shirt, which was much the worse for wear after her hectic day, and her espadrilles. "I can see that. Come up. We're planning Edward's slap."

"His Slap Down, she means." Clarissa stood at the top of the staircase. "Hi, Quill. Rose Ellen said you were in the thick of things this morning at the high school."

"I suppose I was."

"Citizen's arrest. Don't you love it? I wish I'd been there, but I was stuck with a cooking class."

Quill followed both women up the stairs and onto the second floor. The area in the farthest recesses of this floor was dedicated to restoration. Quill's sensitive nose detected solvents, oil paint, and carbon tet.

It wasn't as crowded as downstairs, but the pieces were arranged with the same eye for elegance. There was a very nice Victorian love seat with a carved mahogany frame that would look terrific in the Victorian suite at the inn. The needlepoint footstool next to it would have been perfect, too.

A large piecrust table had been pressed into service as a desk behind the love seat. Rose Ellen sat down in a Regency armchair next to it and picked up a manila folder. Clarissa sat in a folding chair across from her. Rose Ellen settled a pair of horn-rimmed reading glasses on her nose and looked up. "There's another folding chair in the back, by the toilet. Why don't you bring it over here and Clare and I can bring you up to speed."

Quill kept her tone pleasant. "I really can't stay. I came down because I wanted to let you know how disappointed the Henrys were that you and Edmund didn't show for lunch.

117

They'd planned that luncheon carefully. I wanted to tell you that I'm putting their lunch tab on Edmund's bill. And to ask that you treat my friends with more respect in the future."

"Those dim little . . ."

"They're my friends," Quill said firmly. "Both of them. And I invited them to the cocktail party as you requested, so this is basically a heads-up."

Rose Ellen waved her hand dismissively. "Fine. Whatever you think. I certainly don't want to interfere with any of your business relationships here. Believe me, I completely understand. Now get that chair and see what we've planned for Edmund and that revolting Barcini."

Curious in spite of herself, Quill got the chair and sat down.

"Now. As distasteful as it is for me to admit—publicity is of value to both *Ancestor's Attic* and my boutique. Word is already around town that Barcini plans to air his 'challenge,' if you want to dignify it as such, on the episode of *Pawn-o-Rama* that's due to air this week." In response to Clare's puzzled look, she said, "Surely you know that episodes can be shot months ahead of the time that they're aired. Barcini plans to edit the tape his sister took this morning and introduce this week's show with it."

"Are you sure about all this?" Quill asked doubtfully.

"Positive. That overly groomed person . . ."

"She means Harvey," Clare said.

"That passes for an advertising man has been very, very busy. It's his duty, he says, to promote the village and apparently this is a prime opportunity for him."

Quill suppressed a smile. Harvey would be in his element.

"Mr. Bozzel seems to feel that an appropriate challenge would be a . . ." She turned to Clare. "What did he call it?"

"A cook-off."

"Correct. I think it's a feasible idea. Cooking is . . ." She paused and bit her lip ruefully. "Safe. Edmund is not, as you may have noticed, the kind of man to square off and punch Barcini in the nose, however much I would like him to."

For a moment, Rose Ellen was very likeable. Belter had come by his nickname honestly.

"So. Barcini and Edmund will meet in one of Clare's kitchens at Bonne Goutè and each will prepare a dish. A panel of judges—professionals like Clare herself, and Meg—will vote on which dish has been prepared the best. We'll have the audience vote, as well. So there will be a popular choice and a judge's choice."

Belter didn't look like much of a cook. "Has Belter agreed to this?"

"You've got to be kidding. He'll fall over those disgusting flip-flops in his race to do it. We'll air the segment on our show the moment it's done. We're going to release ten-second spots to the media to run as a promo. Belter couldn't buy that kind of exposure no matter what he did. The man's trailer trash, pure and simple and that's not news. He'll jump at the chance to be in the same studio with someone as prestigious as Edmund."

"Then why does Edmund want to be on the same show as him?" Clare asked innocently.

Rose Ellen flushed. "Barcini does have a certain share of the market," she said evenly. "Do I have to say it again? I find this sort of exhibitionism distasteful. But in today's environment, it's absolutely necessary. Now, have you made Madame LeVasque aware of this opportunity? It'll be advantageous for Bonne Goutè, of course."

"Madame talked about it after you called, yes." Clare's voice was reluctant.

"Then I assume that's clear. Now." She turned to Quill. "You understand why the Inn isn't suitable. Of course we considered you as a venue. But we require an audience of at least one hundred, and there just isn't enough room."

"Thank Go . . . goodness," Quill said. "I mean that you considered us, at least."

"Good. This is Tuesday. I'd like to get this out of the way before the wedding. So shall we plan on Thursday to do the shoot?"

"Thursday?" Clare said. "We can't possibly be ready by Thursday."

"Why not?"

"We've got to get enough supplies in so a hundred people in the audience can taste the recipes, for one thing."

"So you're saying there's a problem you can't handle? Perhaps I should turn this over to Madame LeVasque."

Quill winced. Madame had been dubious about Clare's ability to handle the directorship of the academy. She had a hunch Rose Ellen knew that very well.

"We can handle it just fine," Clare said defensively. "It's just . . . so fast. No, I guess there's no problem. We have a soups and stew class scheduled for that evening, but if the students can be in the audience and we move the class to another date, I guess that'd be okay."

"Of course it will." Rose Ellen made a few notes, then closed the manila folder and tossed it on the table. "That's all then. Thank you very much for coming. And I'll see you both at the engagement party tonight?"

"We're dismissed then?" Clare said with an ominous cheerfulness.

Quill knew that look in Clare's eye. She'd clearly reached her limit. "Yes. Well. We'll be off," Quill said hastily.

Clare's eyes glittered. She was taking deep, steadying breaths. Clare was nowhere near as volatile as Meg, but she was, after all, a chef. Quill got up and put her hand on Clare's arm. "It's close to four o'clock and I need to get back to the Inn. Walk down with me, Clare."

She led the way down the stairs, Clare stamping along behind her.

To her credit, Clare waited to explode until they were both well clear of the store and at Quill's Honda.

Then she flipped.

"That witch!" She dropped her voice in a ferocious imitation of Rose Ellen's breathy whisper. "Of course you'll love having your kitchen invaded by two Visigoths, Clare. Of course you'll jump through any hoops I roll out, Clare. Gaah!"

"Visigoths?"

"Edmund is as phony as a three-dollar bill. Barcini at least is an honest thug. They're both raiders and plunderers."

"My gosh," Quill said mildly.

"Sorry. But that woman just gets up my nose."

"She does at that."

"Cooking contest my . . . left foot. Did you notice the conspicuous absence of anything?"

Quill thought a moment. "Nothing was said about what they're going to cook?"

"Who cares? Not me. Except that I have to order enough

supplies to feed a hundred-plus people." Clare shuddered and shook her head. "Ugh. Poor Meg. Poor me. And we have to judge this thing? I'm going to look like a horse's ass."

"It's not a live show or anything. It's a shoot. So they can rewind, or whatever, or cut." Quill was rather vague on the details. "Have you said anything to Meg about this?"

"Poor Harvey left the store just before you got there. *She*"—the venom Clare invested in that inoffensive pronoun was remarkable—"sent him up to the Inn to talk to Meg."

"I'd better get up there, then."

"Right. I'll see you at this engagement party tonight, I guess. Celebrity chef on call." She adjusted her tote on her shoulder with a casual air. "What's Meg planning on serving, do you know? We never did settle on a final menu."

Quill thought with dread of the choux pastry. "I'm not sure. You know how menus go—she's considered a couple of things. Edmund asked for a 'sophisticated country house weekend' theme using local produce."

"That'll mean pears, I expect. Pears are all over the farmer's markets right now. I've got a great recipe for pears in cream. By the way, where is he in all this, anyway?"

"Who?"

"The fraud, the fiancé, the sucker-sophisticate. Edmund Tree."

"Up at the Inn, I think. In his rooms. The Provencal suite."

"He's not staying with her?"

"No."

Clare narrowed her eyes. "I know that look, Quill. You're being discreet. Why isn't Tree staying with his sweetie? Why isn't she staying with him? The Provencal suite is nine hundred percent nicer than those apartments over there. I know.

I checked them out as a place to live when I thought I would have to leave the academy and live on my own."

One of the rules of innkeeping—Quill couldn't remember which number it was—stated very firmly that what went on at the Inn stayed at the Inn. It didn't do to gossip about the guests.

"Rose Ellen is staying pure for Edmund."

"Say what?"

"Or maybe it's the other way around. Maybe Edmund is staying pure for Rose Ellen."

"Fruitcakes," Clare said darkly. "And I'm not talking Christmas, here."

9

~Choux Pastry Puffs~

SAVORY:

- 1 pound chopped fresh, steamed shrimp, crab, or clams
- 3 tablespoons finely diced celery
- 1 tablespoon finely diced leek
- 1 lemon
- 3 tablespoons fresh minced parsley, chives and dill, combined
- ¼ cup freshly made mayonnaise
- 36 baked choux puff pastries

Blend all ingredients. Chill. Fill puffs.

SWEET:

- 1 cup Pecans Quilliam
- 4 cups English Cream, flavored with curaçao
- 36 baked choux puff pastries

Mix all ingredients. Chill. Fill puffs just before serving.

PECANS QUILLIAM:

> 4 ounces butter
> ¼ cup dark brown sugar
> 1 cup whole pecans

Melt butter and sugar over medium heat. Add pecans. Over high-medium heat, toast the pecans until caramelized. Cool. Place in blender and chop fine.

Quill came through the back door of the kitchen curious about her sister's reaction to the chance to judge the relative merits of Tree and Barcini, chefs for a day. Her curiosity was satisfied almost immediately.

"Have you ever heard of anything as stupid in your whole *life*?"

"Probably not," Quill said cautiously.

The kitchen was usually hectic at four o'clock and today was no exception. Bjarne seared beef tenderloin at the grill. Elizabeth chopped tomatoes. Devon and Hilary, students from the nearby Cornell School of Hotel Administration, scrubbed pots.

Meg stood at the twelve-burner stove over a large sauté pan. She dumped a wad of butter and a bowl of brown sugar into the pan and turned on the heat.

"Are you going to judge the contest?"

"The Slap Down, you mean? In your dreams. I'd rather eat a rat." She shook the pan, and then dumped a bowl of whole pecans into it. "Harvey says they're going to have the whole pitiful performance at Bonne Goutè. What's Clare thinking? She's going to look like a horse's ass."

"She didn't say so—well, she did say she thought she'd look like a horse's ass—but I think Madame is forcing her hand."

"Yeah, well, Madame's a trip, that's for sure. It has to be hard not to be boss in your own kitchen." Meg looked smug.

"You know she'll be here tonight?"

"Clare? Yeah, I know that." Meg peered into the sauté pan. "How come these darn nuts aren't caramelizing?"

"You're still serving choux pastry."

"So what if I am?"

"Clare's specialty. I'm just asking for a little clarification."

"You ought to be asking for caramelization. Ah! There we go." She lifted the pan from the burner and set it on the prep table. "We'll let it cool off a bit. Then, Elizabeth, pulverize them in the blender, would you? And then start on the cream filling. Go easy on the curaçao. People will want to taste pecans, not liquor." Meg untied her apron and took it off. "There. We're good to go. I'm off to the lounge. I want to check Kathleen's setups."

The short way to the lounge was out the back door and around the side of the building, and Meg invariably took it. Quill followed her outside. Meg glanced over her shoulder. "Are you coming with me?"

"No. I wanted to talk without risking a big hoorah in the kitchen."

"So you're risking a big hoorah out here?"

"What I'm doing," Quill said with a flash of temper, "is trying to make you see reason. Why are you behaving like this? Are you trying to start a fight with Clare?"

Meg ran her hands through her hair, so that it stood up in short spikes. "I am a peaceful kind of person. I always have

126

been. But I will respond when provoked beyond reason. I am not trying to pick a fight."

Quill let this astonishing piece of mendacity pass. "This doesn't make any sense. You know as well as I do that the average person can't tell the difference between choux pastry and a wad of laundered Kleenex. So who's going to be able to tell the difference tonight? Clare, that's who."

Meg scowled. It was the sort of scowl Quill hadn't seen on her sister since she was five years old and trying to bluff about being bullied at preschool. "She sure will. And then she's going to eat her words."

They'd gotten around the building to the rose gardens. The gardens were one of the loveliest parts of the grounds in good weather, and even now, with fall coming on, the roses made a brilliant show of color against the emerald grass. Quill stopped and sat down on the nearest bench. She patted the space next to her. "Sit down here, Meggie. Tell me about it."

~

"Edmund Tree told Meg that Clare Sparrow thought her pastry was a joke." Quill sat curled up in one corner of her living room sofa. Jack was busy on the floor at her feet, gleefully stacking his wooden blocks in a tower and then knocking them over. Doreen was in Quill's tiny kitchen, making macaroni and cheese. Quill, still flushed with indignation, looked up to see Doreen's reaction. She paused, cheese grater in one hand and went, "T'uh!"

"They were going over the menu for his engagement party tonight and he asked for sweets and savories. Meg said if he wanted pastry, it'd be better to get Clare to cater."

"She's right, from what I hear about Clare's pies."

"Of course she's right." Quill was furious, and trying to keep it from Jack. "My sister is a good person. A great person. She acknowledges greatness in others, and Clare is a great pastry chef. Anyhow, so then Edmund tells Meg that Clare was telling anyone who would listen that Meg's pastry was a joke."

"You think Clare really said that?"

"I do not. I think Edmund Tree is a troublemaker. I have no idea why. Grr. I can't wait until the whole pile of them get out of my Inn."

"Grr," Jack said. *"Grrr!"*

Doreen grated another couple inches of cheddar cheese. "Why would he make trouble? Just for the sake of making trouble?"

"Who knows? Maybe he's malicious by nature. Maybe he thinks he can get Meg and Clare to start a feud in front of the cameras on this Slap Down. They're both coming to the engagement party tonight, you know. I'm really worried that there's going to be a scene."

"You were thinking of skippin' the party, weren't you?"

Quill looked wistfully at Jack. "I have to drop in for about half an hour. I was hoping Meg could handle the hostessing part."

"Not darn likely. So much for delegating. You might better stick through the whole thing in case there's another riot. You may not be much at delegating, but you're pretty good at handling scenes." Doreen thought a moment, then added, "Unless you start one yourself."

Jack toppled his block tower with a shriek of joy. "All done!" He jumped to his feet and clambered into Quill's lap. "I pushed them over a billion times, Mommy."

"Good work, my darling boy. Very, very good work." She wrapped her arms around him and rubbed her cheek over the top of his head. Life could be sweetly uncomplicated if she didn't have to deal with guests.

Doreen gave her a shrewd glance. "Want me to get after this Tree with the mop?"

"I'm tempted. But no. I'll just have as little to do with them as humanly possible."

Doreen took Jack's plastic dinner plate out of the cupboard and heaped it with the macaroni and cheese. She added a pile of cooked carrots and a sliced tomato. "They going to live in Hemlock Falls after the wedding?"

"Who? The Trees? Oh my word. I hope not."

"What's she going to do with the store, after she gets married, then? Hasn't been open but a few months, and she's been raking it in, from what I hear."

"She certainly wants people to think so."

"What, you think she's broke?"

"I don't know. There was something about the shop that bothered me. And Clare said the apartments are tiny and not very nice. You think Edmund would have given her money for a better place."

"Maybe she's thrifty. You look at that Marge Schmidt. She's got more money than God and buys them chinos at Walmart."

This was true.

"If Rose Ellen is planning on moving here, she never said a word to me. I hope not." Quill shook her head. "It's nuts. There's no way an urbanite like Edmund would live here. He's rich. He lives all over the world. She'll probably sell the place and we'll never see either one of them again, thank goodness."

"Marge Schmidt said they was looking to buy a couple of acres down by the river."

Quill closed her eyes and leaned her head against the sofa back. "You know what? I don't have to think about these people for another hour yet, until I make an appearance at the flipping engagement party. And I won't. Come on, Jack-a-rootie. Gramma Doreen has your mac and cheese all set up."

"Mac and *cheese*!" Jack hugged himself ecstatically.

"Okay, pal. We're going to forget all about Mr. Tree and his shenanigans for a bit." Quill picked him up and headed for the small dining room table. A thunderous knocking at her door interrupted her progress halfway.

She handed Jack over to Doreen and answered the door.

"They're gone!" Edmund Tree stood there, teeth clenched, eyes bulging in rage. He was half-dressed in a tuxedo: fine wool trousers and a starched white shirt. The sleeves of his shirt flapped wide.

"Hello to you, too," Quill said mildly. She stepped out into the hallway and closed the door behind her. "How can I help you? What's gone?"

"Rose Ellen's rings. Both of them. Her engagement ring, a three-carat blue white diamond set with sapphires. And her wedding ring. Both in platinum. And my cuff links. They're vintage, rose gold. I was getting dressed and I couldn't find the cuff links. The jewel box with the rings was gone, too. I've called the police. What the hell kind of place are you running around here?"

"Good grief." Quill took a moment to collect herself. "I'm so sorry. When did you last see them?"

"Day before yesterday, I guess. I don't know. Goddammit. Goddammit. Of course they're insured, but Rose Ellen was very particular about this diamond. It belonged to Elizabeth Taylor. I picked it up at Sotheby's for her. I want all of the housemaids searched. All of the other rooms, too. Right now!"

Quill's cell phone rang in her pocket. She took it out and flipped it open. "Hey, Dina."

"Davy's here," Dina's tone was perplexed, "and it's not to take me over to his house to eat pizza, either. He said Mr. Tree reported a burglary? Davy says he thought the burglaries would all be over because . . ."

"I'm with Mr. Tree now," Quill interrupted. "We'll come down and meet in my office, okay?" She shut the cell phone and slipped it back into her pocket. "If you'll just give me a moment, Mr. Tree, I'll settle my son and be right down."

"You're thinking about some brat at a time like this?"

Quill looked at him levelly. "I'm definitely thinking about a brat, yes. Go right into my office. Sheriff Kiddermeister is already there."

10

~Meg's Country Pâté~

½ cup diced sweet onions
20 ounces sweet pork sausage
¾ pound chicken breasts
½ pound beef livers
1 cup panko bread crumbs
1 extra large egg
1 cup cream cheese
1 chopped clove garlic
¼ cup Five Star or Hennessy brandy
¼ cup sweet cream butter
2 tablespoons kosher salt
¼ teaspoon each thyme, rosemary, ground bay leaf,
    and pepper
¼ cup shelled pistachios, sliced thin

Combine all ingredients except pistachios in a food processor. Mix in pistachios by hand and mold into a well-greased loaf pan. Bake for seventy-five to ninety minutes in a 350-degree oven. Cool. Remove from pan and wrap in cheesecloth. Store in refrigerator for at least twenty-four hours before serving. Serve with

ground mustard, cornichons or other pungent pickles,
and wafers of toasted sourdough bread.

"Quite a party," Howie Murchison said. He and Quill stood
at the far end of the Tavern Lounge bar. Quill sipped halfheartedly at a glass of wine. Howie nursed a Manhattan. The
engagement party swirled around them. Although it wasn't so
much a swirl as a sluggish eddy, Quill thought glumly. Word
of the theft of the wedding rings and the cuff links had spread
like a California wildfire. By the time she'd finished her statement to Davy Kiddermeister, showered, and changed into an
evening gown, she bet the farmhands at Peterson Dairy five
miles out of town were discussing the thefts over the nightly
milking. Rose Ellen sobbed, Edmund cursed, and the *Ancestor's Attic* crew of assessors and staff had tsked-tsked with the
kind of repellant satisfaction mean-spirited people take in the
misfortunes of others. Nobody was in much of a party mood.

At least the lounge looked good. The Tavern Lounge
glowed with the firelight from the big stone hearth and the
antique sconces on the wall. All of the waitstaff had been
called out, and they circulated among the guests with trays
of beautifully presented savories and sweets. Everyone was
dressed up. Quill herself wore a close-fitting tea length gown
in washed bronze velvet. Edmund had changed his tuxedo for
one of his three-piece suits—because he was missing his cuff
links, she supposed. Rose Ellen was a slender vision in a
dramatic black-and-white gown with a huge taffeta bow at
the neck. Her eyes were red and swollen. Edmund's eyes were
slits of suppressed rage.

Most of the wedding party was unfamiliar to her with the exception of Jukka Angstrom, whom she had met once at an art gallery opening years before. The others had checked in that afternoon and Quill was nerving herself up to go meet them.

Howie set his Manhattan down on the mahogany bar top and smiled at her. "Place looks good. Just the venue for a party like this, Quill. A photographer from *Vanity Fair* is here—did you meet her? A couple of the fashion magazines are here, too. This should be very good publicity for the Inn."

Quill thought the Tavern Lounge was one of the handsomest parts of the Inn. The floor was flagstone dating from the days when the Inn was the refuge of a notorious barkeep named Leaky Peg. Quill had rescued the ash wood floor of the old high school gym when it was remodeled and made tabletops. The bar top was a long sweep of mahogany that Nate the bartender kept meticulously maintained. "It will be great PR, if the news about the wedding rings doesn't spoil it," Quill said rather wistfully.

Howie fished the cherry out of his drink and ate it. "I heard about the burglary."

"Everybody's heard about the burglary."

"Does Davy have any leads?"

Quill thought about her lightbulb. "I hope so. We'll see. I think I may have actually heard the burglar leave the Inn down the fire escape. Edmund talked about suing the Inn for the value of the rings. Not enough security, he said. You have a legal opinion on that?"

Howie shrugged. His great-grandfather, grandfather, and father had practiced law in Hemlock Falls and he was content to continue the tradition. Quill suspected he enjoyed his role as town justice more than lawyering for a living; Howie had an equable temper and avoided contention. "Let the insurance companies duke it out. Either way, you don't have to worry. It won't come out of your pocket."

Quill sighed and got to her feet. "I'd better go do my hostessing thing." She scanned the crowd, trying to decide who to tackle first. "Miriam's not here?"

"Just me. And the Henrys over there." He nodded at them. Elmer beamed in a rented tuxedo. Adela was resplendent in a sequined floor-length gown with a red boa. "The only noncelebrity Hemlockians to be invited."

"You're both celebrities in my book," Quill said warmly. "But was there a reason you were invited all by yourself? It's a social occasion, isn't it? Didn't Miriam want to come along?"

"Actually, it's more of a business meeting. Rose Ellen invited me. Insisted, really." He ran one finger around his dress tie. He didn't like dressing up. Quill wondered how Miriam had talked him into a tux. She swore Howie had worn the same pair of Florsheim loafers for ten years until the shoe repair shop refused to resole them one more time. "I wish I'd stayed at home with Miriam."

"Rose Ellen insisted you come?" A sudden qualm hit her. "They aren't buying real estate here, or anything?"

"If they are, they haven't mentioned it. No. She'd like me to talk Edmund into making a will before the wedding."

"He doesn't have a will?"

"A man that wealthy—it's not smart. I know. Rose Ellen says he's phobic about it. A lot of people are, you know. You'd be surprised. It's a very familiar superstition. I can understand it—making a will is an acknowledgment of your own mortality. But . . ."

"It's dumb not to have one?"

"Very dumb. In any event, she thought Edmund would feel easier about setting up an appointment if we met beforehand, socially. So that's what I'm doing, being sociable."

Quill picked up her wineglass. "I suppose I'd better start being sociable, too. I'll see you later."

"Maybe not. If she doesn't drag Tree over here to meet me pretty soon, I'm out of here." He smiled and looked at her over his wire-rimmed glasses. "Great party, though. Love that pâté Meg does. The savories are pretty good, too. I take it Clare contributed those?"

Quill surveyed the crowd again. Clare was in one corner, a plate of choux pastry in her hand, a set expression on her face. Meg was in another, chatting feverishly to a sleek-looking couple. The male—mid-fifties, with the look of someone who spent a lot of time indoors—was dressed in a tuxedo. The female, who was extremely thin, with white hair drawn back into a severe knot at the back of her head, was in a tight red dress that was more skirt than dress. She was younger than her partner, but not by a lot. Both of them were familiar types from Quill's art gallery days.

"This is Sarah McHale," Meg said as she came up to them. "Quill, this is Andrea and Phillip Bryant. They're scouts for *Ancestor's Attic*."

Andrea Bryant drew herself up with an icy glare at Meg. "We're consultants to the show, Mrs. McHale."

"Sure you are," Meg said breezily. "If you three are all set, I'll be off, then." She turned her back to them, grimaced at

Quill, and headed to the buffet table and a clutch of other guests.

Phillip Brant lunged forward, his hand extended, "Mrs. McHale. Call me Skipper."

Quill shook hands. "Welcome to the Inn. I'm sorry that I wasn't here to greet you when you checked in."

"You know Edmund," Skipper said. His voice was extremely nasal. "We dropped our bags and rushed right over to the high school. Doesn't waste time, our Edmund."

"You rushed, darling," Andrea said, with an undertone of spite. "It is true, though, Mrs. McHale, that the auditions can't be held without either one of us, so there was a certain degree of urgency when we checked in."

"I hope you're comfortable in your rooms. Please let us know if there's anything you need."

Skipper glanced around the room dismissively. "It's a nice enough place. Not quite as top drawer as I'd been led to believe, but what can you expect from a village inn?"

"The beds are comfortable," Andrea said reluctantly. "I wouldn't mind a decent showerhead in the bath, though. You really ought to look into the spa showerheads. You know what they are? Pricey, of course, but worth it."

Quill gave them a professional innkeeper's smile "I do. Actually, it's an excellent suggestion. We've been thinking about doing just that. Now, you're the expert in North American paintings, aren't you, Skipper? And you're pottery and American crafts, Andrea. Those are wonderful areas to explore. I suppose you follow the show all over the country?"

Andrea lifted her skinny shoulders. "You would suppose right. We find ourselves in the damndest places, chasing after what turns out to be junk, more often than not." She turned to her husband and said in a confidential tone, "Although there's quite a nice piece of work hanging in the office. The receptionist took me there when I signed us in. The one of the two women sitting by the falls? I know you weren't all that impressed with it, but there'd be a place for it in our New York apartment. The guest room." She smiled at Quill. "You know the one I mean?"

"Yes, I do." She'd painted that soon after she and Meg had arrived in Hemlock Falls. The two sisters sat with their backs to the viewer, looking into the water as it spilled over the lip of the gorge outside.

"I don't know where you picked it up, but . . ." Andrea leaned toward her willing her to answer. Her eyes were pale blue and lined with kohl pencil. They gave her face a feline intensity.

"The oil comes from right here, actually," Quill said.

Andrea relaxed into a half smile. "Hm. I suppose you're wondering what it's worth. That's the downside of what Skipper and I do—everyone's convinced they have an unknown Rembrandt in the closet, and they want you to value it for free, and then they want to sell it to you." Quill opened her mouth. Andrea placed a hand on her arm. "I'm sorry to disappoint you. What you have there is a nice enough little piece. Some local yokel imitating a Quilliam is my guess. But it's not a bad effort. Not a bad effort at all. We'd take it off your hands for two or three hundred if you like."

"Thank you," Quill said. Out of the corner of her eye, she saw Clare set the plate of pastry down with a bang on a nearby table. "I'll think about that offer. Will you excuse me? One of my friends seems to be leaving."

She caught up with Clare just as she was about to exit through the patio exit. "Hey!"

"Hey, yourself." Clare was a little pale.

"You're not leaving already?"

"Work," Clare said vaguely, "You know."

"It's not work. It's the pastry, right?"

Clare took a deep breath. "Okay. So it's the pastry. All I have to say to your sister is, I thought we had an unspoken agreement to respect each other's area of . . . of . . ."

"Expertise," Quill said.

"Exactly. And what do I find here? Choux pastry. *And* Meg's pâté." Clare blinked away tears. "And the pastry wasn't bad. Not bad at all. Your average yahoo isn't going to be able to tell the difference between my stuff and hers, you know. I mean, her stuff is okay." Clare's face was pink and Quill couldn't tell if the tears were from frustration at the quality of the pastry or anger over Meg's betrayal. Quill bit her lip so she wouldn't laugh. It really wasn't funny. But chefs seemed to feel about food the way she felt about her painting and she knew how mad she was at Andrea Bryant right now. "I know. I'm sorry. But there's a reason—no, it's not a reason, it's an explanation because for the life of me I can't think of a good reason. Anyway. Edmund Tree told Meg you told him that her pastry was terrible." Quill bit her lip. "You didn't, did you?"

"Of course I didn't," Clare said, astonished. "I would never . . . Terrible? He said I said it was terrible? It's not terrible. It's . . . pretty good. Why did he do that?"

"I don't know. Edmund's a snake. That's clear. He may be stirring up trouble just because he can, or he may have an ulterior motive. I don't care. What I do care about is the two of you getting into a squabble that could be terrible for both our restaurants." She bit her lip. "And it's an awful thing to do to friends."

"Tree told her I thought her pastry was terrible?" Clare repeated wonderingly. "He's a liar."

"His crew's not much better. The Bryants over there just offered me a couple of hundred dollars for the painting that's over the couch in my office."

"For a Quilliam? My God. Meg told me you've turned down twenty thousand for that painting."

Quill blushed. "Well, yes. I did. I like that painting. It's one of the few . . . never mind. That's not the point. The point is Meg introduced me as Sarah McHale and they didn't know who I was. As Quilliam the artist, I mean." She grinned. "It won't take them long to find out, but never mind that. What's interesting is they thought they could scam me. Reputable dealers don't do that."

"These guys," Clare said indignantly. "Do you suppose they're all like that?"

Quill shook her head. "I doubt it. If I had to guess, I'd say that Edmund hates being number three in a four-horse race and he's trying to pull ahead any way he can. Look, I've got to keep circulating." She nodded in the direction of a tall man seated at a table next to the fireplace. He was broad-shouldered, with white blond hair and a face that looked as if it had been carved with a hatchet. His companion was small and very buxom in a simple black dress and strappy heels. "That's Jukka Angstrom, from Sotheby's. I've met him before and it would look very odd if I didn't go over to say hello." She touched Clare's shoulder. "Are you still bent on leaving? I wish you wouldn't. It'd be wonderful if you could bring yourself to go talk to Meg. Tell her what you really think of her pastry. Tell her that you didn't say anything about it to Tree."

"And never would," Clare said indignantly. "How could she think I'd be that much of a jerk?"

"She didn't think at all. She just reacted. You don't mind trying to clear things up, do you? I don't think she'll pitch a fit, but she might. Would you like me to go over with you?"

"No." She squared her shoulders. "No. I'll go talk to her. Just to make sure—all the eight-inch sauté pans are in the kitchen, right? I mean, she's not armed or anything?"

Quill looked at her sister, who was chatting up the two security guards who'd been at the high school that morning. The short one still had his sunglasses on. Tree had called him Marco. The other one darted suspicious glances around the room, which was a good reason, she supposed, to wear concealing sunglasses even indoors. He looked guilty. Both had changed into tuxedos. Meg wore her favorite pair of black leather pants and a bright green satin top. "I doubt it. She couldn't conceal a hairpin in that outfit she's got on."

"She looks cute, though."

Quill rolled her eyes and walked across the room to talk to Jukka Angstrom.

He rose to his feet as she approached the table and held out both hands in greeting. "My dear Quill. How nice to see you again after all this time." He kissed one cheek, and then the other.

"It's good of you to remember me, Mr. Angstrom."

"I could not forget so beautiful a woman. That auburn hair! Those amber eyes! I hope you remember me well enough to call me Jukka." He pulled out a chair. "Please. Sit down with us. Melanie, I would like to make known to you one of the finest artists of our generation. This is Sarah Quilliam, known to her friends as Quill. And this is Melanie Myers."

"Hi." Melanie extended one hand, which was tipped with scarlet fingernails and loaded with rings. Her black dress barely contained a pair of exuberant breasts. A deep breath would have dislodged them both. "I'm Edmund's personal assistant. He speaks very highly of your work. Very highly. That last show you had . . ." She raised both hands, as if appealing to the artist gods. "Fantastic."

"You would have been thirteen years old at the time of her last show," Jukka said gently. "Quill is known for her reticence. And perhaps even better known for producing very little in the past ten years. The art scene misses you, dear Quill."

"We certainly do," Melanie said, unabashed. Her eyes narrowed suddenly, to icy green slits. She poked Jukka with her elbow. "Will you look at what that woman's doing now?"

Quill followed her stare to see Rose Ellen picking a bit of lint, or something, off Edmund's lapel. She tucked her hand under his elbow and whispered in his ear.

"He hates being touched," Melanie confided. "She just won't leave him alone." She snorted and took a big swallow of her drink and emptied it. From the look of it, it was either pure vodka or straight gin.

"Oh, well," Jukka echoed. "Melanie, perhaps you would go to the bar and ask that very nice bearlike man for another glass of wine for me. You should probably not have any more yourself. Quill, may she fetch something for you, as well?"

Quill raised her glass. "I'm fine for right now."

"Ah, the hostess must always keep her head clear. Very well then, off you go, Melanie. Do not," he called after her, "hurry back." He shook his head and chuckled. "A dear child. But quite spiteful."

"She's an expert in vintage clothes?"

"You have been reading up on us, again, the perfect innkeeper. Yes. She is. Amazingly enough. A graduate of the Parsons School of Fashion and not at all bad at evaluation. It doesn't hurt that Edmund has known her family for years, of course. You know what the antiques world is like at all levels. It's all in who you know."

Quill admitted this was true.

Jukka wriggled his eyebrows. "You are wondering, perhaps, what has happened to my career that I am relegated to the somewhat distasteful duty of trailing after a reality show?"

"My goodness, Jukka. I wouldn't quite put it like that."

"You were always too nice for the game, my dear. But of course you are aware why I am here. There was this little item that made the newspapers a while ago . . ."

"The . . . ah . . . kerfuffle with Sotheby's?"

"Price-fixing, yes." He winced at his own use of the term. "Please. My dear. It is best forgotten. The bill has been paid, as it were. Our poor director was relegated to a prison term, and I, alas, to this. But it will not be forever." He crossed one elegantly trousered knee and regarded the tip of his shoe. "No, indeed. A few marvelous finds, and I will be back in the good graces of my employers again." He shot a surprisingly vindictive glance in Edmund's direction. "If that son of bitch allows it."

Quill couldn't think of a response to this. If Edmund had some sort of hold over Jukka, she'd rather not know about it.

"Did anything of worth turn up at the audition this morning?"

"A tactful change of subject. That's always been your forte, my dear. That, of course, and your skill with using light and dark in your painting. Yes, something of worth turned up at the auditions. Your marvelous Ms. . . . Schmidt, is it? I was in the auditorium and so missed much of the festiveness. But I would say that she indeed is a find of worth. She is your mayor?"

Quill laughed. "She is terrific, isn't she? Is Marge our mayor? No. She'd like to be." Quill took a sip from her glass and set it on the table. "Jukka, how long have you been on the *Attic* circuit?"

"Three hundred and ninety two days," he said promptly. "The prison term of my director was three years. I am hoping that my own exile will not last that long. Why do you ask?"

"I was wondering how much you knew about the way they operate."

He shrugged. "As you see. They select a small town, bring a team of experts in to scout items of value, and then feature the interesting pieces on the show."

"The Bryants just made me an offer on *Sisters*."

He drew his eyebrows together. "*Sisters*. Wait a moment. Ah. That very delightful piece you had on loan at MoMA. Ah, yes?"

"I was introduced to them as Mrs. McHale. I hadn't met them before."

"And?" The perplexed look vanished suddenly. "Ah. I see. The offer was for how much?"

"Two or three hundred."

"Thousand? You are delightful as an artist, my dear. But—if you will forgive me—not at that price."

"Dollars."

Jukka threw back his head and laughed so hard the party noise quieted momentarily. He patted her hand. "If your question is, has your worth in the market fallen to that extent, I can assure you, it has not."

"It flashed across my mind," Quill admitted, "but only for a second. Mostly because Andrea said it was an effort by some hack to imitate a Quilliam. I guess that's good, right? That she would say someone is trying to imitate me. So the second question that crossed my mind was whether or not Tree encouraged this sort of thing."

"Mm." Jukka's rough-hewn features became totally expressionless. "Why do you want to know? If you are thinking of selling *Sisters*, you'd better leave it to me. I will get a decent price for it, you can be sure."

"No, no. I won't sell the painting. It's not about the painting at all. It's about what kind of man Edmund Tree is. He's been here two days, and he's already causing trouble, and I have no idea why. What can he possibly gain by pitting my sister against one of our best friends, for example. And those darn wedding rings . . ."

"I'm afraid you've lost me, my dear."

Quill tried again. "Is Edmund Tree a quarrelsome sort of man? For example, when did this flap with the Barcinis begin?"

"Flap? Barcini. Wait. The pawnbroker from New Jersey. Is that who you mean? You know, the fellow is not bad at valuing certain kinds of antiques. Not bad at all. What flap are you talking about?"

"You know. The insults traded back and forth."

"I wasn't aware that they were. At a guess, I would say it would be jousting for market share. Edmund is offensively interested in market share. The reason is because the man is a—there is a wonderful expression in English. Wad of tight?"

"Tightwad."

"That's it. The show will feature a clip of the wedding, and therefore, the show is carrying all the expenses for this very lovely and very expensive trip to Hemlock Falls. Like many very wealthy people, Edmund is cheap. Stingy. A miser. An *Ancestor's Attic* that is number three in the ratings does not have the money to spend that a number one show would have."

"So this feud with Belter Barcini is about ratings?"

"It would seem so. As for your interest in when it began . . . I do not know when it began. I can, however, tell you that it is about to continue."

Quill had been sitting with her profile to the French doors that led to the patio. Jukka took her chin gently between his fingers and turned her head. "Voilà, as my friends in Amiens are wont to say."

Belter Barcini stomped through the doors. His black T-shirt was imprinted with a scarlet dress tie, a red cummerbund, and a violently purple dress shirt. He'd replaced his khaki shorts with black bicycling shorts. He hadn't changed his flip-flops.

Josephine was right behind him, her Steadicam at the ready.

Behind them both was Mrs. Barcini, resplendent in gold

lamé and acrylic high heels. Bringing up the rear was Hemlock Falls's best (and only) advertising executive, Harvey Bozzel.

"*Buon notte!*" Mrs. Barcini shouted. "You doughheads!"

~

"I'm telling you, Myles . . . It was stranger than the invasion of all those people from the Church of the Rolling Moses," Quill said some hours later. She was curled up in her bed, her phone at her ear. "Belter insulted Edmund and Edmund insulted Belter and Mrs. Barcini insulted everybody. And through it all, Josephine is whirring away with her Steadicam, recording the whole thing. Harvey claims it's all in aid of this Slap Down Thursday night. You know what else he said? That reality shows are scripted. Does that make any sense to you at all? I thought a reality show would be . . . I don't know. Real."

"You sound worried."

"I *am* worried. I'm really worried. This Slap Down thing Thursday night. Something nasty's going on. I can feel it. I wish I could shake the feeling that the burglaries have something to do with it. There's an escalation factor, for one thing. The burglar seems to have stopped scouting attics and basements for forgotten items and moved into the big time. Tree claims the rings and the cuff links together are worth over one hundred thousand dollars. What's more, Jukka Angstrom didn't come right out and say it—I mean, this is a man who survived a case tried in the media during that Sotheby's thing, and he's not about to give anything away to someone like me—but there was a very strong inference that Tree has a scam going on the side." She stopped. She realized she was sputtering with indignation.

He paused for so long that she thought she'd lost him. "Myles?"

"I'm here. I'm just lining everything up, in case you've decided to put your detective hat back on. We've agreed that it's been permanently retired? The detective hat?"

Quill made a noncommittal sort of noise.

"Because we've talked about this before. Law enforcement isn't for amateurs. You're going to leave it to the professionals."

Quill made another noise. Then she said, "I know you recommended Davy for the sheriff's job. You said he'd grow into it. But he doesn't seem to be growing into it fast enough. I think he needs help."

"Quill."

"From you, I mean, as the older mentor. Shouldn't you be giving him some tips, or something?

There was a very long pause. Quill didn't think she was imagining that it was skeptical. "I just thought I could tell him I talked with you about the missing jewelry, and the attic and basement burglaries and that you had some observations. I won't even bring up my suspicions about the scam."

"I'm not sure what you mean by scam, but it wouldn't necessarily come under his jurisdiction. So forget about that, please. The burglaries are another matter."

Quill didn't say anything. But she wanted to.

"Okay, my darling. If they've actually been stolen and the rings were recovered, it'll lift some of the pressure from you. Which would be good. So let's look at the theft of the rings and cuff links. Ask Kiddermeister if this is the first time something of value has been stolen. There's a pattern with repeat offenders, and if the jewelry's an anomaly, that's significant information. Can you find out if anyone's actually seen the ring in Tree's possession?"

"An insurance scam, you mean?"

"That's my good quick girl. Sorry, sorry. No, I'm not being condescending. Trying hard, anyway. But yes, an insurance scam."

"Good grief, Myles. The man has an American Express black card. He's been spending money like there's no tomorrow. He paid to have the whole restaurant closed down so it would be private for his engagement party." She bit her lip. "On the other hand—Jukka did say the show budget is paying for all of it. So maybe you're right."

"Have Marge check Tree's net worth. While she's at it, check out Rose Ellen Whitman's, too."

"Okay, I can do that. What about the fact that Tree's entourage consists of a bunch of scam artists? That seems pretty suspicious to me."

"Well." This time the pause was even longer. "It's not going to get us anywhere. The Bryants are obviously bargain hunting . . ."

"Bargain hunting!" Quill said indignantly.

"Bargain hunting isn't illegal."

"But, Myles!"

"I know. Immoral maybe, but not illegal. Now—Jukka Angstrom? I think you should keep an eye on him."

"You do?"

"Yes. Because he's clearly making moves on my wife."

"I wouldn't call them moves, exactly."

"Yeah. Well, my advice is to keep a frying pan handy. As

for Clare and Meg—they're just going to have to work things out on their own, my darling."

"That's it?"

"That's it. Unless you want to tell me who you're going to vote in for mayor."

"Oh my word. I'd forgotten about that. I told you both of them want me to endorse them? I'm going to tell them we're Swedish, you know—neutrals. And I'm not going to borrow trouble, either. I'm going to take things one day at a time."

"Excellent plan."

"So the next thing to worry about is the Slap Down." Quill slid down the bed until she was lying flat on her back. "Ugh. I'm getting a headache. A three-day headache. I'm going to stay in my room with Jack until Friday morning when the Slap Down will be all over. You know that Harvey's called a planning meeting for it tomorrow morning at the academy. I told you that, didn't I?"

"My poor Quill."

"Don't laugh at me, Myles. It isn't funny. I have to be there because Meg and Clare have called a temporary truce, and Meg's agreed to be a judge. Phooey! And every single one of these awful people is going to be there."

"It's clear you've got an unpleasant set of guests, but that's happened before and it's going to happen again."

His voice was warm. There was an ache in her heart from missing him.

"Give Davy a nudge. As for the rest of it? Wait it through, my love. It's not as though there's been a murder."

11

~Belter Barcini's~
Brunswick Stew

3 red, gray, or black squirrels, skinned and
    quartered
¼ cup lard (leaf lard from hogs, preferred)
4 pig hocks
2 quarts water
¼ cup salt
3 bay leaves
4 stalks celery, chopped
4 large yellow onions, chopped
4 large carrots, chopped
4 large potatoes, peeled and quartered
2 turnips or rutabagas, peeled and cut into 3-inch
    pieces
4 cups peas
¼ cup cider vinegar, or more, to taste

Fry squirrel parts in a frying pan with the lard. Put
squirrel parts, pig hocks, salt, bay leaves, celery, and
onions in a large pot with water and simmer for four
hours on low heat. Add carrots, potatoes, and rutabagas/

turnips and simmer thirty minutes. Add peas and simmer another thirty minutes. Add vinegar to taste.

*Serves six to eight. Serve with molasses corn bread,
fresh corn on the cob, watermelon, and fried peach pie.*

"Squirrel?" Clare said. "Where the heck am I supposed to get
squirrel by tomorrow night? Is it even legal to eat squirrel?
What's with this guy Barcini, anyway? I've never even tasted
Brunswick stew. I'm supposed to supervise a dish for a hundred people I've never even tasted?"

"I'm sure you'll do it *brilliantly*," Harvey said eagerly. His
face was pink with excitement. He smelled faintly of cologne.
He'd spiffed up even more than usual. Quill was sure his
cashmere sports coat was new. "Mrs. Barcini says it's been
in the family for years. It's a huge favorite at holiday time."

"Easy for you to say—you don't have to cook it." Clare
began to pace around the kitchen.

The kitchens at Bonne Goutè were huge, which gave Clare
a lot of room to pace. Clare was looking thin. The last couple of days had been hard on her. Or maybe it was the fact the
kitchens were so big. Quill wondered if there was some kind
of ratio between chef size and kitchen size. The bigger the
kitchen, the skinnier the chef?

It was nine thirty on Wednesday morning. Meg and Quill
were there. Clare and the academy staff were there. Harvey
was there.

Everybody else was late.

"Where are Tree and Barcini?" Clare demanded. "Where
are their people? We have to get started."

"I'll make some calls." Harvey pulled out his cell phone and wandered off to the corner.

"Use beef instead of squirrel," Meg said briefly. "It's either that or send out the volunteer firemen to shoot a passel of the poor animals."

"Let me see that recipe again," Raleigh Brewster said. Raleigh was in her mid-forties. She had what used to be called a matronly figure and a sprinkling of cinnamon-colored freckles across her nose. She was Bonne Goutè's expert in soups and stews.

"Harvey brought copies." Quill picked up a handful of the recipes from the counter and began distributing them. Pietro Giancava, the slender, devastatingly handsome man who was both sommelier and Clare's expert in sauces, folded it in half and tossed it over his shoulder contemptuously. Jim Chen (fish and seafood) read it carefully and started to laugh. Jinny Franklin, who had replaced the late (and unlamented) Mrs. Owens in jellies, fruits, and vegetables, jotted notes in pencil in the margins. She was a cheerful woman in her twenties and had come to Clare from Cornell. She paused and nibbled the end of the eraser. "Fresh corn is going to be a bit of a problem. The season's way over. Peas, too. But it's prime time for the root vegetables. You want me to start placing orders?"

"Please," Clare said. "Go frozen if you can't get fresh. This sucker stews so long it's not going to make any difference."

"You'll want to substitute bison or even deer meat for the squirrel," Raleigh said. "Beef is going to add too much fat."

"As if anyone could tell, with this mess," Clare said crossly. "Yeah, fine, see what you can get shipped in. What time is this stupid Slap Down, anyway?"

"Seven in the evening!" Harvey bustled back to the group assembled at the counter. "I wanted to give everyone time to prepare." He looked happily around him. "Belter is on his way. And Marco said Mr. Tree is just leaving to pick up Rose Ellen. Everybody overslept. There was," he explained to Raleigh, "quite an exclusive party at the Inn last night. We partied hearty."

Clare glared at him. "Right. Okay, people. So that means we have to start the Slap Down thing by ten o'clock tomorrow morning at the latest. I hope you're prepared for hefty delivery fees."

Harvey waved airily. "No problem. I've already received a retainer against expenses."

"It'd better be a big one. Have you found out what Edmund Tree is going to make? Has it got exotic ingredients, too? Zebra, maybe? South African elephant?"

"You can get that in cans," Raleigh said. Then, in response to the appalled looks, "Not that I would order it or anything."

"Mr. Tree will prepare zabaglione," Harvey said. "There was a voice message on my phone this morning."

Clare put her hands to her cheeks and groaned.

"It's a very simple recipe," Harvey protested. "I thought you'd be pleased."

Pietro Giancava broke his long silence. "The ingredients are not a problem, Signore Bozzel. A quarter cup of sugar for every four egg yolks, plus a third of a cup of Marsala. It's the preparing that is the difficulty. The entire recipe depends on the technique. So while Mr. Edmund Tree is in front of the camera whisking away, those of us in the background will have to prepare the cream for one hundred people? Meg and Clare cannot aid us—they are judges. That leaves Raleigh,

154

Jim, and I myself." He shook his head and folded his arms across his chest. "It cannot be done."

Harvey waved his hands excitedly. "You could put the eggs in a blender."

This time the appalled looks were directed at Harvey.

Meg finally broke the silence. "You'll have to, you know. There's no way you guys can whisk two hundred egg yolks in the time it'll take Tree to prepare his version for the camera."

Clare nodded. "Spoken like a true executive chef. Blenders it is. We'd better practice, then. I've got six on hand. It'd be better if we had ten. Could I borrow some from you, Meg?"

Quill saw her chance to get out of the meeting and on with the rest of her day. "We've got two. I'm sure I can scout out a couple more. Why don't I pick them up right now?"

"So you're going over the wall," Meg muttered. "If you don't come back, I'll send the posse after you."

She let herself out and walked around the building to the parking lot. Meg was right. She felt exactly like an escapee. But after her talk with Myles last night, she needed to do more than nudge Davy Kiddermeister about the burglaries. She needed to get actively involved in the case. She and Meg had solved several murder cases in the past, and however some professional law enforcement types might feel, she was pretty good at detective work. Burglary would be a snap after murder.

The municipal buildings were two blocks away from Nickerson's Hardware, off Maple and not visible from Main Street. They had been built in the late fifties, a time when the village had enjoyed another surge in prosperity, by the same architect who had designed the high school.

All the buildings were brick. The courthouse was three

stories high. It sat between two smaller one-story wings. The south side contained the county clerk, the tax assessor's office, and the Department of Motor Vehicles. The north side contained the sheriff's department and a two-cell holding pen for criminals on their way to somewhere else. Davy's black-and-white cruiser—with a bumper sticker that read: SHRF #1—was parked in its designated spot. Quill parked one spot over and went inside.

The front office held two desks: one for the sheriff and one for the dispatcher. The back half of the building contained the two cells and a small meeting/interrogation room where the deputies gathered for meetings. Davy was clicking intently away at his computer. He looked up as Quill walked in. His hair was as light as his sister Kathleen's was dark. But like all of the Kiddermeister clan, he had very fair skin and pale blue eyes. He blushed more easily than anyone she'd ever met.

"'Lo, Quill."

"Hi, Davy." She sat down in the metal chair that faced his desk. "How are things going?"

"Pretty good. And you?"

"I'd like to see the back of Edmund Tree as soon as possible," she said a little helplessly, "but I don't seem to be able to get rid of him. Other than that, I'm pretty well, too. I don't suppose you've had any results from forensics on that lightbulb?"

Davy ran his hands over his crew cut and leaned back in his chair with a sigh. "Budget."

"Budget?"

"It's a county expense to ID any evidence on that bulb. Couldn't find a way to justify it."

"Even though we discovered a loss after I heard those feet going down the stairs?"

"How am I supposed to link that up with the lightbulb? And it's not like I can find anyone to back your statement up. No offense meant."

"None taken." Quill thought for a moment, trying to think of a tactful way to bring up Myles's suggestions.

"Dina says you talk to the sheriff every night; is that right?"

"You mean Myles." She decided not to remind Davy yet again that he was sheriff and Myles wasn't anymore. "Yes. I do. And I did mention the burglary to him."

"So what'd he have to say?"

"That repeat offenders follow a pattern. So maybe our first task is to take a look at all the burglary reports and see if we can find any similarities."

Davy sighed, smacked open his lower desk drawer, and withdrew a thick green folder. "These are the incident reports. We have a computer record, too, of course."

"How many incidents have there been?"

"Of B and E and petty theft? Since when? It's the most common crime we have. The most routine stuff you read about in the *Gazette*. Stuff taken out of cars, stuff swiped out of gas stations, computers and TVs stolen out of offices and living rooms. But the A and B started a month ago, just after you and the sheriff left for the Adirondacks."

"A and B?"

"Attics and basements. There's one significant fact that sticks out a mile."

"They started right after *Ancestor's Attic* announced they were coming into town to do the show?"

"Right."

"What kinds of things were stolen?"

"Nothing you could really put your finger on," Davy admitted. "This is all forgotten stuff. Think about it. Can you give me a definitive list of what's in your basement or your attic?"

"A definitive list?" She shook her head.

"So we have evidence of somebody breaking in—a busted lock here, a broken window there—and of somebody rummaging around. Boxes have been emptied, a lot of green garbage bags with the stuff inside pawed through—but nobody's sure for certain what's gone." Davy tapped at the computer keys. "Mrs. Nickerson reported the theft of a couple of antique vases belonging to her grandmother. Turns out they were a couple of ceramic pots her grandma made in a ceramics class and they turned up in the garage when the Nickersons were looking for stuff for the Attic audition. Rory Kelleher's missing a painting but the description of it's so vague I couldn't write down much more than 'big painting of ocean or maybe pond.'"

"All the thefts are like that?"

"Most of 'em."

"So if a stolen item was brought to the *Ancestor's Attic* assessors, the genuine owner might not be able to prove ownership?"

"That thought did occur to me."

"Well, it didn't occur to me until just now," Quill said frankly. "This is very interesting."

"As far as the pattern is concerned, I don't think I can rule out the Tree burglary. Seems to me once a criminal gets a taste for it, it's pretty easy to graduate from petty stuff to the big time. Lot of them get a thrill just from the secretiveness of it, and they get so they need bigger and bigger thrills."

"This all makes a huge amount of sense to me. It's exactly what I told Myles." Quill looked at Davy with renewed respect. "Tell me, do you have a gut feeling about who it could be?"

"The law doesn't go with gut feelings now, does it?"

"No. Nor should it." Quill tugged thoughtfully at her hair. "You've got all the data on the computer, right? Can you run a search for any commonalities between the victims?"

"Why not? Any idea what you'd expect to find?" He grinned suddenly. "Don't say it. I can tell already. You have a gut feeling, right?"

"I haven't a clue. But it might help us see things in a different light." She sighed. It was nice and quiet here in the sheriff's office. If Jack were here, she could jump into a nice cozy cell and come out after the Slap Down was over. "I'd better be off. You wouldn't happen to have a spare blender around would you? You know, a food processor?"

Davy didn't blink. "Not at the office. You might try Marge. The diner and the Croh Bar couldn't function without blenders."

"She's next on my list." Quill got up to leave. "Thank you, Davy. Will I see you at the Slap Down tomorrow night?"

"You kidding me? Everybody in town wants to be invited and I heard they're only letting the bigwigs in. No way in heck I'm getting an invitation."

"You just did. I'm allowed a guest or two and that'd be you and Dina."

~

She found herself repeating the invitation to Marge some twenty minutes later at her realty office.

The offices were pleasant, if rather utilitarian. Hunter green indoor-outdoor carpeting covered the floor. Two artificial ficus stood in one corner. A brass coat tree stood in another. Marge's desk was a good quality maple and an impressive row of metal filing cabinets lined one wall. Marge was in the middle of one of her periodic cleanups. Her desk was piled high with manila envelopes and her shredder was whirring away in the corner. Quill found it all oddly soothing.

Marge raised one ginger-colored eyebrow. "You sure about the invitation? I heard the invites are scarcer than hen's teeth."

"Of course. They need a hundred people in the audience. Clare's arranged for a loan of folding chairs from the Church of the Word of God. I just hope enough people turn out to fill them up."

"I don't think you have to worry about that. Everybody and his brother wants to watch Belter and Tree duke it out."

"Let's hope it doesn't come to blows. Anyhow. Bring Harland, too, if he can stand to sit through it."

"He'd like it, but he's getting a third cut of hay in. Doubt that he can get away."

"Then just come yourself. I just dropped by to see if I could borrow a couple of food processors. I've got to get them back up to the academy."

"I don't see why not. Walk with me over to the diner and we'll see what Betts can spare." She looked at the wall clock. "Maybe get some lunch, too."

"I'd like that." Although she was perfectly aware that she and Marge were alone in the office, she couldn't help glancing around to make sure no one was listening. "Before we go, I'd like a favor."

"Ay-uh."

This was a classic Hemlock Falls response. It meant: I'm listening, but I'm not committed.

"This wouldn't be about this restaurant association, by any chance?"

"No. But I still think it would be a good idea."

". . . Because if it is, it's all about Carol Ann Spinoza and her maybe getting that food inspection license."

"Well, yes, it . . ."

"You really think there's anything going on in this town that I don't know about? Restaurant association, my foot. You want me to scare Spinoza off. All I can tell you, missy, is that you don't have to worry."

"I don't?"

"Nope. I'm going to fix her little red wagon but good."

Quill considered this statement for a moment. "Do I want to know?"

Marge grinned in a sharklike way. "I dunno if you want to know, but I'll tell you if you keep it to yourself."

Quill debated with herself. Marge wasn't above a bit of blackmail when the circumstances warranted it. "If it's anything illegal . . ."

"Pooh. Of course it isn't." Marge leaned back in her chair and laced her fingers across her belly. "You know when this town was incorporated? Of course you don't: 1825. You know what I found when I looked up those articles of incorporation? That you have to have a residence *within* the village of Hemlock Falls to run for an elected office. You know who doesn't?"

"Carol Ann?"

"Got it in one. She lives two hundred feet over the village boundary. I checked."

"But she's still within the township."

"Doesn't matter. So I'll be giving her a choice; she can still run for mayor but she's got to keep her squeaky clean little paws out of village restaurants. If she does get her license, and that's by no means a cakewalk, she's going to write a letter to the state authority that due to the potential conflict of interest of poking her nose around restaurants where she has dear friends and neighbors, she will not be taking any assignments in her hometown."

"Do you suppose the state will honor that?"

"Do I have a lawyer who'll sue Carol Ann and the state for the union pension fund if they don't?" Marge slapped her desk top in satisfaction. "You bet your sweet patootie I do."

~

"So it's still a three-way race for mayor?" Myles said.

"Looks like it." Quill yawned. It'd been a long day and Myles's call was later than usual. She'd fallen asleep waiting for it and her head felt fuzzy. "I pointed out to Marge that this wasn't the most honorable way to handle the situation, and Carol Ann is bound to plot some kind of revenge, but she just looked smug and laughed to herself every time I tried to bring it up. I'm not sure who I'd back in a contest between Marge and Carol Ann. Marge is tough, but Carol Ann's mean. And can a town stipulate how long a person has to live in a place? You said five years. Five years seems excessive."

"A town can pass any ordinance the town board approves.

It can be challenged, of course, but that's a lot of time and expense on the part of the plaintiff."

"Anyhow. Marge was in such a good mood at the thought of settling Carol Ann's hash, she agreed to make some calls concerning Tree's creditworthiness. I told her I was concerned about the huge bills he was running up at the Inn. That's one of the nice things about Marge. She's always ready to lend support if finances are involved." She didn't mention the rather knowing look Marge had given her when she'd made the request—or the comment: "Detecting again, huh? Well, lemme know if you need to break in anywhere. Kinda got a taste for it the last time we detected together."

"We had a good idea about looking for commonalities among the victims," Myles said. "Did Davy come across anything yet?"

"He left a voice mail for me. Said he'd bring the information he found to the Slap Down tomorrow night."

"I'm going to try to get back earlier than I planned."

Quill sat up. "Oh, Myles. Do you think you could?"

"We'll see. Things are pretty well in hand here, considering."

Quill closed her eyes. She bet it was Libya. But she wouldn't think about that now. She made an effort and kept her voice light. "I'll keep my fingers crossed. How soon, do you think?"

"A week or two."

"Darn. You realize, don't you, that you're going to miss the Slap Down tomorrow night. Although according to Dina, you don't have to. She can set up her computer so you can watch with the rest of us."

"That might not be a bad idea," Myles said agreeably. "I'll look in from time to time."

"Getting all of this in place is like herding cats. Hissing, cranky cats."

"I thought you and Dina had discussed the joys of nonintervention."

"The no busybodying rule? That was two days ago. I'd forgotten all about it. I'm going to write it on my bathroom mirror with a piece of soap and look at it every morning when I brush my teeth."

"Hm."

"That's a very skeptical 'hm'. You just watch. I'm taking most of tomorrow off. Jack and I will go to Peterson Park. We'll wade in the Hemlock River. I will refuse to make campaign posters. I will leave the Trees and the Barcinis strictly alone. What's more, I will refuse to be made indignant, discomposed, or dismayed by any of their hangers-on. Unless an event directly affects me or mine, I'm out of it."

"That's a promise?"

"It's more than a promise. You can't see it, but I'm raising my right hand. It's a solemn oath."

12

~Zabaglione~
2 servings

4 egg yolks
¼ cup superfine sugar
½ cup heavy sweet red wine, such as Marsala
    or port

Place egg yolks in a metal chafing dish, either copper
or stainless steel. Place heat source beneath the dish,
either Sterno or a similar high-temperature heat. Whip
yolks to a creamy froth. Add sugar in a thin stream,
whisking continuously. Mixture will begin to emulsify.
When custard is smooth and thick, remove from heat.
Beat in wine. Serve warm or chilled with mint leaves
and sugar wafers.

Quill's new policy of nonintervention lasted until six forty-
five Thursday evening when she arrived at the academy for
the Tree-Barcini Slap Down.

She'd spent most of the day with Jack, having little to do
at the Inn other than ask Dina to set up a Skype connection

to stream the Slap Down to Myles. Everyone was caught up in Slap Down fever. Nobody called. Nobody dropped by. Nobody asked her for her endorsement for their mayoral campaign. Even the kitchen was free of squabbles since Meg spent most of the day at Bonne Goutè with Clare.

The peace and quiet were absolutely wonderful.

She was in a relaxed and happy mood when she turned Jack over to Doreen for the night and began to prepare for the event. She wasn't sure how to dress. Belter would be in his shorts and flip-flops. Edmund and Rose Ellen would look like they were ready for a photo montage in *Vanity Fair*. Everybody else would be somewhere in between. She settled for a calf-length black skirt, boots, and a cream wool turtleneck sweater.

Bonne Goutè was lit up like a cruise ship. The parking lot was full. So was the lot around back, where the staff parked. After a fruitless five minutes looking for a parking spot, she tucked the Honda under an oak tree off the road and walked up the circular drive to the front doors. Marco was waiting for her as she stepped inside. He held a clicker in his hand and punched it. "Two hundred," he said. "That's it. You're the last."

"There are two hundred people in those kitchens?"

Marco jerked his chin down in a curt nod. The bulge in his sports coat told her he was armed. The ideal security guard, complete with a no-smile policy. At least he wasn't wearing sunglasses. "Not counting the ones who tried to get in through the kitchen. I sent Bruce back there about half an hour ago to make sure we don't get too full. We don't want to violate any fire codes."

"No, indeed."

Marco locked the door and followed her as she headed to the back.

The long hallway to the kitchens held an overflow of people. The air was humid. It smelled sweaty. Quill didn't like subways, elevators, or crowds very much, and she stopped. "You know, they don't really need me in there, and one of my employees has her computer set to stream the event, which I can watch just as well from back home as here."

"No can do. Ms. Whitman's set up a spot for you at the judge's table." He grabbed her elbow and marched her forward. Quill caught a glimpse of Elmer and Adela, Nadine Peterson, and the Nickersons. All of them waved hopefully at her. Quill couldn't get her arm raised to wave back. Marco pushed her through the thickest of the crowd—which was clustered at the entrance—and she emerged into the kitchens with a gasp.

Despite the chaos outside, the room was calm and well ordered. Somebody—probably Rose Ellen, who had a genius for design, had made excellent use of the space available.

The kitchen had six work areas; each area was a square formed of four stoves, with a prep sink at each end. The work areas faced one another, leaving a large open space in the middle, where Clare and her chefs stood to teach. The open space had been set up with two metal prep tables, angled so that Tree and Barcini could face each other and the cameras. Quill was surprised to see how little equipment seemed to be required to shoot a TV show. There were two small cameras on tripods, a monitor on a stand, and two tall skinny lights, all placed discreetly out of the way.

Eight of the twenty-four Viking stoves were set up with twelve-inch sauté pans, ready to heat the zabaglione. Bottles of Marsala stood at the ready and the eight food processors were stocked with egg yolks. Brunswick stew bubbled away in pots on the others.

The metal folding chairs were placed in four long rows around the walls. They were all occupied.

Meg, Clare, and Raleigh Brewster sat in a row behind a third prep table off in the corner by the refrigerators. Dina sat at one end, her laptop open and pointed center stage. An empty chair was at the other end. Still holding her by the arm, Marco dragged Quill over to the judge's table. Clare smiled at her and nodded at the empty chair. "Last seat in the house."

Quill sat down, tucked her tote beneath her feet, and said hi to everyone. She looked at Dina. "Is Myles on there?"

"I'm streaming it to his computer, but he's not on, no. I got an email from him. He'll try to catch us later."

"When he comes on, let me know so I can say hey. Wow. I can't believe how . . . efficient this all is." She looked around. "Where are the Trees? Where's Mr. Barcini?"

Raleigh rolled her eyes. "Squashed in the office with Madame. They're going to roll out one after the other as soon as the shoot begins. There was a whole lot of squabbling over who was going to host the thing. Barcini wanted Josephine to do it, since she's his producer and Edmund flatly refused. Edmund wanted Skipper Bryant to do it, and Barcini flatly refused. So they were at an impasse for a while. Barcini threw a punch at Edmund, but he ducked. Then Marco and Bruce—you know, the security guys—puffed up like a couple of male turkeys in mating season and things got a little dicey. But everyone settled down eventually."

"So who's going to host the show?"

Meg smiled. "Harvey."

Quill laughed. "Hooray for Harvey. I'll bet he's over the moon."

"He's the only one," Clare said. "Edmund said Harvey was too 'unpolished.' Barcini said Harvey was . . ." She stopped for a moment, clearly thinking of a more tactful word—"too effete. Then there was another squabble about who was going to whip up the zabaglione for the masses. Edmund insisted that his staff do it and Belter pitched a fit about how much air time they'd have because it'll be very dramatic, seeing all those whisks flailing away, so we ended up with a bunch of nonprofessionals making one of the toughest desserts there is."

Quill was happier than ever about her day spent in the park. "I'm glad I missed all that. So who's going to whip up the cream?"

Clare held up her hand and counted off on her fingers: "Skipper Bryant, Andrea Bryant, Jukka Angstrom, that walking advertisement for Victoria's Secret . . . you know, the blonde with the big boobs."

"Melanie Myers?"

"Right. And then Rose Ellen, Josephine Barcini, and Mrs. Barcini. One for each of the food processors. Harvey's going to pinch-hit. He's the only one who is neutral."

"How'd it go today with the prep? Did the practice recipes taste okay?"

Raleigh snorted. "The Brunswick stew's a joke. Fatty, overcooked, no subtlety of flavor at all."

"It's supposed to be fatty and unsubtle," Clare said. "It tasted delicious, if you want to know the truth. And actually, the amateur cooks practiced whipping up zabaglione all day and they weren't too bad." She sighed. "I just wish this was all over. I want my kitchen back."

Meg patted her on the shoulder. "An hour or two, at most. Then we can all go home and have a nice bottle of wine. Or maybe two."

Somebody clapped their hands with the imperial smacks of a gym teacher calling students to order: "People! People!" Harvey emerged from the director's office and clapped his hands again. "People! Pay attention, please!"

"My Lord," Meg said. "What the heck happened to him?"

"The chance to be on national TV," Quill said. "Oh, dear."

Harvey's well-cut sports coats, Brooks Brothers long-sleeved shirts, and Countess Mara ties had been replaced by a look Quill could best describe as Producer Gothic. His blond hair was clipped short. Sunglasses perched on his head. A small gold ring was in his left ear. A day's worth of beard stubbled his chin. He wore black jeans, tennis shoes, and a slouchy sports jacket. He took the sports jacket off and slung it over his shoulders, revealing a tight black turtleneck and a very nice set of muscles.

"My goodness," Raleigh said. "I never knew the guy was built like that."

"He's a regular at the Y," Meg said.

Harvey flung his arms out and addressed the camera grip. He snapped his fingers. "Mic?"

The grip hustled over and attached a clip microphone to his turtleneck.

"Testing, testing!" Harvey's voice boomed around the room. The tech at the monitor clapped his hands to his earphone, held up one finger, and fiddled with the monitor. Then he shot his forefinger forward."

"Testing," Harvey said. "There. That's better. Now. Is everyone in the audience ready for . . . the Slap Down?!"

The grip held up a sign that read APPLAUSE. A scattering of handclaps followed.

"People! I said are you ready for the *Slap Down*!"

The applause increased. Followed by a few whistles.

"Slap. Down!"

The grip put his fingers to his lips and whistled sharply. The tech rattled a large cooking whisk against the metal monitor cart.

Harvey moved across the floor like a dancer, swinging his arms. *"Slap. Down. Slap Down!"*

A thunder of shouts, yells, and catcalls followed him.

"Are you ready for this? Are you ready for this?! Men! Ladies! A joint production of *Your Ancestor's Attic* and *Pawn-o-Rama* brings you . . . Dr. Edmund Tree and Mr. Belter Barcini!"

Edmund and Belter came out of the office and jogged to the prep tables in the center of the room. The applause was tremendous.

"Cut," the tech said. "Let's do it again."

Quill sat back in her chair and sighed.

~

"Nuts," Meg said several hours later. "I should have brought something to read."

It had turned into a very long night. Dina played solitaire on her laptop. Clare and Raleigh had dug up a deck of cards and played gin rummy. Quill herself was in a half doze when

Meg reached over and nudged her. "They're getting to actually serve stuff in a minute, so we'll have to do our judging thing. Are you ready?"

Quill rubbed her face briskly with both hands. Edmund sat at one end of the stage prep table, legs crossed. He looked amused. Belter leaned forward at the other end, brawny arms extended, intent on the action at the stove. Pietro Giancava (scowling) and Jim Chen (exasperated) stood with some of the Bonne Goutè waitstaff. All of them held large trays filled with small plastic glasses and small plastic spoons.

"The serving's going to be the messy part," Clare observed. "The waitstaff has to hand the samples down the rows to the audience. We'll be mopping up eggs and stew for weeks. Edmund ordered a tray of punch to go round, too. He says people are going to need to clear their palates."

Meg groaned and rubbed her eyes. "I can't stand much more of this."

"Pietro doesn't look too happy," Quill said. "Neither does Jim."

"Pietro's furious he wasn't asked to be one of the whips. Jim's just disgusted. This isn't cooking. It's, it's . . . I don't know what it is. A three-ring circus. I wish I'd never agreed to this."

"It'll be over soon," Quill said.

Jukka, Skipper, Andrea, Melanie, Josephine, and Mrs. Barcini stood at the stove, whisks at the ready. Rose Ellen had a long white apron wrapped elegantly around her slender figure. Harvey's TV host grin was a little rigid by now, but he stood next to Rose Ellen, his hands on his hips and his eyes on the tech at the monitor.

The tech nodded.

Harvey's voice was slightly hoarse. "Now folks, we're going to bring the cameras over here so we can catch the action as our guest chefs whip Edmund's dessert into shape. We'll take a short break, so that we can dish it out, and then I hope you'll all be ready to vote." He took a breath, waited for the tech to countdown from five, and said excitedly, "We've been waiting for this, folks! Edmund—you've seen Belter sauté and chop. Are you ready to whip?!"

Edmund was. He stood up, gave the camera a superior kind of smile and poured the egg yolks into the chafing dish. Behind him, the assembled amateur chefs punched the blenders into action. It was fascinating, in a weird kind of way, and it was all over pretty quickly. Edmund whipped the eggs in a very professional-looking way. The crew at the stove flipped on the food processors, then poured the eggy results into the sauté pans and whipped away.

Edmund gave his eggs one final whip and held up his dish of zabaglione with a graceful flip of his wrist. He offered it to Belter, who hunched over the chafing dish for a long moment, then looked up and blew a loud raspberry.

"Cut!" the tech said, unperturbed. "Okay—get the samples out here, please."

The waiters sprang into action and ladled stew and cream into the cups with astonishing rapidity. The punch was passed around. The audience was served.

"Take it from the top, Mr. Tree," the tech said. "Offer the pudding . . ."

"It's a cream," Edmund snapped.

"Whatever. Anyhow, offer it to Barcini. Take a taste yourself. Then you're going to sample a little of each of the pud—creams your amateurs chefs prepared, right? We're going to

173

do this in one take, because it's been a long night and we're all getting freakin' tired."

Edmund offered the cream to Barcini, who declined with another even louder raspberry. He sampled his own pudding, frowned, and added the Marsala and whipped it again. He sampled the cream and smiled triumphantly into the camera. The camera followed him as he tested each of the creams from each of his amateur chefs in turn.

Edmund stopped a passing waiter and took a cup of punch and drank it down.

Then he died.

Horribly.

He stiffened, suddenly, as though something large and awful had grabbed the back of his neck. He clutched at his throat and gasped for air with great, whooping screams of effort. Foam bubbled from the corners of his lips. He went into another spasm and then another.

By the time Quill was on her feet, he lay contorted on the floor, his body curved in a final throe that looked like a question mark. She couldn't make herself heard through the shouts and the screaming. Rose Ellen was on the floor in a faint. Jukka knelt by her side. Melanie was in hysterics. Belter's mouth was wide open in astonishment. Mrs. Barcini tapped her wire whisk against her teeth and looked interested.

"The punch!" Quill shouted. She did her best to make her way through the mob. "Don't throw out the punch!"

The grip kept the cameras rolling. The tech sat at the monitor his mouth agape. Most of the audience crowded around the doors to the hallway, struggling against the tide of people trying to get in.

Everyone stayed clear of the body.

"The punch!" Quill shouted again. "Don't touch it!" She felt her cell phone vibrate in her pocket, and took it out with the feeling that all of this was unreal, but that she'd known something was going to happen. She'd known it from the beginning.

She looked at the screen.

Myles.

She held her phone to her ear. "Not the punch, Quill. The zabaglione. Make sure that no one throws out Edmund's zabaglione."

13

~Bonne Goutè's~
Between-Course Punch
Clears the palate of 8 diners

6 cups grapefruit puree
Juice of 1 lemon
1½ teaspoons grated ginger
Dash of grenadine

Combine puree, lemon, ginger, and grenadine in a bowl. Taste and adjust seasoning if necessary. Place in a glass thirteen-by-eleven pan and put in freezer until mixture is slushy, about one hour. Divide into cups and serve with mint leaves.

GRAPEFRUIT PUREE:

⅔ cup fine sugar
Zest of 2 well-scrubbed grapefruits
8 grapefruits, peeled and sectioned

Place sugar in blender and puree with zest. Add the grapefruit sections and puree until the texture of oatmeal.

"You're sure Myles wants all that pudding sent to forensics?" Davy Kiddermeister asked.

"It's a cream, an Italian cream," Quill said automatically. "And yes, he does. Everything Edmund tasted. All of it. If he tried the Brunswick stew, you'll have to test that."

"He didn't eat any stew," Davy said. "I checked."

They were seated in Quill's office. The late morning sunshine spilled through the window, illuminating the patterns on the Oriental carpet. Quill was as tired as she'd ever been in her entire life. "He said to put it in separate batches. Labeled with who made which batch. You did do that last night, didn't you?" Quill said anxiously.

"In a manner of speaking. We kept the pots in the same places on the stove. Two of them tipped over, you know. There's pudding all over the floor. Stew, too."

"I know." Clare's kitchen was a mess. It looked like a riot had been staged there. Actually, Quill thought, there *had* been a riot staged there.

Davy brightened. "We've got Dina's digital tape of the whole thing plus the footage from the shoot. I haven't had a chance to go through it yet. I can't believe we got the whole murder on tape. So if anybody switched the pots' positions, it might have been recorded."

"Dina doesn't have much. She jumped up when the rest of us did and forgot all about the laptop."

"We'll see," Davy said optimistically. "She got a good record of Tree drinking the punch. Myles wants the punch sent to forensics, too, you said."

"I was the one who told you to save the punch. It's because strychnine . . ."

"We don't know that it was strychnine."

"I'll bet you one of Meg's meals it was."

Davy scratched the back of his neck with his pen. "The ME tends to agree with you. Provisionally, of course."

"Anyhow, strychnine isn't necessarily instantaneous. If you've had a meal beforehand it can take up to twenty minutes to take effect in your system."

"How do you know all that? Oh. There was that newspaper guy that bought it here, years ago."

"His sister," Quill said. "And I learned more about strychnine poisoning then than I ever wanted to." She ran her hands through her hair, and then re-knotted it on the top of her head.

"Any idea where the perp got hold of it? If it is strychnine?"

"I have a very good idea. Rose Ellen Whitman cleans and restores paintings on the second floor of Elegant Antiques. Strychnine compounds are used in cleaning old oils sometimes. You need to check that out."

"The widow, huh?" Davy smiled a little and made a note.

"They were to be married soon. And yes, we all know that murders are usually committed by a close relative, but she isn't a relative yet. She never will be, given the circumstances." Quill shivered. Dina had brought coffee and scones in on a tray. She'd had two cups of coffee already, but wasn't able to touch the scones. Davy had eaten three. She waved the coffeepot in Davy's direction and refilled his cup when he nodded yes. "I don't think finding the murderer is going to be that easy. Maybe the burglar was the murderer and stole the stuff from her inventory. Which opens the suspect field way up. Anybody can wander through that shop and does. Maybe you can charge her with keeping a poisonous substance on hand without due regard for security or whatever, but I doubt you can charge her with murder."

"You know, strychnine compounds are still used in a lot of products found on farms hereabouts," Davy said. He made another note. There were dark circles under his eyes and his skin was pallid. "I don't even know why I'm writing this down. We don't even know what killed him."

"Strychnine," Quill said glumly. "You can count on it. Are you going to call in the state investigators? You look exhausted. This case is getting major attention and it's got to be a strain on department resources, Davy. Not to mention on you."

He hunched his shoulders defensively. "I can handle it."

"Yes, well, let me know if I can help."

"There is one thing."

This was so uncharacteristic that Quill sat up, her own fatigue forgotten. Davy had been even more intransigent than Myles about accepting amateur help on cases.

"Motive isn't something I can take to the DA's office—but you know that already."

"True. Cases are all about hard evidence these days." She'd wondered about that. She didn't have much time to read her favorite mysteries anymore, but times had certainly changed. Nero Wolfe would be laughed out of the courtroom. Perry Mason would receive a letter of censure from the American Bar Association. Belgium would suspend Poirot's police pension for improper evidence gathering before all the suspects gathered in the library.

"But motive does have everything to do with why somebody's been offed. You know these people pretty well. Is there anything you know that could point me in the right direction?"

Quill smiled at him. She couldn't refuse a direct request from the sheriff's department, could she? Myles couldn't possibly get upset over that. "I'll make a list. I'll ask some questions."

"Thanks. The sooner you get it to me, the better. You know, don't you, that everyone here at the Inn is going to have to stay on for a bit. At least until we get the underbrush cleared away."

Quill pinched herself on the knee, so she wouldn't scream. "Yes. I'd thought about that."

Davy eased himself off the couch with a grunt and a creak of his leather belt. "By the way, I had Delores Peterson fiddle with those burglary statistics for you. Actually, she had her son Tim do it. He's a programmer and she says he's faster than a speeding bullet at this stuff. I'm trying to get the department to take him on as a consultant." He worked at his shirt pocket and handed her a crumpled printout. "I'm putting the B and As on the back burner for the next week or two while we get this case sorted out. If you include the stolen wedding rings, there's zero crossover. If you take 'em out, there's maybe three. They all have the same homeowners' insurance, that being Schmidt Realty. But Marge insures sixty percent of the homes in this area. Plus, she's been turning down every claim she can. You know Marge. So that's meaningless. There's nobody that hasn't lived here for a while, but newcomers don't usually haul their attic and basement junk with them, so that's meaningless, too. Couple other things, but they're more coincidences than not. Like, everybody on the list is a member of the Hemlock Falls Historical Society. Meaningless." He took a deep breath. "I did send that darn lightbulb into the lab to check for prints, but I'd say the chances of getting anything other than Mike's prints on it are zero to none. So."

"So," Quill echoed. She tucked the printout under her desk blotter. The burglaries were the least of the problems on hand.

"You'll get that list of motives for me?"

"I'll start right on it."

He went out the office door just as Dina came in. She twined her hand in his for a brief moment. "I can download the final ten minutes from last night onto a CD if you let me have my laptop back. Then I can email the file to you."

"DA's office told me no. The laptop's entered in evidence and it's not coming out soon."

Dina looked at him coldly. "Is that so? My whole life is on that laptop, David Kiddermeister. I want it back."

"You'll get it back. Just not yet."

"Oh yeah? Fine. Fine." She sat down on the couch with a flounce. "Don't let the door hit you on your way out."

Davy's face was bright red. His jaw jutted out at a stubborn angle.

"We can find you another one, Dina," Quill said hastily.

"Where? Where are you going to find an extra computer? All my lab notes are on my laptop. All my thesis notes."

"C'mon," Davy pleaded. "You know as well as I do all that stuff's backed up. The thumb drives are in your bedroom."

"A place you'll never see again, if you don't get that laptop back to me."

Quill didn't think it was possible for Davy to get any redder, but it was. He muttered under his breath, and banged out the door.

"You were kind of harsh just now, I think," Quill protested. "Last night was hard on him, too."

"Last night was hard on *me*," Dina said flatly. "And yes, I

181

know all that stuff about how you have to make concessions when you're involved with a cop, but really. I've never seen such a horrible thing in all my life."

"It was pretty bad."

"Did you see how that poor man just lay there? All of his so-called friends and coworkers left him to die alone. Nobody went to help him, Quill! By the time we got there, he was . . ." Dina shuddered. "Ugh, I'm going to have nightmares for the rest of my life."

"All the more reason to let poor Davy back in your bedroom," Quill said sadly. "It's nice to have somebody there for you in the dark."

"He knows I didn't mean it." She sat up straight, her face alive with interest. "So. Are we investigating the case?"

"*We* aren't investigating anything. You are going to do your job and your schoolwork. I am going to make a list of suspects for Davy."

Her face fell. "Why did I expect to hear anything different from you? You never let me in on the cases."

Quill deliberately avoided looking at the scar on Dina's neck, a terrible consequence of the last murder investigation at the Inn. "It could be dangerous. There's a murderer running around loose, don't forget."

"I'll bet that's all they're talking about at the Croh Bar and Marge's diner." She smiled, and Quill softened at the sight of her dimples. Jack had dimples, too. "Which is better than arguing about who's going to be elected mayor, I guess. So there's a murderer running around loose and we're going to nail him."

"Or her."

"Or her." Dina's eyes widened. "Do you think it's Rose Ellen?"

"First rule of investigation, dating all the way back to Cicero . . ."

"Cui bono." Dina jumped up, took two yellow pads out of the filing cabinet next to the couch, and handed one to Quill. "Rose Ellen inherits the big bucks, right? Perfect motive for murder. Direct and unambiguous."

"Let's find out." Quill took out her cell and speed-dialed Howie Murchison. Their conversation was brief. She shut the cell phone off.

"Well?"

"Rose Ellen, Edmund, and Howie had a preliminary conversation about setting up a will, but nothing's drawn up yet. Howie said Edmund has a half sister somewhere but he hasn't seen her for years. Everything was to go to Rose Ellen. Now it goes to the half sister." Quill had jotted her name on her yellow pad and she looked at it. "Devora Watson."

"Is it a lot of money?"

"Howie doesn't know. But Marge was going to check into that for us. Me, I mean." Quill bit her lip. "Howie's not sure, but he guesses it's north of twenty million."

"Dollars?"

"Yep."

"Jeez." Dina closed her eyes for a minute.

"What are you doing?"

"Trying to figure out how much my weekly paycheck would be if I had twenty million dollars invested at four percent."

"Too much," Quill said firmly. "I guess the timing lets Rose Ellen out."

"Unless there's something we don't know, but I can't imagine what it would be. I mean, why not wait until the will's signed? I would." Dina blushed. "If I were a murderer, I mean. Which I'm not. Okay. Who else?"

"There's a certain ruthlessness to Jukka Angstrom."

"The big guy?" Dina tapped her teeth with the point of her pen. "I know what you mean. He's got a tough sort of face."

"He's in a tough sort of business. We had a talk at the engagement party. He was . . . tied, I guess is the best way to express it, to *Ancestor's Attic* until Edmund decided to let him go back to Sotheby's."

"That doesn't seem like much of a motive for murder," Dina protested.

"It does if you look at the financial facts. Jukka was extremely successful as Sotheby's rep. Which means he enjoyed an annual income of seven figures, at least."

"A million dollars a year? Selling antiques?"

"Probably closer to two. Now he's reduced to scouting out the leavings from people's attics and basements. I'd say a dramatic cut in your lifestyle would be a motive for somebody like Jukka. I wonder if we can get some background on him. Marge might help." She set her own pen down. Her conscience was pricking her. "Ugh. I feel like such a snoop."

"These people deserve to be snooped on," Dina said dismissively. "I'll tell you what I think of all this. It's not snooping. It's justice. I think we're just like those investigative reporters seeking out crime and administering justice."

"We're snoops," Quill said rather gloomily. "Okay. I can live with it if I don't think about it too much. I'll ask Marge to check on Mr. Angstrom's financial well-being."

"Who else? Wait. That Melanie. She's a pretty good suspect."

"Clearly in love with her boss," Quill agreed. "But don't you think her preferred target would be Rose Ellen?"

"I don't know. Maybe Melanie figured if she can't have him, no one can. Maybe she figured Rose Ellen would suffer more alive and missing out on that twenty million dollars. Wait! Maybe Melanie's really his half sister and she's just waiting to inherit."

"Good idea, but it's a no-hoper. She comes from a nice Upper West Side family in New York. Jukka said Edmund knew the family."

"I still think we should keep her on the list."

"All right. But very far down. It'd take a real psychopath to kill for those reasons. She didn't strike me as a psychopath. More of a Mean Girl."

"You'd be surprised," Dina said, rather obscurely. "I've known some psychopathic Mean Girls in my time. Okay. What about Belter Barcini?"

Quill threw her pen on the desk. "The obvious suspect. But I'm beginning to see why motive is such a nonstarter in the court system. He had everything to gain, apparently, from the airing of this TV show and keeping Edmund alive so they could snipe at each other. On the surface, he doesn't really have a motive—other than that he and his family hated Edmund Tree. And it never struck me as a hatred grounded in *who* Edmund was so much as *what* Edmund represented."

"Class war," Dina said. "Belter hated the suits, the attitude, the first-class degree from Cambridge, but not Edmund the person so much. Yeah. I can see Belter as revolutionary, getting hot over ideas rather than individuals."

"This strikes me as such a personal murder. Somebody wanted Edmund himself out of the way."

Dina raised her eyebrows. "On the other hand, just look at what the French did to Louis the Sixteenth. Chopped his head right off. There's a guy that was murdered for an idea."

"You might be right. I don't know. We certainly have to move him close to the number one spot, if not at the top. Myles is convinced the poison was in Edmund's zabaglione. We don't know that for certain, and we won't until the lab gets through testing all that stuff. But if it was—Belter had the best opportunity to drop whatever it was into the chafing dish. More important, Belter set this whole thing up. The Slap Down. The challenge. And whoever did this, Dina, had to plan for it ahead of time. The murderer had to get the poison and know for certain that there'd be access to the chafing dish just as Edmund prepared it. Otherwise, the murderer would be risking killing whole piles of innocent—or relatively innocent—people. On the surface, Belter's motive looks thin. But the hard evidence may point to him after all."

"So what do we do now?"

"Wait until the forensics come back. If we have any luck at all, we'll be able to narrow down the source of the poison itself. If, for example, it has the same chemistry as the solvents in Rose Ellen's shop, we can talk to her about who might have had a chance to steal it."

"So we leave Belter with a big fat star next to his name."

"I think so."

"Anybody else?"

Quill's eyes flew to the painting over the couch. She'd drawn two slender women, one a head taller than the other. They had turned to look at the waterfall in the distance. The faces were obscured, but she'd concentrated on the language of their bodies. The older, taller woman had her arm around the younger. The small sister was vulnerable. The tall sister was protective. Some local yokel had painted that, huh?

"The Bryants," she said. "Skipper and Andrea."

There was a tap at the door. It opened. "Hello," Andrea Bryant said coyly. "Did we just hear our names? I hope you aren't taking it in vain!"

14

~Meg's Scones~

2 cups flour
1 tablespoon raw sugar
2½ teaspoons baking powder
4 tablespoons salted butter
2 eggs
⅔ cup whipping cream
1 teaspoon grated lemon peel
½ cup golden raisins

Blend flour, sugar, baking powder in bowl. Cut in butter. In a separate bowl, stir eggs and cream to a smooth liquid, then add to flour mixture. Add lemon peel and raisins. Mix with a fork until all liquid is absorbed. Knead on a floured surface for about ten seconds. Divide dough into an eight-section scone pan, or shape into eight wedges. Bake at 400 degrees for fifteen minutes. Serve with butter, lemon cream, and the jam of your choice.

"Quill, my *dear*." Andrea Bryant wore tight black jeans, an oversized men's white shirt, and blown glass earrings that caught the sunlight in a distracting way. She'd pulled her white hair back with a tortoiseshell clip. She walked into Quill's office with an apologetic twitch of her hand. "I hope we're not disturbing you."

"Hello," Skipper Bryant said. He wore gray wool trousers and a striped Brooks Brothers long-sleeved shirt. The sleeves of a navy blue cardigan lay over his shoulders, as if the sweater had hopped on his back for a ride. Quill wondered if they'd discussed the proper attire for a post-murder Friday before they'd come down for breakfast. She looked at her watch. Ten o'clock. Brunch, then.

Andrea settled herself on the sofa arm next to Dina and dangled her Hermès bag over Dina's lap in a pointed way. "Do you mind?"

Dina flushed and got to her feet. "Maybe we can talk about this later, Quill."

"Sure thing." She smiled. "I'll keep you posted."

Dina left with a soft click of the latch.

Skipper pulled a chair away from the small Queen Anne table Quill used as a conference center, spun it around, and settled himself backward, legs out to either side and chin in his hands. He gave her a boyish smile. "We wanted to come and apologize."

"About that wonderful piece." Andrea tilted her head backward and gazed up at the painting. "We'll be candid with you. We recognized it at once for the marvelous piece of work that it is . . ."

"A genuine Quilliam," Skipper said, with just the proper degree of awe.

"Exactly," Andrea said.

". . . And yes, we admit it," Skipper said. "We thought we

could acquire it from the small-town innkeeper. We had no idea it was you."

Andrea shot Skipper a look filled with dislike. "Cut the crap, Skip. She's not buying it." She looked at Quill and smiled sourly. "You know what the antiques business is like. Everybody fantasizes about coming across the deal of the century. This was as close as we've come at striking it big in quite a while. So, yeah, we made you an offer we thought you couldn't refuse. We should have recognized you, but your sister introduced you as Mrs. McHale, and the penny didn't drop until later. I'm sorry. I figure you must be used to it by now, the way this business runs, I mean. You're too much of a realist to hold our little dodge against us."

"You didn't do anything illegal," Quill said uncomfortably. "And yes, art can be rough. On the business side, at least."

"Okay, then. I don't suppose you would be interested in selling it? At a price more commensurate with its worth, certainly. No? I thought not. Too bad. There are two galleries we work with in New York that'd kill to get their hands on it." She put her hand to her mouth. "Oh my God. I've shocked myself. I didn't think that was possible anymore. Terrible thing last night, wasn't it?"

"Terrible," Skipper echoed. "Great loss to the community, Edmund's death. Very sorry to see it. You'll be glad to know that we're already planning a tribute."

"I'm sure Rose Ellen will welcome it," Quill said politely.

"We'll have to speak with her about it," Andrea said vaguely. "Something just occurred to me, though. I don't know, Skip, do you think Quill might want to come on the show and say a few words about Edmund?"

Skipper nodded. "You'd be quite a draw as far as the art community goes. Of course, the average viewer isn't going to know you from a hole on the ground, but you're pretty enough. And we could feature *Sisters* in the background." He waved a forefinger in the direction of the painting.

Quill blinked. "You'd like me to come on the show? What show?"

Andrea's smile was catlike. *"Your Ancestor's Attic.* Oh. You didn't know? Yes. Well. News of Edmund's death got around pretty quickly, as you might imagine, and before you could say 'Henri Matisse,' the producers from New York were on the line demanding that we take over."

Quill took that with a grain of salt. She was willing to bet Andrea had had her cell phone out and put a call into the producers before Edmund's body was cool.

Skipper blustered. "They were pretty insistent. It took some convincing, especially with Andrea, here. But we figured we'd give it a trial run."

"We agreed to a five-year contract with options," Andrea said. "She's not an idiot, Skipper. Look at her face."

Quill adjusted the cloisonné bowl on her desk from one side to the other.

"Yes," Andrea said flatly. "The show will be good for us. As a matter of fact, it's just what we needed right now. Our finances have been a little less secure than I'd like, Quill, as I'm sure you'll find out if you snoop around." Her eyes were cool and calculating. "You should know, Skip, that not only does she have a reputation as artist-that-was, she's developed a bit of a reputation as an amateur detective. You don't want to be pulling the wool over her eyes, or even be seen trying to." She got up, with an abrupt, decisive movement. "So. We just wanted to let you know that we realized our gaffe almost immediately and wanted to apologize once more for our mistake."

"It looks like we're stuck here for a bit," Skipper added. He paused on his way out of the office. "Your local sheriff as good as told us not to leave town. So we're going to go ahead with the Hemlock Falls segment of the show, just as Edmund had planned. He would have wanted it that way. You're sure about not appearing on the show? It'd be good advertising for the Inn."

"I'm sure. Very, very sure." She added, silently, *And don't let the door hit you on your way out.*

Dina came back in as soon as they were gone. "Well?"

"Another motive," Quill said with satisfaction. "A good one. They're taking over *Ancestor's Attic*. Plus, they're broke. Well, not broke. Just not as rich as Andrea would like to be."

"They told you all that?"

"It could hardly be kept a secret. And they're not idiots. Well, Andrea isn't, anyway."

"What now?"

"I've got two more people to talk to. Mr. Barcini and Rose Ellen."

"I'll go with you," Dina said promptly.

"Who's going to mind the front desk?"

"I'll ask Mike. He's done it before. And he's really good about telling the media to piss off. Sorry. I meant bug off. He's really good about keeping the media at bay. So can I come? All the best amateur detectives have sidekicks, and I know Meg is usually yours, but you argue about which one of you is Sherlock and which one is Watson, and it's pretty obvious who the senior detective is." She fluttered her eye-lashes.

"Flattery," Quill said, "will get you everywhere. Let's go see the widow."

~

"Edmund would have wanted that phony Bryant and his witch of a wife to take over the show?" Rose Ellen threw back her head and said, "Ha!"

Mike Santini had been more than willing to take over the desk. He had been the Inn's groundskeeper for more than twelve years. Quill had sketched him once, in charcoal. His tough, wiry body resembled the roots of a banyan tree, so she had drawn a banyan in the background and ever since, he'd tried to find a variety that would grow in upstate New York with no success at all. At Dina's insistence, Quill also stuck an extra wad of tissues and a small pint of brandy in her tote, "In case Rose Ellen is a basket case," Dina said. "Because, my gosh, she must be devastated."

Nothing was further from the truth. Quill thought she might need a nip of the brandy she'd brought, herself, just to adjust to the behavior of Rose Ellen, the non-grieving widow. "Edmund didn't see the Bryants as suitable successors as hosts on *Ancestor's Attic*?"

Quill and Dina sat in the narrow living room of Rose Ellen's third-floor apartment. Clare was right. The rooms were small and shabby. Rose Ellen had concealed the peeling wallpaper with a collection of prints and photographs, and draped the shabby windows with graceful swoops of muslin, but the dreariness of the place was inescapable. The cramped space was reduced even further by a collection of empty cardboard boxes. Rose Ellen was leaving Hemlock Falls as soon as the sheriff allowed it.

Rose Ellen's face and voice were acid. "Suitable successors? Edmund was cheap. Edmund was tight. Edmund thought he was going to live forever. He wasn't going to let the show go to anybody, much less Skipper and Andrea. And he wasn't about to leave any money to me. Not before I slept with the bastard anyway, and I was so careful to insist that we waited until we married. And when I think I might have gotten something out of him if I'd just . . . damn it all." Rose Ellen tossed a couple of throw pillows into a cardboard box, then sank into a chair. It was a reproduction Louis XIV, reupholstered in satin brocade. Rose Ellen smoothed the edge, lost in thought. "I redid this myself, you know. When Edmund and I became engaged, I thought all of that was over. Scrabbling through other people's leftovers, spending hours with those ghastly paint thinners and horrible restoring fluids." She held out her hands. The nails were polished and well cared for, but the palms were calloused and there were faint acid scars on her wrist and the backs of her hands. "We had a prenup, you know. He was going to settle two million dollars on me the day after we were married, and then give me twelve thousand a month—for my very own—as long as the marriage lasted. And now . . . I'm back to this." She swept a bitter gaze around the room.

Quill didn't know what to say. "I'm sorry" seemed inappropriate.

Dina's eyes were shocked and she blurted, "You didn't lo . . ." She blushed fiery red. "Sorry, I meant um . . . you didn't . . ."

"Didn't get a thing?" Rose Ellen said. Her smile was ugly. "Not a dime. Not a centavo. Not a sou."

"That's not what Dina meant," Quill said.

Rose Ellen clasped her hands together tightly. "He only agreed to the expenses here because it would have been so much cheaper than a wedding in the Seychelles or the Hamptons, which is where I wanted to be. He said since the wedding was part of the shoot we could expense it out. Damn. *Damn.* He was so afraid he was going to outlive his money. That's a common fear of the rich, you know. You see it all the time. It's ironic. He was such a tightwad, and it killed him."

"Excuse me?" Dina said.

"If we'd been in the Seychelles or the Hamptons, he wouldn't have gotten those bad eggs or whatever. He wouldn't have been doing the TV show at all."

"He didn't die of bad eggs," Dina said. "You don't die the way he did from bad eggs."

Rose Ellen bit her lower lip. "What are you saying?"

"The coroner hasn't filed his report, but the sheriff's department is treating it as murder," Quill said.

"No."

"I'm afraid so."

She sat very still for a moment, looking down at her hands, rubbing them over and over again. Then she nodded, as if in response to a voice only she could hear. "Wonderful. Just wonderful. You know what? I try and try, and I just never catch a break." Then, "Who killed him? Barcini?"

"We don't know."

"I suppose you'll find out?"

"The sheriff is very experienced," Quill said loyally. "I'm sure we'll get some answers soon."

"If the bastard who did it has any money, will you let me know? Maybe I can sue him."

Quill glanced at Dina. Bewilderment had replaced shock. "I think we'll be getting along now, Rose Ellen. We just dropped by to see how you were doing."

"I'll be fine, thank you. It was good of you to call." The mask had slipped back into place. "Let me walk down with you." She rose fluidly to her feet, looking just like Audrey Hepburn in slim black pants and a black turtleneck. She opened the door for Quill and Dina, and then followed them onto the landing. "I'm having a fire sale at the store. I haven't had a chance to price anything yet—I think I may just leave it in the hands of what's her name, the sales girl . . ."

"Delores Peterson?"

"Yes. She's perfectly capable of selling up the shop, isn't she?"

"I'm sure she is."

"I'm going back to New York. I've got some friends on Fire Island who will let me crash there for a while, until I decide what to do next. At the moment, I just want to get away from this godforsaken place. So much for trying tourist towns." She stood at the head of the stairs and looked back at them. "Come down with me. You liked that trompe l'oeil of the fountain, didn't you?" She tucked her arm beneath Quill's and led her downstairs. "You've been such a dear friend to me, Quill. I can let you have it at a discount. Say, two hundred dollars. In cash, if you wouldn't mind. Delores can run it up to the Inn, and you can pay her then. That'll be all right with you, then?"

They reached the bottom floor. Rose Ellen pushed the door open. Quill and Dina found themselves on the sidewalk.

"Bye," Rose Ellen said.

She closed the door.

Outside, the day was brilliant with sunshine. The maple trees along Main Street were just beginning to show the faint rosy flush of fall. Elmer and Adela Henry drove past in their Cadillac. Elmer had affixed large signs to the rear passenger doors that read, HENRY FOR MAYOR: YOUR HOMETOWN HERO! Two of the ladies from the Fireman's Auxiliary walked by, giggling. The scent of roasting coffee drifted on the air.

"It looks so normal out here," Dina said. She zipped her gray hoodie up. "It's a little chilly out, though, don't you think?"

Quill didn't say anything. It was seventy-two and sunny.

"Rose Ellen . . ." Dina tried again. "She was . . ." She stopped and shook her head, as if to clear it, as if to brush the episode away. "My goodness."

"Goodness has nothing to do with it." Quill put her arm around her. "That coffee smells great. Let's get a cup. And let's not think about Rose Ellen Whitman ever again."

15

~Josephine's Corn Pone~

1⅔ cups yellow corn meal
1⅔ cups flour
½ cup sugar
2 tablespoons baking powder
1⅔ cups milk
4 large eggs
⅔ cup salted butter, melted
¼ cup raw sugar
⅓ cup butter, chopped into one inch squares, for
    topping

Mix all ingredients except for last two. The batter will be lumpy. Butter an eight-by-eight square pan and pat the batter into it. Sprinkle the raw sugar and chopped-up butter over the top. Bake in preheated 375-degree oven for twenty-five to thirty minutes. Let stand for twenty minutes. Remove from pan. Serve with maple syrup.

A latte at the Balzac's Café brought Dina back to her sunny self.

The café was very pleasantly laid out, with posters of Honoré de Balzac on the walls and a wide selection of coffee beans in clear glass bins. The tables and chairs were made of pine. The floors were terrazzo tile. It felt Parisian.

"I guess she didn't murder him," Dina said. "I guess she didn't love him, either, but she sure didn't want him dead." Dina poked at her latte with the plastic straw. "This sidekick stuff is pretty amazing." She stared absently into space, and then shook herself, as if getting rid of horrible thoughts. "Who's next? Belter Barcini? His people-whomping mom? Melanie Vampira Myers? Are they going to turn into monsters before my very eyes, like Rose Ellen Whitman?"

"Are you sure you don't want to go back to the Inn? It's been an eventful twenty-four hours." Quill checked her watch. "Not even that. Eighteen."

"I'll say. Edmund Tree dropping dead right in front of my eyes, and then Rose Ellen Whitman dancing on his grave. Stomping, actually, since she's so pissed off he's dead. She's not even going to stick around for his funeral. Who's going to bury the poor guy?"

"The family, I guess."

"All he's got is a half sister he hasn't seen for years. What do you want to bet she'll show up speedy-quick? Twenty million dollars is a lot of money. I figured it out, you know. My paycheck if I had twenty million dollars invested at four percent. It'd be eight hundred thousand dollars a year divided by fifty-two, which is sixteen thousand dollars a week, minus taxes. The sister could pay for the funeral and not even notice."

"His lawyers will take care of the funeral and the sister. In any event, we don't have to worry about it. If you don't want another latte, I think we should go back to the Inn. I want to give Marge a call about the umm . . ." Quill glanced around a little nervously. Why did she feel guiltier about snooping into suspects' financial backgrounds than about the rest of the detecting?

"The money part? How broke the Bryants are? How much Edmund Tree is really worth? Yeah, I'd like to know that, too."

Marge would tell her that finances profile a person. That you could get a good sense of who someone was by how they saved, how they spent, how they earned.

"Quill?"

Maybe a financial profile was a matter of character. Which should be private. Unless you'd murdered somebody.

"Quill?"

"Sorry. I was thinking about something else. Did you want another coffee?'

"You should have some. The caffeine would perk you up. None of us got to bed before three last night. I don't think Davy slept at all."

She *was* tired. Maybe the ugly scene with Rose Ellen wouldn't have been so awful if she'd gotten a good night's sleep.

"I don't want another latte, although thank you very much for buying me this one. I see it as a sidekick perk. Balzac lived off coffee, did you know that? And he died after drinking fifty cups in one day."

"He did?" Quill said, startled.

"It's a fact. Which is why I'll pass on the second one, and you should, too, come to think of it."

Quill left two dollars on the table for a tip and followed Dina out to the car. Dina fastened her seat belt with a cheerful air, and was quiet until they reached the bottom of the Inn driveway.

"So when are we going to interrogate the Barcinis?"

"The thing about amateur detecting is that you have no official standing and you can't appear to be interrogating anybody. I've got to think of some good excuse to drop in on the Barcinis in a casual way. You'd be surprised what people will tell you if you're an interested listener without a badge."

"If the Barcinis stayed at the Inn, that would give you a good excuse to chat them up, wouldn't it?"

"Yes, but they're out at the Marriott, and to tell you the truth I'd rather they stayed there. Belter's so . . . noisy. And Mrs. Barcini keeps whacking people with whatever's at hand. Very disruptive. "

"They're not at the Marriott anymore. Isn't that their bus?"

Quill braked abruptly. Yes, that was the Barcinis' bus, gleaming orangely right in front of the Inn and blocking all the traffic. Not that there was any traffic, but still, the bus was blocking prospective traffic.

Quill leaned her head against the steering wheel and groaned.

"And there they are," Dina said in a pleased way. "You know what I think? I think now that the Provencal suite is free because Edmund Tree is dead, they're going to move right in."

Dina was right.

Quill arrived at the reception desk a few minutes later to find Mike hauling an assortment of suitcases up the staircase and the Barcinis headed on in to the dining room. Quill had a moment's confusion identifying Josephine because she didn't have the Steadicam on her shoulder.

"It is Signora Quilliam," Mrs. Barcini said with a broad smile. "Finally you got our reservation right."

There was something different about Mrs. Barcini, too. She didn't glitter, glow, or fluoresce. She had on a navy blue pantsuit, tennis shoes, and a rather attractive print blouse. Belter was still in shorts and flip-flops, but he wore an Izod golf shirt in dark green that was almost flattering to his rubicund complexion.

Belter noticed her discreet surprise. "We're here to kick back some. Don't figure we'll have to deal with my fans, like we do at the Marriott. Can't keep up the glamour twenty-four/seven. Poops Ma out."

"We are also here to try some of your food," Mrs. Barcini said. She bypassed Kathleen, who ran after her with a fistful of menus, and sat down at the one empty table in the dining room. It was by the kitchen, and it was where Quill sat herself when she wanted to keep an eye on the guests. "I hope there is no poison in this food, as there was at Bonne Goutè last night," she said loudly.

A pair of tourists at the table nearby looked nervously at their entrees.

She looked down at the pale blue tablecloth, which was clean but bare of cutlery, glasses, or flowers, and announced, "This table has no forks."

Kathleen rolled her eyes at Quill. "We don't usually do a setup here, Mrs. Barcini, but let me . . ."

"You know who I am?"

"Certainly. If you'll just take these menus, I'll go get . . ."

"It's because I have a famous son." She slapped Belter on the shoulder. "A very famous son. Although, as you see, we are not here in our shiny clothes, which attract the fans. We are here to relax and prepare for the tidal wave of attention that is sure to follow the airing of the TV show about the slapping down. After last night, Joey is going to be a bigger star than ever before. Do you know about last night?"

"Ma," Belter said. "Just cool it, okay?"

"See?" Mrs. Barcini beamed. "I embarrass my boy. Good. Keeps him on his toes."

Belter raised his arm and headed off another slap. "Okay, Ma. Okay."

"It's very nice of you to let us stay here, Mrs. McHale," Josephine said.

Quill looked at her more closely. Groups always had a member quieter than the others, and Josephine was definitely quiet. Other than the indignant squawk she'd let loose when Marco the security guard had grabbed her camera at the high school, Quill didn't think she'd ever heard her make a noise. Maybe the camera served as her voice, and without it, Josephine had to speak up.

She rubbed her forehead. Dina was right. She was overtired. She was so overtired she was hallucinating.

"She's not letting us stay here, Sis. We're paying her."

"She could always say there's no room," Josephine said serenely. "But you didn't. Thank you."

"Has that hap—" Quill cut herself off. If the Barcinis had been kicked out of other inns and hotels, it wouldn't be kind to ask about it. "I mean, what's been happening since the tragedy last night?"

"That's what it is, a tragedy," Belter said, with the air of someone who's gotten the answer to a puzzling question. "Here Edmund and me had a nice little feud going—good for market share, feuds are, and someone goes and knocks him off. Right in front of me. Oh, well." He shook his head and opened the menu. "So what's good to eat here?"

"Everything," Josephine said. She smiled a little shyly. "I Googled you guys. Ma and Joey wanted to keep staying at the Marriott because of the stewardesses but I wanted to come here." She patted Quill's arm again. "I was pretty sure you wouldn't turn us away like the last time."

"We didn't have any rooms, the last time." Then, a little desperately, she asked, "Stewardesses?"

"Air hostesses," Belter said. He grinned widely. "There's a convention. Most times, we're stuck in Trenton with the pawn show, and I don't get out much to meet women."

"Grandchildren," Mrs. Barcini said. "Joey's heading on toward forty and Josie here's thirty-five and there are no grandchildren."

"Order anything, Joey," Josephine said. "Her sister's specialty is charcuterie, which is French for really good meat with white beans."

"Beans make me fart."

"Me, too. So order anything with meat in it."

"Osso buco," Mrs. Barcini said. "I will forgive anybody anything for a good osso buco."

Quill felt as if she was herding cats. "We don't serve osso buco at lunch. Do you mind if I give you some suggestions?"

"Whatever," Belter said with a wave of his hand.

Quill turned to Kathleen, who had been standing patiently by. "Bring the country pâté for starters, the steak frites for Mr. Barcini, the pasta Quilliam for his mom, and the mushroom-bacon quiche for Josephine."

"Hot damn," Belter said. "Steak. Tell her make it rare. If I stab it with my fork, I want it to move."

"Will do." Kathleen winked at Quill, then turned and pushed open the doors to the kitchen.

"Is that where she cooks, back there?" Josephine asked.

"Yes. Would you like to see the kitchens? Are you interested in cooking?"

"That Brunswick stew recipe's hers," Belter said. "She makes a hell of a corn bread, too. But we figured that wasn't flashy enough for the show. Shame about Edmund getting whacked like that, Josie. We could have made something out of that stew once the audience tasted it. Oh, well."

"Oh, well," Josie echoed.

"Last night was pretty awful," Quill offered, figuring it was as good a prompt to an amateur investigation as anything, "Had you known Edmund very long, Belter?"

"Me? Never met the guy before this week. Watched his show, is all. Crook."

"I beg your pardon?"

"I said he was a crook. And his ratings were higher than mine, too. Can you beat that? Just goes to show, in today's world, it's the crooks that get all the face time. You'd think the media would have better morals, or whatever."

"No character, that Edmund Tree," Mrs. Barcini said. "That one, he would steal from his grandmother."

"I'm in the business, see," Belter said. "I get all kinds of people in my pawn shop and all kinds of stuff comes across that counter. So you got to know a little bit about everything, right? Or you end up either cheating the customers or cheating yourself. Maybe both. So I know a little bit of this, and a little bit of that, and I hear things. Basically, what Eddie does is swoop through a town like this one, full of nice folks, full of people who should be watching my show, and he creams off the top. Makes an offer on the good stuff and resells it for the bigger bucks. Now, he keeps just enough of the pricey stuff on the air, 'cause that's what the audience is looking for. It's a fantasy, like. That they might own something worth a million bucks and they don't even know it." He shook his head. "Crook. And it's legal crookery, if you get my drift, because it's not illegal to make somebody an offer if they don't know what they got."

It took Quill a moment to work this last sentence out. Then she said, "I see what you mean."

"Now let's take what I got on hand for a minute. I got me a guy brought in a Colt .45 belonged to Buffalo Bill Cody. I know a bit about guns. I check the firing pin. I check the grip. Colt didn't make the kind of grip this sucker's got till two years after Buffalo Bill bought the farm. Not touching that with a ten-foot pole, believe you me. So I tell the guy to take the gun somewhere else. I got me another guy, comes in with a whacking big sword supposed to have belonged to the emperor Hirohito. I get that checked out. Nope, not touching that, either. So I tell them what they got isn't worth a plugged nickel and they think I'm robbin' them blind." He shook his head regretfully. "I tell you another thing about Fast Eddie. He likes to embarrass folks on the air. That little old lady with the Italian trompe l'oeil?" He pronounced it correctly, with just a hint of his drawl.

"I'm afraid I don't watch the show."

"You could tell it was a fake from ten feet away. Does Eddie give a shit? No. Just decides it be a grabber to slam her down." Belter picked up a toothpick and explored his back molar. "'Course, an old painting like that, something else might be under it. Artists do the darnedest things. You're broke, you need to paint, you grab an old painting out of an attic somewhere, and paint right over it. You know they found a couple of Rembrandts that way?"

"Yes, I did know that, as a matter of fact."

"Creepola, that Eddie, definitely," Mrs. Barcini said. "But it's too bad he's dead."

"Oh, well," the Barcinis chorused.

Kathleen brought out the pâté and the entrees all at once, accurately guessing that this particular party wanted a lot of food and fast.

Quill rose from her seat. "I've got to go up and be with my little boy right now. I'm sure I'll see you all later. And we'd like to offer you the lunch as a courtesy, for . . . umm . . . confusing your registration."

~

"So there it is," Quill said to Myles that night. "The Barcinis are rude, disruptive, annoying, and I'm mortally certain they're going to give some of our quieter guests heart attacks . . . but they're the good guys, Myles. Or at least they seem to be." She fought to keep her eyes open. She'd missed talking to him the night before and she wanted desperately to talk to him now, but she was so tired she couldn't see straight. "So this morning I started out with five major suspects—and the two I've talked to in depth turn out not to be suspects at all. I haven't seen Melanie Myers around all day—Doreen told me she's been holed up in her room ever since Edmund died. If she doesn't come down to breakfast, I'll knock on her door. To see if she's all right, if nothing else. As for Jukka Angstrom . . ."

"Quill." Myles's voice was firm. "You know how I feel about this—" He paused. She could tell he was struggling with both his temper and the right words. "This curiosity you have about this case. I don't have to say it again, do I? You're dealing with someone who's taken the life of another human being. It's dangerous. You are a mother. My wife. We need you, Jack and I. Please, please, do not continue with this. Leave it to the professionals. Wait until I come home."

"But Davy asked me . . ."

"He was out of line," Myles said harshly. "I love you. Leave this case alone. If you want me to beg, I will."

Quill didn't say anything. Her own temper was up. She made it a rule not to quarrel with Myles during these phone calls, not if she could help it. He was too far away. His absences stressed their marriage, as much as she liked to think they didn't.

"Okay," she said finally. "I'll leave it alone. Unless . . ."

"Unless *what*?"

"Unless I run across something accidentally that Davy needs to know." She waited, and then asked, "Are you grinding your teeth?"

"Of course not," he snapped. "I'll live with that, I suppose. I have to."

"Hey, here's something I know you aren't going to go ballistic over." She got out of bed and went to her dresser, where she'd left the computer printout Davy had given her that morning. "We have the results from the cross-check on the burglaries. You want me to read it to you? Myles?"

"Yes. I'm here. Just struggling with my temper."

"Me, too. Listen, now. The only things that the burgled homes have in common are that they were all insured with Marge, so we can discount that, and that every householder was a member of the Hemlock Falls Historical Society."

"Run those names by me again?"

Quill read them out, beginning with the Ackermans and ending up with the Petersons.

Myles didn't say anything for a very long minute. Then he started to laugh. He laughed so hard that Quill heard him put the phone down.

He picked it back up again, "Okay, supersleuth. I don't have any proof. But this is what must have happened."

16

~Quiche Quilliam~

3 extra large eggs blended with enough heavy cream
   to make 12 oz
2 teaspoons combined kosher salt, freshly ground
   pepper, and freshly ground nutmeg
½ cup grated Gruyère cheese
6 strips maple-cured bacon, fried crisp
9-inch baked pie shell

Blend eggs and cream with a wire whisk. Whisk in sea-
sonings and cheese. Place fried bacon in the baked pie
shell. Pour the quiche mixture into pie shell. Top with
grated Parmesan or Swiss cheese. Bake for thirty to
thirty-five minutes in a preheated 375-degree oven.

Quill marched into Schmidt Realty the next morning and
slammed her tote down on Marge's desk.

"Marge Peterson-Schmidt, you are a shameless woman.
And a burglar. If I had any actual proof, I'd rat you out to
Davy Kiddermeister so fast it'd make your head spin."

Marge opened her mouth and then closed it. Her face turned red. For once, she was speechless.

The speechlessness turned out to be momentary.

"I don't know what you're talking about."

Quill leaned over the desk. "You most certainly do. Every single burglary committed in Hemlock Falls in the last four weeks has been you rummaging around for fifteen-year-old records from the historical society. Just before Meg and I moved here, when Myles had just arrived as sheriff, the historical society put on a push to redistrict the village. They won. As it stands right now, the house you live in with your legal spouse, Harland Peterson, is within the town tax rolls but outside the village tax rolls. You are *not a* legal resident of this village."

"I am, too." Marge shouted.

"You are not! Want me to go to Albany and check the tax registry?"

Marge growled like an attack dog.

"I won't," Quill said mildly. "I just wanted you to know I can. You can't run for mayor."

"Carol Ann's not a resident, either," Marge said, rather feebly.

"As you pointed out yesterday. Which is what put me on to you. Why in the world would you be checking on eligibility requirements to be mayor, unless it was on your own behalf? So neither one of you can run for mayor. Ha."

Marge ground her teeth, an activity Quill had read about but never actually witnessed. "Nobody's going to remember that redistricting stuff."

"Probably not. But you had to be sure that nobody would

211

come across those old records while they were rummaging around for artifacts for *Ancestor's Attic*. Certainly not Carol Ann, who wasn't even around here then."

Marge eyed her suspiciously, "So what are you going to do?"

Quill sat down in the visitor's chair. "Nothing. I just wanted you to know that I know." She added, in a prim way, "I will leave it to your conscience."

Marge brightened. "Well, then. No problem."

"Well, then, nothing. I'm assuming that your conscience will preclude you running for office."

"I'll think about it. I can do this town a lot of good, you know."

"I'm sure you can. But I'm just as sure you'll do the right thing and let Elmer run unopposed."

"You're going to make Carol Ann drop out, too?"

Quill tugged at the curl over her ear so hard it hurt. "I have to. It's not right to make you drop out and let her run."

"That means she's going to be poking around my kitchen. Yours, too."

"I realize that."

"But you're going to wreck things anyway. Figures." She slammed the metal desk drawer open and shut several times, maybe to calm herself down. Quill wasn't sure.

"How'd you figure it out?"

"I didn't. Myles did."

"You got no proof. About the burglaries, that is."

"No. Myles said it was a wag. A wild-assed guess. He was sheriff when the redistricting was such a hot item, and he was pretty impressed with you scouting out Carol Ann's ineligibility to run, and he was really curious about why nothing was actually taken from the homes that reported the burglaries. If you'd paid out on some of those claims, he might not have leaped to the conclusion he did. But he knows you, he knows Hemlock Falls, so he did."

"Like I said, prove it," Marge said doggedly.

"We don't need to prove it. Nobody was harmed, nothing was taken except some old records, and you aren't doing it anymore, are you? So we'll drop it. But why did you think swiping those old records would keep your residency from coming to light?"

Marge shook her head. "No reason why it should. I live in the town. Won't occur to anybody I don't live in the village, too." She slammed open the file drawer again and took out a thick folder. "Got all the records except those in the tax office. Anybody wants to check, they'll have to truck on up to Albany. Figured that's far enough away so nobody'd take the time and trouble." She dropped the files back into the drawer. "So there's your proof. Arrest me, already."

"You know I'm not going to do any such thing."

Marge pursed her lips. "You sure?"

"I am not a snitch."

"You're a snoop."

"I grant you the snoop part. I am bringing this to your attention. That's all. From here on in, it's your call."

Marge muttered something under her breath.

"Just one thing. Myles is sure you didn't take those wedding rings out of Edmund Tree's room. I don't think you did, either, unless you were trying to make the whole burglary thing more convincing?"

Marge scowled ferociously. "Of course I didn't steal any wedding rings."

"I didn't think so. As a matter of fact, I have a pretty good idea of who did, now that this has been cleared up."

Marge ignored her, caught up in her outrage. "You actually thought I was a thief! What the heck do you take me for?"

Quill felt the need for some tact. "A great resource for information to help Davy Kiddermeister find out who murdered Edmund Tree," she said promptly. "Did you come up with any background information that would help him? I'm not investigating, or anything, but Davy's always up at the Inn to see Dina, and I could pass this along to him, if you like."

"If I like? I thought Quilliam Snoopers Inc. was back in business. You asked me for this." Marge motioned to the briefcase by her feet.

"Only on behalf of the sheriff's department. As a concerned citizen."

"I suppose Myles has his knickers in a twist again. Can't say as I blame him. Look what happened to Dina the last time you started poking around."

Quill did feel incredibly guilty about that. "Maybe you ought to take that straight to Davy. Leave me out of it altogether."

"No, no. Davy's growing into the job, but you're not so bad at this detecting business . . ."

Quill made a polite noise of demurral.

". . . Though we all know Myles is the real brains of the outfit."

"That is not true."

Marge smirked. "Gotcha. I owe you one for this mayor's business."

"Excuse me," Quill said hotly. "But was I the one sneaking around Miriam Doncaster's basement in the middle of the night? I think not."

Marge waved both hands, as if flagging down a speeder. "Hello? Can we put this behind us, please? You want the stuff I got on Tree or not?"

"Yes," Quill said. "I do."

"Shut up for minute, then. I got your message about adding the Bryants and Angstrom to the list. I didn't have time to get actual records, you understand, but the info is solid." Marge reached down, put her briefcase on the desk, and rummaged a bit. "Here we go. Tree's assets total twenty-three million, give or take a couple million depending on the stock market. Liabilities are almost none. The guy paid as he went. He's got some tax shelters set up so there's depreciation and what have you, but it's minimal. Stupid way to be wealthy, but there you are. Has a reputation for being tighter than a tick. Expenses out everything he can on that TV show. If he lived, you could have turned him in for suspected tax evasion. There's a bounty, you know."

"There is?"

"You betcha. Check it out. Anyhow, moving on to Jukka Angstrom . . . Angstrom is upside down on his Park Avenue condo and behind on his mortgage. He's gonna lose it unless he tap-dances pretty darn fast. Had a pile of legal expenses on that price-fixing charge, and the Sotheby's board refused to pay his legal bills. The Bryants, on the other hand, are not so rich, but not so poor, either. Not a lot of debt, or no more than they can handle. Guy I talked to said the Feds inquire once in a while about Andrea's offshore accounts, but there's no ongoing investigation into them." There was a trace of admiration in Marge's voice when she added, "That Andrea's no slouch, when it comes to the money side of things."

"So Angstrom's the only one who might be desperate?"

Marge shrugged. "Depends on what you mean by desperate. He's negotiating to turn the condo back to the bank. He's got a good set of lawyers. He'll probably pull that off. He's got too much in other assets to declare bankruptcy at the moment, but you never know. I've been in tighter spots myself and sailed on through okay." She tucked her notes back into her briefcase and plunked it on the floor. "So what's all this tell you?" She squinted at Quill. "You look funny. Not funny ha-ha. Funny peculiar."

"I don't believe it."

"Believe what?"

She looked at Marge with dismay. "Nobody's got a real motive. I've only got one suspect left. If I were investigating, that is. Which I'm not."

"Yeah, well, you need anything else, don't call me."

Quill picked her tote up and prepared to leave. "You're not permanently mad at me are you?"

"Nope."

"Are you still going to run for mayor?"

"That's for me to know and you to find out."

When Quill went out the door, Marge was busy at the shredder. She sighed and drove back to the Inn to find her sister.

~

"I suppose it doesn't matter," she said to Meg half an hour later. "If the historical society had missed the notes on that old redistricting battle, somebody would have hollered by now. But there goes any solid proof that Marge was the burglar."

"Let me get this straight." Meg stretched herself out on Quill's office sofa and stared at the tin ceiling. "Carol Ann doesn't meet the residency requirements to run for mayor. Marge is blackmailing her into staying out of our kitchens by threatening to torpedo her campaign."

"Right."

"You found out Marge doesn't meet the residency requirements, either. If you tell on Marge, you have to tell on Carol Ann."

"It's only fair."

"And then Carol Ann's inspecting our kitchens?"

"Maybe she'll flunk the state exam."

"Carol Ann studies to go to the *hairdresser*!"

"It wouldn't be fair, Meg."

Meg sat straight up and shouted: "Are you crazy? Let them both duke it out!"

"If I don't tell Davy about Marge being the B and A burglar, what if he arrests someone else for the burglaries?"

Meg kept on shouting. "What if he does? Whoever it is didn't do it!"

"Meg, innocent people get convicted of crimes they didn't commit all the time!"

"Once in a while, maybe!" She was still shouting. "I'd hardly call it routine!"

Dina opened the office door and peeked in. "We can hear you in reception."

"Who cares!" Meg roared.

Dina pushed her spectacles up her nose with her forefinger. "I don't, since you do it all the time. But it might disturb the guests. Which might be a good thing, now that I think about it. That Melanie Myers hasn't been out of her room since Edmund Tree died right in front of us, and housekeeping's starting to worry. Maybe all this shouting will get her out in the hallway to see if the Inn's on fire or something."

"You think I should check on her?" Quill asked.

"You'd better," Meg said. She got to her feet and tucked her T-shirt into her sweatpants. She wore clogs on the days she was in the kitchen. Quill looked at the color of her socks; volcano red. She should have waited to tell Meg about Marge and the mayor's race. Meg's socks were a reliable indicator of her mood. "If you don't go up and see if she's still alive, I suppose I'd better."

"Oh my God." Dina's face was pale. "I didn't even think of that. You don't suppose she'd actually . . ."

"No," Meg said flatly. "That girl is way too self-involved to do anything silly. Besides, she's ordered room service five times since the hoorah at Bonne Goutè, and potential suicides don't eat pasta, eggs, beef Quilliam, and every variety of dessert we make, all within a thirty-six-hour period."

"Oh my god," Dina said. "She's eating herself to death."

"She's fine," Meg said. "I think."

Quill wasn't so sure, either. "How long has she been in her room, Dina?"

"Doreen says the DO NOT DISTURB sign hasn't gone down once, and housekeeping hasn't been in at all. They knock and she shrieks 'go away.'"

"I'll go on up right now. Dina, make sure we can get her home phone number if we need it. And see if you can track down Jukka Angstrom. He seems to know her pretty well. If she won't let me in, she might respond to him."

"Should I call the hospital? See if Dr. Bishop's on call?"

"Not yet. Make sure you've got the number handy, though."
She patted her pockets. "I'll need a house key, in case she
won't open up."

"Right here." Dina held it out.

Quill took the key and went out and up the stairs. She was
anxious. And remorseful. She should have checked on the
poor girl sooner than this. Melanie's over-involvement had
been obvious to everyone. She remembered Rose Ellen's malicious dig at the girl: *Edmund's little dog.*

She'd never forgive herself if Melanie had given in to her
grief and harmed herself.

Melanie was registered in room 226, a room Quill particularly liked. The color scheme was deep rose, celery, cream,
and hunter green. There was a fine Adams-style mantel over
the small brick fireplace. All the even-numbered rooms overlooked the Gorge and the waterfall. But 226 was a corner unit,
and the balcony wrapped around the side of the building, so
that there was a view of the rose gardens, too.

The DO NOT DISTURB sign dangled from the doorknob.
Quill put her ear to the door panel, knocked loudly, and
called, "Melanie?"

No answer.

Quill knocked again, and then grabbed the doorknob.
"Melanie? It's Sarah McHale. I'm going to come into your
room now. I want to see that you're all right."

Somebody stirred behind the door. Then, Melanie's voice,
angry and hoarse: "Go away!"

"I'm sorry, but I have to come in. We're concerned about
you. Are you ready? I'm putting the key in the lock."

She opened the door to the scent of fresh air. The French

doors to the balcony were open. Quill felt a stab of fear—the girl wouldn't have flung herself over the side, would she? She hurried in, and then stopped. Melanie was on the bed, the duvet pulled up around her shoulders. The red dress she had worn the night of the murder was flung onto the bureau. Wadded Kleenex littered the floor. A service tray piled with dirty dishes sat on the small round table near the balcony. The air near the bed smelled of shampoo.

"Leave me alone!"

Quill went into the bathroom. Used towels littered the floor. She took a washcloth from the wicker basket on the sink, rinsed it in cool water and wrung it out. She went back into the bedroom, drew the occasional chair up to the bed and sat down.

"Are you deaf? I said leave me alone!"

"I can't do that, Melanie. I'm very concerned about you." Quill drew the duvet down around the girl's shoulders. Melanie's face was clean. Her hair was combed. She wore a long T-shirt with a unicorn on it. Quill patted her cheeks with the washcloth.

"I know you feel terrible about Edmund's death."

Melanie closed her eyes. "She did it," she hissed. "That bitch. She knew he wanted me. He was going to marry me, not her. She knew it. She couldn't stand it. If she couldn't have him, she wasn't going to let anyone else have him."

Quill wiped her face, then took Melanie's hands one at a time, and ran the cloth over her closed fists.

Rose Ellen's wedding rings were on her third finger, left hand.

Quill unfolded her fingers gently one by one. Melanie stared down at her palm. "He bought them for me, you know."

"Here, let me help you sit up."

Quill put her arm around her shoulders and eased her up against the headboard.

"The thing is, they don't fit." Melanie tugged at the rings. "They're too tight."

"Rose Ellen's fingers are pretty small."

Melanie stared at her. "He didn't buy them for her. He bought them for me. Edmund was always forgetting things like my ring size. I'm his assistant. I had to do things like that for him."

"Did you order the rings for him?"

"No." Her eyes shifted away from Quill's steady gaze. "They were supposed to be a surprise for me, I think."

"How did you find out about the surprise?"

"We were all at dinner. Rose Ellen started talking about rings, rings, rings to Jukka Angstrom, and she was whining that Edmund wouldn't give them to her to wear so she could show them off. He was just stringing her along. He meant to give them to me the whole time. So I got up to go to the bathroom, only I went to his room and took the rings. So she wouldn't get them. The cuff links, too. As a keepsake until we were together."

"Why did you go down the fire escape?"

She darted a glance at Quill. "Who says I went down the fire escape?"

"I heard you."

She shrugged. "Edmund hated not having the elevators come right away when he wanted them so he kept propping them open on the second floor. He insisted that I always use the stairs. There was somebody on the inside stairs when I left, so I ran up one floor and got stuck when the people below kept on coming up. The fire escape was the best way out."

Quill studied the clean hair, the fresh T-shirt, and remembered what Meg had said about Melanie's frequent use of the room service menu. "You know that Edmund was murdered, don't you?"

The big blue eyes welled over. Melanie wailed, "Yes. She did it! She slaughtered him."

"Actually," Quill said coolly, "the police suspect you."

Melanie froze with her mouth open. Then she shoved herself upright. "What!"

"It's a pretty familiar motive," Quill continued, "and you know small-town policemen. Wealthy girl from the city. Crush on her boss. Boss falls in love with somebody else. She poisons him. How did you express it? 'If she couldn't have him, no one else could.'"

"Who, me? Don't be ridiculous!"

"If they find your fingerprints on the bottle, the jig's up."

"What bottle? What are you talking about?"

"Did Rose Ellen give you anything to hold when you were up on the second floor of her shop? She's pretty clever and I wouldn't put it past her to try and set you up."

"I've only been in the shop once, I swear to God. And that bi—"

"Rose Ellen," Quill said a little sternly.

"Fine, Rose Ellen, then, never even gave me a cup of tea, much less a bottle of poison." Melanie jumped out of bed and paced around the floor. "Oh God, oh God, let me think. What did I touch when I was in there? I picked up some of the Depression glass. Is that it? Was the poison in a Depression glass? Because she must have, like, wrapped it in tissue paper or something. But I didn't kill him, Mrs. McHale. I swear to God I didn't."

Quill looked at her for a while. Then she said, "Give me the rings." Melanie scowled, but dropped them into Quill's palm.

"Thank you. Now, tell me about Edmund Tree."

Melanie stopped pacing and started biting her fingernails. "It's older guys, you know? They're so much smoother. They make things so much easier."

"Things like intimacy?"

"Well that, sure." She looked down at her generous breasts with a terrifying combination of world-weariness, innocence, and an unpleasant glee. "These puppies get all the guys going. Have since I was twelve years old. But it's the other stuff. Nice cars. Great restaurants. Cool clothes. Edmund was locked into all the good clubs. I mean, with that kind of money, who wouldn't be? He got me the job on the show because he could take me out, get me stuff, and it was all in the budget."

Quill resisted the temptation to put her head in her hands and howl.

"He liked it, that I was so jealous of Rose Ellen," she said with another flash of that too-adult cynicism. "So I kind of played it up. Then he'd take me somewhere really cool, just to piss her off, or he'd have the show budget spring for something extra nice. You wouldn't believe the wheels he got for me back in New York. I suppose I'll have to give the car up now." She tossed her hair over her shoulder with a flick of her hand. "All the stuff belongs to the show. I guess that's over, now that he's dead. I could say the clothes and car are part of my salary. They were. He told me they were part of my salary."

"The Bryants are taking his place," Quill said dryly. "You'll have to talk to them."

"That Skipper?" Melanie made a face. "Yuck. Well. Whatever. Are they still around?"

"Everyone's still around. They will be until the police are finished with the interrogations. You'll be able to leave after Sheriff Kiddermeister has talked to you."

Her eyes flashed white with alarm. "I had nothing to do with the murder. I swear to God!"

Quill got up, went into the bathroom, and tossed the washcloth into the sink. When she came out again, Melanie clutched her hand. "I'd better get myself a lawyer. I've gotta call my parents. God! This is like, so ironic. I mean, the man was basically my meal ticket. Why would I want to kill him?"

Quill wanted to say what she thought: that Melanie had nothing to do with it. Instead, she slipped the rings into her skirt pocket and pointed toward the phone on the nightstand. "Give your mom and dad a call."

Melanie stared at her, unseeing. "Okay, so, like, my mom's off with her boyfriend for that Hawaii thing. Dad's . . . where? The Hamptons maybe. You know what? I'll call the lawyer myself."

"You do that," Quill said and left.

17

~Madeleines~
Makes 24 cookies

2 large eggs
$\frac{2}{3}$ cup sugar
1 cup flour
5 ounces salted butter, chopped
Grated rind of lemon
$\frac{1}{2}$ teaspoon vanilla
$\frac{1}{4}$ cup powdered sugar, for topping
Madeleine pan, or any cookie pan with 3-inch molds

**Beat eggs, sugar, and flour together. Melt butter. Blend
all ingredients. Grease the molds. Put one tablespoon
batter in each mold. Bake at 375 degrees in a preheated
oven for about fifteen minutes.**

Quill went down the one flight to the first floor in the elevator, mainly because Edmund Tree hadn't propped it open for his own personal use, and it took longer than walking down the stairs. She resisted the impulse to punch the up button, which would take her to her own rooms and a much needed break with her beloved, innocent son. She could use some of Doreen's decent, straightforward view of life, too.

Instead, she found herself on the main floor, facing Davy Kiddermeister, Dina, and Jukka Angstrom. She stepped off the elevator.

"You didn't call," Dina said. "And the more I thought about it, the more freaked out I got, so I called Davy and I found Mr. Angstrom in the Tavern Bar. Is she okay?"

"She's fine. Well, she's not fine, exactly, since she thinks she's going to be arrested at any moment for murdering her meal ticket, but she's okay." She met Angstrom's eyes. The corners of his lips lifted in a cynical smile. "I apologize for that remark," she said. "She's only what, twenty-two, twenty-three?" She took a deep breath. "A confused kid, basically."

"Twenty-three going on forty-three," Jukka said. "So? There is nothing I can do at the moment?"

"I don't know. You could tap on her door and see if she needs a familiar face."

"Hmm. An hysterical young woman who has just lost the source of a fine car, expensive clothes, and the entree into various top-shelf city clubs? I think not. She is well able to take care of herself, that one. If she does need me, she can find me in the lounge. A pleasant place to pass the time, Quill. You have done well." He nodded to Davy and Dina and walked down the hall to the bar.

Quill sighed. "Okay. That crisis is over. Anything else I should be aware of, Dina? No dead bodies on the lawn or mobs picketing the Inn?"

"Just me," Davy said. "Could we go in the office and talk?"

"Sure. Absolutely. Dina, if you could ask the kitchen to

send in some coffee and cookies, I would love you forever. As a matter of fact . . ." She looked at her receptionist, with her oversized, red-rimmed spectacles, her shiny brown hair in its usual neat ponytail, and her unflagging commitment to the life cycle of small pond creatures. "I'd love you anyway."

"But coffee and cookies would help. Got it."

"Thank you. All right, Davy. You know the way."

She followed him into her office and closed the door. "Let's sit at the conference table. Marge gave me some information I should turn over to you."

He pulled out a chair and she sat down across from him.

"The ME's got a cause of death."

"That's pretty quick. Was it strychnine?"

Davy rubbed the back of his neck, in an evasive gesture. "County doesn't have a lot of murder cases to begin with, and this here is what they call high profile, which is why I got the results so fast. But I've decided not to make the cause of death public for a while yet, so I guess I can't confirm it to you. The thing is . . ."

"Myles called you," Quill guessed.

"He did. I'm sorry. I shouldn't have involved you in this. The sheriff is right. Not just about bringing civilians in, but about getting you mixed up in it, in particular."

"Fine. Just to clear the air, I'm not investigating. As a concerned private citizen, I have collected some information that might be useful to the police. So I'm going to turn that over to you." Quill fiddled with the curl over her ear. "Which will be okay with Myles. Just so you know. And even if it weren't, I would do it if I thought I should. You see?"

"No," Davy said. "But I'm up the creek without a paddle with this thing, and I'm going to take what I can get."

"So I'll tell you what I know, if you tell me what the ME's report said."

Davy hesitated, clearly torn between the thought of an angry Myles—several thousand miles away—and an importunate Quill with information to share. "Strychnine, like we thought."

"Any idea where it came from?"

"He sent the compounds off for analysis. But it's not like it is on TV. We're not going to get a chemical breakdown for weeks. Maybe months."

"Did the medical examiner know how Edmund ingested it?"

"The wine, he thinks. Something to do with the residual sugar."

"The Marsala? Good grief, Davy. Everybody had access to the Marsala. It stood open on the prep table for hours." Quill bit her lower lip. "Wow."

"Yeah, well, the good news is, as soon as they confirm the strychnine in the wine, they can dump all that pudding."

"Cream," Quill said automatically.

"Whatever. I'm still up that creek. You have anything else that might help?"

"First off, there are these." Quill dropped the rings into his hands. "The cufflinks are up there, too, I think, but I didn't feel like spending one more minute with that dreadful girl than I had to."

"Where'd these come from?"

"Melanie. She took them. She thought Edward had really bought them for her. She's all mixed up. But there they are. You can close the burglary case."

"She did the basement burglaries, too?"

"No, no, no. I know who did the basement burglaries. You can forget about them."

"I can't forget about them. It's an open case."

"You can close it without solving it, can't you?"

"Sure, I guess. There's a procedure for that. It's not going to look real good on my record."

"Fair enough. How's about if I tell you who burgled what and you decide if you want to keep it open. I mean, it'll be up to you. But I am hoping like anything that you will give this person a break. For one thing, there's no evidence to speak of, and for another . . . never mind the other. This is what happened."

He listened intently. By the time she was finished, his face was bright pink. "You're kidding, right?"

Quill held her hand up, palm out. "I swear."

"And she shredded the evidence?"

"The last of the paper was disappearing into the shredder as I walked out the door."

Davy muttered a word he didn't usually use. "And Ms. Schmidt, of all people."

Quill waited, filled with hope. Davy rubbed his chin hard. Finally, he shook his head. "Well. Shoot. Okay." His jaw stuck out in a way that was becoming increasingly familiar. "I'll tell you one thing though. Neither one of those ladies is going to be running for mayor. So. We close out the burglaries. What about the murder?"

Quill let out a long, pent-up sigh. "Marge looked into the finances of some of the people you're interested in. I've talked with a few more." She got up, the better to pace around the room. She felt a little bit like Poirot, except the suspects weren't gathered in her office. "Here's the deal. I couldn't find anybody with a credible enough motive to kill Edmund Tree."

By the time she finished going over the results of her interviews, Dina had brought the coffee and the cookies and Davy had filled up his small incident book and switched to a yellow pad. He flipped back through the pages of his notebook to the beginning. "Let me see if I got this right. Rose Ellen Whitman lost out on big money when Edmund died."

"If she was going to murder him, she should have waited until after the wedding," Dina said. "I would have."

Davy looked at her a little uneasily. "Right. And this Melanie Myers lost out on a car and some clothes . . . do you have the make of the car?"

"Does it matter?"

"Just curious. Not to mention all the fancy clubs this guy took her to. So she lost out on that. Barcini lost out on . . ."

". . . A potentially lucrative feud."

"Right," Davy repeated. "So all these folks lost something."

"That's right."

"Now the people who gained were the Bryants . . ."

"In a way. I couldn't take it to court, but Andrea seemed to feel that they'd be under a lot more scrutiny as hosts of the show. They've been making some money on the side. That's going to stop."

"So they have a weak motive."

"If it's a motive at all."

Davy tossed his pencil on the table. "Which leaves Angstrom."

"If Marge is correct, his motive is weak, too. Yes, he does get to wind his way back to Sotheby's, but he wasn't desperate." She hesitated. "I know what I'm about to say isn't good police work. Jukka's a tough guy. No question about that. But he's too . . ." Quill bit her lip while she searched for the right word. "Sane and balanced to kill for gain. It's certainly possible. But I don't think it's probable. It bears looking into, though."

Davy tried to look optimistic and failed. "That's something, anyway."

"How long do you plan on keeping them here?"

"The suspects? Not much longer. We've collected all the evidence, done all the interviews. Unless I come up with something in the next twenty-four hours, I'll have to let them all go home. That Rose Ellen has a lawyer on my case already. She wants to get out of Dodge and she wants out fast."

"She sure does," Dina said. "You know that Delores Peterson brought that painting you liked up to the Inn, don't you, Quill? Yep. Told me she couldn't go back to the store without two hundred bucks in cash."

Quill raised her eyebrows. "You're kidding."

"I am not kidding. So I looked in petty cash and we had one hundred and forty-two dollars."

"Then what did you do?"

"Gave it to Delores." Dina fidgeted. "I kind of like the painting and poor Delores was in a state. I asked Mike to put it in the Provencal suite. You aren't mad, are you?"

"No. I'm not mad. And it will look really nice above the fireplace. Besides," Quill added wryly, "trompe l'oeil is the coming thing."

Davy tapped his pencil impatiently on his notebook. "Does this have anything to do with Edmund Tree's murder?"

"Not a thing," Quill said. "It sounds to me like forensics will be the only thing that's going to help us solve that. You think there'll be anything back from the crime lab before all these people leave town?"

"No flippin' way. It'll be weeks. Months. No clues, no evidence. No motive. Just one dead guy. If you ask me . . . this is one case that we're never going to solve."

~

Davy Kiddermeister moved the Edmund Tree murder case to cold-case status two months later.

18

~Heaven and Earth~

5 large potatoes, peeled and cut into 1-inch pieces
1 teaspoon salted butter
¼ cup cream
1 tablespoon chopped parsley
3 apples, peeled and cut into 1-inch pieces
¾ cup sugar
2 slices bacon, diced
2 sweet onions, peeled and sliced into rings
Salt and pepper to taste

Boil potatoes in salted water for fifteen minutes. Mash the potatoes with the butter, cream, and parsley. Cook apples and sugar until soft. Add the potatoes to the apple mixture. Puree the mixture by hand. Fry the bacon to a crisp. Add onions to bacon and sauté the onion for a few minutes. Combine bacon/onion mixture with potato mixture. Serves six, as a side dish to a meat entree.

"I'm not closing the case, exactly," Davy Kiddermeister said to Myles McHale. "Just moving it to the back burner."

"Might be the best thing to do."

Davy looked as depressed as Quill had ever seen him. "I don't know what else to do. What kind of leads do I have? Where can I go from here? I'll be darned if I know who killed Edmund. I asked you to stop by the department for advice. Maybe you could look over the file again, see if there's anything I've missed."

Myles was a tall, big-shouldered man in his late fifties. His skin was weathered. His eyes were gray and turned to silver in certain slants of light. He'd been home in Hemlock Falls for a month. He was about to leave again.

"You, too, Quill," Davy added with a self-conscious blush. "If you have any ideas at all I sure could use the help . . ."

Myles leaned against the filing cabinets. He wore jeans, a denim shirt, and a baseball hat with a John Deere logo on it. Quill sat in the visitor's chair across from Davy.

It was mild, for November in upstate New York, and she wore a heavy sweater, a long wool skirt and boots. Jack careened around the peeling linoleum floor. Quill had made him wear his *Sesame Street* parka and he kept pulling it off and giving it to her. Davy kept the sheriff's office in the low sixties, so she kept putting it back on again.

"It's a miserable case," she offered, by way of comfort. "The forensics weren't any help at all."

The strychnine had come from a common rat poison that could be purchased at Nickerson's Hardware and the CountryMax feed store. Both stores had reported petty thefts of the poison. Both stores had computerized inventories, and Davy had patiently traced down each logged purchase to buyers with no connections at all to Edmund Tree and the *Ancestor's Attic* TV show. The light bulb she'd carried so carefully around in her pocket had two sets of fingerprints: hers and Mike the groundskeeper's.

Myles and Davy had watched and rewatched the available footage of the Slap Down event. During the course of the evening, everybody had passed by the bottle of Marsala. The only person to come near Edmund Tree and his zabaglione was Belter Barcini.

Davy confiscated all of the Barcinis' luggage, searched the *Pawn-o-Rama* bus with a team of forensic scientists from Syracuse, and came up with nothing. The Barcinis complained loudly and delightedly to the swarms of media that descended on the village. Belter took advantage of their enforced stay to ask Nadine Peterson out on three different dates. Nadine restyled Josephine Barcini's hair into a startling mass of curls with a couple of maroon streaks at the sides. Mrs. Barcini bought a knitting kit from Esther West's Country Crafts and made two pairs of booties, one pink, one blue, and looked hopeful. Nadine started spending weekends in New Jersey.

The bottle of Marsala itself had come from a cardboard box of twelve that had remained unopened until Clare set the bottles out at ten o'clock in the morning the day of the Slap Down shoot.

Davy got a search warrant for Clare's apartment at the academy and brought the forensics team back to go through every personal item she owned. Clare was so mad she spent the day of the search in Meg's rooms at the Inn. They each downed a bottle of Keuka red and swore eternal sisterhood, a détente Quill hoped would last until the year-end holidays were over, but she didn't think so.

Davy had compiled thick background files on Edmund Tree, which turned up no useful information, but verified

Rose Ellen's reading of his character. He was miserly, arrogant, and rich. Rose Ellen had made an abortive attempt to sue Edmond's estate for the two million dollars—the suit squashed and tossed out of court by an impatient circuit court judge—and was rumored to be living in a studio apartment on West Twenty-fourth in New York in impoverished circumstances.

The lawyers handling the Tree estate had finally turned up his half sister—the only offspring of Edmund's mother's second marriage. Her name was Devora Watson. She lived in California.

"Once in a while one gets away," Myles said. "There doesn't seem to be a lot more that you can do."

"I still like Angstrom for it," Davy said.

Myles raised his hands slightly, in a "maybe" gesture.

"Every time I look over those videotapes, I feel him sneering at me. Cocky, like."

Quill had seen all the interview videotapes, too. Jukka Angstrom had been amused, unhelpful, and finally, contemptuous. She suspected that Davy was influenced by what she herself felt; Jukka was the only suspect who had the toughness to kill.

"But he didn't have much of a motive," Quill said. "He's not back at Sotheby's, but he didn't lose his place in Manhattan, and he escaped bankruptcy. I can't see that it was to his advantage to kill Edmund."

"He lawyered up right away," Davy argued. "If I'd been able to get a search warrant to go through his clothes I know I would have found traces of strychnine."

"But there's no why," Quill said. "I know motive doesn't

count much in the courtroom, but it does with human beings. There has to be a why."

Davy slammed his fist onto his knee. "We just haven't uncovered the why. Maybe it has to do with some painting he found that Edmund wanted. I'm thinking he cashed in on whatever it was and he's got a slug of money somewhere. The DA over in Syracuse refuses to get a court order to monitor his bank accounts."

"Not enough probable cause," Myles said, with a trace of sympathy. "Fact is, you lose one once in a while."

Davy nodded. He sat disconsolately at his desk. Quill felt sorry for him.

"Daddy!" Jack shouted. "I am thinking!" He ran to Myles and threw both arms around his father's knees. With a smile he gave to no one else but Quill, Myles bent and swung his son up in the air. "What are you thinking?"

"I am thinking Auntie Marge knows we are very hungry."

"You may be right. Do you suppose Mommy is thinking that, too?"

"Are you, Mommy?"

"The diner sounds like a great place for lunch," Quill said. "Why don't you join us, Davy? There's a Chamber meeting I have to attend at two, but there's time for a nice relaxed lunch."

"Naw. Thanks. You go on ahead. I want to go over this file one more time."

Quill didn't say anything until they were outside, headed toward Marge's All-American Diner. Jack walked between them, one small hand tucked in Quill's, the other clutching his father's pants leg.

It was a gorgeous day, with a beauty peculiar to early November. The pine trees were a rich, dark green against the pale blue sky. The oaks and elms were bare of leaves, and the branches spread their elegant bones with grace. November light was thin and peaceful and somehow hushed.

Myles looked at her. "Do you want to stop and make a sketch?"

"How did you know?"

"You patted your pocket for your charcoal stick."

"Not now. Later, maybe." She glanced sideways at him, at the profile she loved so much. "This case is really eating away at Davy."

"That can happen."

"It's eating away at me, too,"

"Not every case is solved, Quill. Most departments are lucky to clear sixty percent."

They crossed Main Street. The unexpected mildness of the day had brought some people outside. Balzac's Café had a few customers in it. But the street was strangely deserted.

There was a FOR RENT sign in the window of Elegant Antiques and a young couple stood huddled at the door, peering in. Quill hoped somebody nice would rent the space. It had been repainted and the floors refinished and looked very inviting. Nickerson's Hardware had a 10 PERCENT OFF!! sign on a garbage can full of snow shovels. Esther's Country Crafts sported a cheerful harvest display of autumn leaves, gourds, and straw bales near the front door. All the topiary was gone, thank goodness. The village was getting back to normal. Maybe Esther would put the 'K' back into Country Crafts. These sights of Main Street in November were familiar, and dear to Quill, with the exception of the red, white, and blue placards demanding votes for the mayor's race. Elmer was running unopposed. Quill suspected the exuberance of signs was a consequence of his relief at having the job nailed down.

The All-American Diner was almost empty, and Betty seated them in a booth by the window. She brought a paper place mat and a small box of crayons for Jack, jerked her thumb at the chalkboard to alert them to the specials, and trudged off to get coffee and a cup of cocoa. "With just one marshmallow," Quill asked, "if it isn't too much trouble, although most of it will end up on Jack's chin."

"Marshmallow!" Jack shouted. "I am thinking about marshmallow!"

"I should be thinking about too much sugar if I were an all-star mommy and not a big sucker for my lovely boy," his mother said. "You can have one. But it will be a nice, big one, I'm sure. Shall I draw you a picture of Bismarck? You can color him orange."

"And Max!" Jack sucked his lower lip for a moment, which made him look like an elf. "And Daddy!"

Quill drew an orange Bismarck and a green Max. Then she took a black crayon and sketched Myles with a magnifying glass in his hand. She turned the box of colors over to Jack.

Myles looked at the drawing upside down. "Is that a hint?"

"It's horrible to have this murder unsolved. Tell me, Myles. Who did it? You've seen the case files. You even saw the murder happen. You must have some theory of the crime."

"Do you?"

"I think Davy's right. I think it's Angstrom." She frowned. "Mostly because he's so emotionless."

Myles hesitated, as if he were about to launch into his

theory of the case. He looked at Jack. He looked at Quill. Then he said, "Maybe."

"Just maybe?"

He reached across the table and took her hands in his. "I'm leaving tomorrow. I'm going to do my damnedest to be back by Christmas. For the rest of the day, I don't want to talk about murder, unsolved or otherwise. I just want to be with my family.

"Let it drop, babe. Let it go."

"I'll try." She sighed and watched her son scribble purple rings around Bismarck's image. So far he hadn't exhibited any particular talent for drawing. She tightened her grip on Myles's hands. "You're right. I should let it go. But the whole town hasn't felt the same since this happened. Tourism is down for the first time in years, and it's not just the economy. Unless I'm imagining things."

"I don't think you're imagining things. Murder has a fall-out. This may be part of it."

"But if Edmund Tree wasn't murdered by any of the people that came with him, it must have been one of us. Everybody's just a little suspicious of everybody else."

"A normal consequence of a crime so close to home. The town will adjust."

"I hope so. But it doesn't look as if it's going to be anytime soon."

~

Betty had made an unusually good potato side dish as part of the specials, and Quill was in a slightly better mood when Myles dropped her off at the Inn for the Chamber meeting.

Turnout was low. Elmer was in his usual spot at the head

of the table. Adela wasn't with him. Dookie and Mrs. Shuttleworth weren't there, either. Mark Anthony Jefferson from the Hemlock Mercantile Bank glanced repeatedly at his watch. With an apologetic shrug, he got up and slipped out the door. Nadine Peterson and Esther West sat on either side of Clare. All three of them had their heads together, whispering. Harvey was at the far end of the table, with empty chairs on either side of him and a dejected look on his face. He was wearing a depressed-looking tweed sports coat and a henley T-shirt in an uninspiring brown. He freely admitted to being on Prozac.

Marge—without Harland—sat a few chairs away from Elmer, arms folded truculently across her chest.

Quill took the chair next to Miriam Doncaster. "Low turnout today."

"Just like last month."

"What's on the agenda?"

Miriam blinked her big blue eyes. "Quill, you're the secretary. You have the agenda."

"Oh. Of course." Quill took her sketch pad out of her tote and flipped back to last month's meeting. "Christmas decorations? That's it?"

Miriam groaned. "Are we going to have that fight again? All of the merchants want the Christmas decorations up before Thanksgiving. Everybody else wants to wait. We go round and round every year. I hate Christmas decorations. I hate them with a passion I normally reserve for people who vote for privatizing Social Security."

Quill, who rather liked Christmas decorations but agreed that they shouldn't go up anywhere near Thanksgiving, made a polite sound that might have meant anything at all.

"Nuts." Miriam looked up at the wall clock. "I'd leave if I weren't here to ask for a fund drive for the library. Maybe I'll just leave anyway."

"Maybe we'll finish early. I'd like that. It's Myles's last day."

"He's leaving again, is he?" Miriam's voice was warm. "I'm sorry. It's got to be hard on you and Jack. I wish he'd stick around, too. I thought when he got back two months ago that he, at least, would make some headway finding Edmund Tree's killer, but I guess not?"

Quill dodged the implied question. "At least Carol Ann isn't here."

"Oh, but she is." Miriam pointed toward the door. Carol Ann wafted in, trailing the scent of gardenia shampoo. "She said your tabletop is sticky and she went out to wash her hands."

"My table is perfectly clean," Quill said indignantly.

"Life's too sticky for Carol Ann," Miriam said obscurely.

Elmer cleared his throat. "I suppose we'd better get started." He picked up the gavel and whacked it halfheartedly on the table. "Before we have the Pledge of Allegiance I just want to say thank you to the good folks of Hemlock Falls for reelecting me mayor."

"So what? Nobody ran against you," Carol Ann pointed out. "Not to mention that we had the lowest voter turnout in village history. If I had decided to run"—she directed a malevolent look at Marge—"you can bet this town would have sat up and voted. Nobody cares whether you're mayor or not, Elmer, and that's a fact."

"Well," Elmer said uncertainly.

"The low turnout wasn't because nobody cared about Elmer," Miriam said crossly. "Honestly, Carol Ann, I think you sprinkle mean over your breakfast cereal."

Carol Ann raised her voice. "I decided *not* to run because I can serve this town a lot better as a duly licensed food inspector for the State of New York. Which I am, now, because I got the results of my exam in the mail this morning." She looked around, as if waiting for applause.

Quill got out her charcoal stick and sketched a screaming Meg, running toward a bus marked ALASKA TRAILWAYS.

"Who cares?" somebody muttered.

"Who'd you have to bribe to take the test for you?" Marge asked.

Carol Ann's blue eyes were icy spears. "I'll remember that, Marge Schmidt."

Marge snorted. "You think you can take me down, young lady?"

Carol Ann puffed up, giving her a remarkably menacing look. "You'll be first on my list of inspections." She rubbed her forefinger over Quill's tabletop with a sneer. "Right after this place."

Marge leaned across the table and glared at her. "I'll move my restaurants to Trumansburg before I let you in the back door of either one of them."

Quill drew Marge in a panzer tank, aiming straight for a prissy-looking Carol Ann.

"Now, now, ladies," Elmer said. "You're exchanging hard words, hard words, and I know you're going to regret them later. Tell you what. We'll skip the Pledge of Allegiance and the reading of the minutes of the last meeting and move straight on to old business. What kind of old business do we have, Quill?"

"Christmas decorations."

"Right!" Elmer beamed. "Now there's a nice cheery topic

to get us all thinking about the season of peace and goodwill. I'm thinking we might want to get all that nice greenery up on Main Street just a leetle bit before Thanksgiving. Give the tourists a reason to shop early."

"What tourists?" Esther West said. "Since that murder, I haven't had a single tourist in my shop."

"Business at the diner is down thirty-two percent," Marge said. "'Course, booze sales are up at the Croh Bar, so it's kind of a wash."

"We've had three tours cancel in the last month," Clare offered. "One of the booking agents told me nobody wanted to actually eat in the place where Edmund Tree was poisoned."

"What about you, Quill?" Elmer asked. "Business been off at the Inn?"

"Some," she admitted.

Elmer drummed his fingers on the table. "You all getting any further on about finding out who did it?"

"Myles doesn't want her in the detecting business," Miriam said. "For heaven's sake, the woman has a young child. It's not her province anyway. Let the police take care of it."

"Far as I can see, Sheriff David Kiddermeister isn't up to the job," Carol Ann said. "I think we should call the FBI."

The meeting descended into a squabble.

Quill tossed her charcoal on the table.

Miriam leaned over and whispered in her ear: "You've got to get to the bottom of this, Quill. The town isn't going to be the same until you do."

"I'm sorry, Miriam. Myles says this happens sometimes—that you just can't crack a case. This appears to be one of them."

"All I can say is, you picked a fine time to stop being a detective."

~

Myles left early, before the sky had begun to lighten, and Quill spent the rest of that morning moving clothes and toys back into her rooms at the Inn. It didn't take long; by now, she had the routine down cold. She fed Jack, built a Lego tower with him so he could knock it down, and turned him over to Doreen for his nap. She was in the kitchen by two in the afternoon.

"Hey, Sister," Meg said. She stood on one leg in front of the prep sink. Her left heel was propped against her right knee. Her socks were dark blue with embroidered pumpkins. She was absorbed in making out a food order and there was nobody else there. It was clear she was relishing the quiet. "Anything you're longing to eat? I'm trying to work up a harvest menu that doesn't include squash."

"I like squash. Squash is also very locovore."

"Squash is boring. Squash is dull. Squash offers no competitive challenge whatsoever." She looked up. "Clare's having a Celebrate Squash night at Bonne Goutè. Can you believe it?"

So the murder-induced truce with Clare was over.

Quill settled into the rocking chair. Mike had removed the autumn flowers from the grate in the fireplace, in readiness for a wood fire when the nice November weather—as it inevitably would—turned colder. "I don't know. What about something on a spit? Over a wood fire?"

Meg rolled her eyes. "Go play with Jack or something."

"He's down for his nap." Quill set the rocker going with a push of her toe.

"Are you just going to sit there, fidgeting and driving me crazy?"

"I'm not fidgeting."

Meg looked up from her paperwork. Her gray eyes softened. "Myles get off all right?"

"Yes. No. I don't know."

"Did he say where he was going?"

"Same place as before. I just hope it's not . . ."

"It's *not* Libya."

"How did you know I was going to say Libya? I might have said Pakistan. Or Duluth."

"There's no revolution in Duluth that I'm aware of. You know what would make a great food festival? I know. Potatoes."

"Potatoes?"

"I can go nuts with potatoes." Meg picked up her pencil and started to scribble.

"Davy thinks Jukka Angstrom killed Edmund Tree," Quill said abruptly.

"I know he does. I thought Jukka was going to sue the sheriff's department for harassment before it was all over."

"Myles does, too."

Meg lifted her head at that. "He does?"

"He didn't actually *say* so," Quill admitted, "but we were at Marge's yesterday for lunch and he was *about* to say so. I think. Davy's sure that there was something we missed, a valuable painting that Jukka and Edmund were both after, maybe. He can't get the court to monitor Jukka's bank accounts, but I bet Marge would be able to figure something out."

"It's pretty awful, having a case go unsolved like that. I don't know what else we can do."

"It was an odd one that's for sure. Nothing was as it seemed, did you notice that? All of the motives that looked so solid at the beginning just sort of melted away. Like the trompe l'oeil painting. Everybody fooled the detective's eye."

"The detective being you, of course." Meg scribbled furiously for a moment, then said, "Elizabeth says everyone in town was expecting us to solve the case. They are mega disappointed. I told her I was too busy hassling over the wedding that didn't come off to play Sherlock but even if I had, we wouldn't have been able to solve it. It's not solvable."

Quill let this aspersion on her detecting ability pass. She might even deserve it. "Everything has a solution, Meggie. We just haven't seen it, yet."

The swinging doors bumped open with a bang, and Dina came in. She held her laptop in both hands. "Hey, Meg. Hey, Quill. I hoped I'd find both you guys here. Look at this."

She set the laptop on the prep table and bent over it. "Somebody was blogging on the *Huffington Post* about the Edmund Tree murder, and it led me to this news item. Look! It's his half sister, Devora Watson. The one from California. She showed up to claim that twenty million dollars."

"I read about her," Meg said. "They ran a picture of her in the *New York Times*. Very hippie-dippy."

Dina sighed. "I read about it, too. She lives near Big Sur in this remote little cabin and weaves her own caftans, or whatever. If I had twenty million dollars, I sure wouldn't wear homemade caftans. Or if I did, they'd be out of priceless cashmere wool. Look. Here she is. Gosh, do you suppose she'll use some of that twenty million to fix her hair?"

Quill looked over Dina's shoulder. The website was running a news clip. A small, shy woman dressed in Birkenstocks, wool socks, and an awkwardly wrapped turban huddled between two sleek looking guys in three-piece suits. She was pudgy, with the sort of overweight that comes from too much fatty food. Her blond hair spilled over her shoulders. It looked in need of a wash. A pair of wire-rimmed spectacles was askew over her nose. Her eyes were brown and frightened. She clutched a wool shawl around her shoulders.

"She's practically in tears," Dina said indignantly. "Those lawyers must be bullying her." She took a breath and leaned into the screen. "You go, Devora!"

Quill stared at the video clip. Her own voice sounded strange in her ears. "Can you rerun that?"

"Sure." Dina tapped the screen. Devora reappeared, walking into the courtroom.

"Can you stop it?"

"Sure." Dina tapped the screen. "How come?"

"That's not Devora Watson. That's Rose Ellen Whitman."

19

~Potato and Leek Dumplings~

2 leeks cut into thin slices
1 pound russet potatoes, peeled and cut into quarters
3 small eggs
Salt and pepper to taste

Blanch leeks for ten minutes in boiling salted water. Pat leeks dry. Puree in food processor. Boil potatoes for fifteen minutes in reheated leek water. Drain the potatoes. Mash all ingredients into a thick dough. Form the dough into egg-sized dumplings. Cook dumplings in boiling salted water for fifteen minutes. Serve as a side dish with a meat entree.

"You are out of your flipping mind," Meg said. "That is a short, dumpy woman with a terrible complexion. Rose Ellen Whitman looked like Audrey Hepburn."

Quill breathed so hard she was dizzy. "Rose Ellen wore three-inch heels. All the time. She didn't eat a thing. Take away the heels. She'd be about that height. And if anybody started eating five thousand calories a day at Burger King, you'd have zits and a potbelly, too."

Quill whirled the laptop around on the tabletop. Dina had frozen the photo in place. Devora Watson had a scattering of pimples at the side of her mouth. "She killed Edmund for the twenty million dollars. She did it."

"I think you should sit down and have a nice cold shot of vodka," Meg said.

"But they were engaged." Dina took her spectacles off and put them on again. "They couldn't be engaged if she was his sister."

"Sure they could. Although Rose Ellen exhibited some sense. At least she didn't sleep with him. That we know of. Wow." Quill wanted to slap her forehead, but didn't. "How could I be so stupid? Cui bono. Who benefits? The sister does. Good grief. Myles is going to be astounded."

Meg squinted at the monitor. "I don't see it. And no jury's going to see it, either. Really, Quill. You've been under a lot of stress, lately. Sit down and let me get you something soothing. If you don't want vodka, I'll make some nice chamomile tea."

"I have *not* been under any stress and I do not need a restorative. Look, do I tell you how to cook?"

"Of course you don't tell me how to cook."

"Then don't tell me you don't see what I see. I see things you don't. I paint because I see bone structure, skeletons, and the way things are put together. I am telling you, as an artist, as a person whose job it is to see the skull beneath the skin, as a person whose eye cannot be fooled for long, that Devora Watson is Rose Ellen Whitman."

They stood together and stared at the monitor. Devora Watson stared at the lawyer bending over her, frozen in time.

"Oh. My. God," Dina said. "I think I see it, too. I'd better get Davy."

"Hang on a minute," Quill ordered. "Let's think this through." She clutched at her hair, which made it fall down, so she scooped it up and rebundled it on the top of her head with her elastic band.

"This will be so good for Davy," Dina said. "He had to close out the basement and attic burglaries because of you-know-who. And just yesterday he put the Tree case into the cold case files. This is going to help his career a lot."

"If Quill's right," Meg said. "Personally, I've never heard of anything as crazy in my life."

Dina's eyes glittered with excitement. "Let's call the lawyers and tell them she's really Rose Ellen Whitman. Then Davy can reopen the case and she'll go to jail. And Davy's career will be saved. It should be easy, shouldn't it? I mean a person can't just turn into another person, just like that."

"Maybe they can," Quill said. "This could be a lot harder to prove than we think."

"It could be hard to prove because she *isn't* Rose Ellen," Meg said stubbornly.

Dina waved her hand. "DNA. DNA would prove who she is."

Meg scowled. "It'd prove she's his sister. How is it going to prove she's Rose Ellen? Rose Ellen doesn't exist."

"Of course she does," Dina exclaimed. "My gosh, her pictures have been all over *Vanity Fair*. She knows thousands of people. She's got friends everywhere. She's in the newspapers. DNA again. Trace evidence." Dina clapped her hand over her mouth for a long second. "Wait. I think I see where you're going. You mean there may be no evidence proving Rose Ellen is a real actual person with a blood type, a genetic code, and a dental chart?"

"Exactly."

"Wow." Dina sank down on one of the stools at the prep table. "She like, totally wiped out the antique shop. It's been repainted and steam cleaned. The apartment, too, I'll bet."

"Her fingerprints are on file with Davy, aren't they?" Meg asked. "She lived in Hemlock Falls for three months—she must have seen a doctor or a dentist during that time." She looked at the monitor again. "You guys are nuts."

"Fingerprints," Dina said. "Of course. I'll call Davy right now. Good grief, Quill. This is just amazing. Oh! Wait! I left my cell phone at the front desk."

Meg pointed at the phone on the wall by the sauté pans. "That one's free."

"I don't know his number. It's on speed dial. Hang on. I'll be right back."

Quill spoke up. She was beginning to doubt herself. "Dina?"

"Yes, Quill?"

"Don't tell him just yet. Just ask him if he's got her fingerprints on file."

"But this is huge! How can I keep it to myself?"

"It'd be good if you could, just for a bit." Quill bit at a fingernail.

"If Quill's wrong, Davy's going to look the fool," Meg said tactlessly. "He's concerned about his record his first year as sheriff. We all are. Just in case Quill turns out to be mistaken you'd better just ask him about the fingerprints. I know you're excited, but don't blow it."

"Good point. Okay. Don't go anywhere. I'll be right back."

Quill stood at the back window and looked out at the gardens.

Mike had tied up the rosebushes and covered them with burlap. The winter parsnips had been harvested and so had the potatoes. Here and there amid the dead and dying leaves were a few bright yellow and green gourds.

"You really think this woman posed as Rose Ellen Whitman?" Meg asked.

"I know she did." Saying it aloud helped. Quill walked over and looked at the computer monitor.

She was sure.

"Okay. I believe you, you know, about what you see that the rest of us don't. Of course Davy's got fingerprints on file, so I guess we'll know for sure pretty soon."

"I'm sure already."

Dina walked back into the kitchen, her cell phone at her ear. "No, D, no special reason. And don't worry about it. We were just hashing things over in the kitchen, you know, things are a little slow this week, and the case came up and Quill wondered about fingerprints. Sure. Right. Of course they won't care. Love you, D. Bye." She flipped the phone shut and tucked it in her shirt pocket. "It's good news and bad news. The good news is that one of the deputies—Neville Peterson, Davy said, went up to Rose Ellen's apartment and got her fingerprints. All ten. The bad news is, paint solvent got spilled on it somehow, and the prints were ruined. All ten. By time Davy sent Neville back to get a new set, she was out of here, back in New York, and he followed up with her to get them done there, but she like, disappeared. The NYPD still has a request on file to get them. It just got lost in the shuffle."

"Hm," Meg said. "If you ask me, that's pretty suspicious."

"This," Quill said, "is a very clever woman."

"I know one thing she left that she had her hands on," Dina said. "That painting. The one of the fountain with the bunch of grapes. You put it in the Provencal suite, didn't you?"

"Dina, you're a genius!" Quill said.

"I have to be. My boyfriend's career is on the line."

"I hate to be the grinch in the group, but if she was clever enough to trick Neville Peterson, would she be brainless enough to leave her fingerprints on that trompe l'oeil? Not only that, but there are bound to be a bunch of other prints on there, too. If we don't have a benchmark for her fingerprints, even if they are on the painting, they'll be useless as evidence."

Quill started to pace. "Rose Ellen told me she picked the painting up at a flea market somewhere. Belter told me *Your Ancestor's Attic* made a practice of buying antiques cheap and selling high from prospects that showed up to audition for the show.

"I'm wondering a lot about that painting and I need to sit down and think." Quill sat down in the rocker and got it going with a push of her toe. "Now, who's more believable? A murderess or an honest pawnbroker in flip-flops?"

"You've lost me, Sis."

"First thing we do is get Devora Watson up here. And the second thing—can you Google an address for me, Dina? I've got an idea."

20

~Potato Crepes with Caviar~

1 pound white potatoes
5 eggs
1 tablespoon flour
1¾ cups sour cream
½ shallot, peeled and crushed
Grated peel of lemon
Sprigs of dill
Salt and pepper to taste
1 tablespoon butter for each crepe
4½ ounces salmon or white fish caviar

Cook potatoes in boiling salted water for twenty minutes. Let cool. Peel and grate in food processor. Add eggs, flour, sour cream, and shallot. Season with lemon peel, pepper, and salt. Mix well. Divide the batter into four parts. Melt butter in frying pan, and spoon the batter evenly into the pan. Sauté until golden on each side.

Serve each of the four crepes with one teaspoon sour cream, a sprig of dill, and a fourth of the caviar.

Ida Mae Clarkson liked the look of Hemlock Falls. There was a lot of snow on the ground. She hadn't dealt with snow for years, not since she and Frank had left Madison, Wisconsin, for Delray Beach, Florida. But it suited this cobblestone village. Christmas was more than three weeks off, but that's what the village made her feel like. Christmassy.

She liked the look of this Provencal suite, too. The blue-and-yellow patterns on the duvet and the old settees were just about perfect. There was a fire in the small fireplace, scenting the air with pine and apples.

And it really was astonishing that Aunt Cecilia's trump loy painting of the fountain had ended up here, of all places, right over the fireplace mantel in this elegant room. That pretty innkeeper had asked her if she wanted it back, but she'd had enough of that painting after being embarrassed by the smarty-pants Edmund Tree on national TV. The innkeeper could have it, thank you very much. As for Edmund Tree—well, he'd gotten what was coming to him, hadn't he?

Ida Mae tweaked the lace scarf at her throat and smoothed the lapels of her Alfred Dunner black velveteen jacket. She'd looked up the Inn on the Internet, right after the phone call that told her she and Frank had won this all-expenses-paid weekend. It was famous for its food and the setting of the waterfall. She'd gone right out and ordered the jacket to celebrate.

"You 'bout done there, Ida Mae?" Frank shrugged into his sports coat with a reluctant frown. He hadn't been happy about leaving his shorts and sandals behind in Florida, but he could hardly go to a gourmet dinner at a five-star Inn in his flip-flops.

"I'm done, Frank. How do I look?"

"Beautiful." He swept her in his arms, bent her over, and gave her a kiss. "My bride."

"Old fool," Ida Mae said fondly. "Let's go on down."

They took the elevator—Ida Mae's shoes pinched a bit, and she didn't want to chance the stairs—and went through the small, delightfully furnished foyer into the dining room.

The dining room was magnificent. There was a full moon out, and Ida Mae made out the faint, silver reflection of the falls outside the floor-to-ceiling windows. The tables sparkled with wineglasses and fine cutlery. Arrangements of white carnations and pine boughs sat in the middle of each table.

There weren't as many diners as Ida Mae had expected, what with the Inn being so famous. A tall, good-looking man with gray eyes and a deepwater tan sat at one table. Next to him was a young, fair-haired guy who blushed bright red when she looked at him. The other tables seemed to be occupied by a different assortment of people. There was a pudgy guy in one corner who looked as uncomfortable as Frank in his sports jacket and tie. She thought the man looked familiar. She poked Frank. "My gosh, Frank, that's Belter Barcini! You know, from *Pawn-o-Rama*!" She wasn't surprised to find celebrities here, not at all. "He got married, you know. To some nice hairdresser who gets to do all of the makeup for the show."

There were three other ladies with him, an older one, who wore a brilliant gold lamé top and a feather boa, and two younger women with very distinctive hairdos. Ida Mae wasn't sure which one was the wife.

"You sure this dinner is with the contest?" Frank hissed in her ear.

"Darn sure," Ida Mae said confidently.

The dark-haired hostess caught sight of them and came up

with a smile. "Mr. and Mrs. Clarkson? I'm Kathleen. I'm glad to say your table's ready."

Ida Mae and Frank followed her across the room.

Kathleen stopped at a table for two. An unhappy-looking man in a three-piece suit sat across from a small, dumpy woman in a caftan that looked homemade. "I'm sorry," she said. "I forgot to bring your salad out. If you'll just give me a moment, I'll be right back. Mrs. Clarkson? This is another one of our guests."

Ida Mae bent forward. "My goodness!" she said. "Why, I know you! You bought that tromp loy off of me after I was on *Ancestor's Attic*. It's Smith. Mary Smith. How have you been, honey?"

Mary Smith jumped, as if Ida Mae had stuck a knitting needle up her backside. "Never seen you before in my life," she whispered.

"Now," Ida Mae said kindly, "I'd know you anywhere from those poor scarred hands of yours, remember?" She took Mary Smith's left hand in hers. "See? Poor Mary got these little scars from putting out a kitchen fire. Remember, honey?" She turned to Frank, beaming. "I remember the name Mary Smith because it's such an ordinary name. It's funny, though, it's so ordinary that not many people have it? You remember that, Mary. We laughed a lot about it. Whatever are you doing here?"

The man with the deepwater tan and his younger partner got up from the table. The younger one had a pair of handcuffs. "What Ms. Watson is doing here," said the young man, "is getting arrested. Devora Watson, also known as Rose Ellen Whitman, also known as Mary Smith. You have the right to remain silent. You have the right to an attorney . . ."

Epilogue

Quill raised a glass of Moët & Chandon champagne and swept a low bow. "We couldn't have done it without you, Mrs. Clarkson."

She had shepherded the Barcinis and the Clarksons into the Tavern Lounge after Myles, Davy Kiddermeister, and his deputies had taken Rose Ellen away to be arraigned for the murder of Edmund Tree.

Quill was shaken.

Mrs. Clarkson was bewildered.

Mr. Clarkson sank his head between his shoulders and looked as if he wanted to be back in Delray Beach.

Josephine Barcini looked grave.

Belter asked for two Molson Goldens from Nate the bartender and drank both of them one after the other. Nadine Peterson Barcini patted his hand and sipped at a Brandy Alexander.

Mrs. Barcini was simply quiet. Then she said, "What you couldn't have done without is my boy."

Nadine Peterson Barcini patted Belter on the shoulder. "That's right."

"I don't understand a thing about what just happened,"

Mrs. Clarkson said. "Who was that woman? She wasn't Mary Smith?"

Quill said sadly, "She wasn't Mary Smith. And she wasn't Rose Ellen Whitman. She was Edmund Tree's half sister, Devora Watson, and she murdered her half brother for his twenty-million-dollar estate."

Ida Mae's eyes widened. "Glory," she said. "I read about that in the *Palm Beach Post*. I'll tell you what I thought. I thought it was that woman chef."

"Clarissa Sparrow?" Quill said, startled. "For heaven's sake. Why?"

"Stands to reason. It was her kitchen. But you say it was Mary Smith? I sold Aunt Cecilia's painting to a murderer?"

"She wasn't a murderer then," Frank Clarkson said heavily. "If I've got that right. So don't you go puffing off to the girls at the coffee club, Ida Mae. When did this Mary Smith decide to turn to crime?"

"My guess is pretty early on. At least two years ago, when the woman we knew as Rose Ellen Whitman showed up as a buyer for *Your Ancestor's Attic* TV show. She is—was—very beautiful and she knew a lot about antiques, and she caught Edmund Tree's eye right away.

"Rose Ellen's real name is Devora Watson. Edmund's birth mother divorced his father soon after Edmund was born and moved to California. She traded her little boy to his father for a generous settlement in the divorce." Quill stopped speaking for a moment and took a sip of the wine. That fact that Edmund's mother had given up her own child for a mass of money had made her ache for Edmund Tree.

"In any event, Edmund's mother didn't keep the money for long. She married a man named Art Watson, who left her soon after she became pregnant with Devora. She made a couple of attempts to extort money from Edmund after that, but he resented her, poor man, and refused to give her a cent. She died when Devora was fifteen.

"Devora grew up hating her half brother. She took up . . . um . . . I suppose you could call it the oldest profession . . ."

"Hooking," Belter said briefly. "Poor gal was a hooker."

"And put herself through UCLA. She has a fine arts degree, you know. If she'd only . . ." Quill sighed. "Anyway. She targeted Edmund as the man who owed her. She got the job on *Ancestor's Attic*. I don't know if she'd intended to kill him all along or not. I do know that she made a practice of skimming off what she could of the undiscovered treasures the show turned up as it traveled across the country. And I know that Edmund must have supported her in that. In any event, her acquisition of your trompe l'oeil painting, Ida Mae, was typical of the way she scooped things up. She'd disguise herself as Mary Smith, an avid fan of the show, and approach owners of all kinds of old and interesting things. Some of them she resold in her antique shop here in Hemlock Falls. Some of them she took to the big auction houses in New York and Paris and Rome. It didn't seem to matter if she was going to make a huge amount of money, or just a couple of hundred dollars. If she thought she could make a profit from a piece, she went after it."

"I've known people like that," Ida Mae said. "I taught sixth grade for twenty-two years in Madison, Wisconsin, and I've pretty much seen it all. There's a few kids—not many—well, when you offer them a straight way to do something or a crooked way, they'll take the crooked way every time."

Quill wasn't so sure about that, so she said, "My goodness."

"So we've got Devora Watson as Rose Ellen Whitman, plotting revenge," Josephine Barcini said. "Go on, Mrs. McHale."

"My personal opinion is that her plan evolved as time went on. My husband Myles isn't so sure. Anyway, Edmund was attracted to her, Edmund asked her to marry him, and Rose Ellen decided it was time to revenge her mother. Time to revenge herself. Myles thinks she picked up the rat poison from somewhere outside of Hemlock Falls, but we don't know for sure. She dropped it into the Marsala in the melee surrounding the slam, conned one of our less alert deputies in the matter of fingerprints, and left Rose Ellen Whitman behind.

"She was clever about that, too. She made an attempt to sue Edmund's estate on the basis of the promises he made to her—and who knows? If she'd been successful, she may have left her real identity as Devora Watson back in San Diego. But she wasn't successful, so Rose Ellen disappeared, and Devora arrived at the lawyers' door, ready to claim her inheritance."

"It's like one of those TV movies," Ida Mae said. "This is amazing. I'm amazed, Frank. Aren't you?"

"How did you catch her?" Frank demanded.

"The artist's eye," Belter said, unexpectedly poetic. "Quill seen her on TV and looked through that disguise right away."

Quill cleared her throat. "That's true."

"You're a genuine artist, you see. Your eyes can't be fooled." Belter burped and patted his belly in satisfaction.

"Yes, well. Devora had covered her tracks really well. There had to be some hard evidence that she was really Rose Ellen Whitman out there, but I was darned if I could figure out a legal way to get it. She sold your aunt's painting to us,

you know, and we checked to see if there were any fingerprints on that, but of course, without a set of prints we knew
to be Rose Ellen's to compare them to, we were up the pro-
verbial creek, paddle-less."

"That's when you called me!" Ida Mae exclaimed. "I
didn't win a grand prize after all!" She slapped the tabletop.
"I remember that clear as clear. You called me up, said I'd
won this fabulous weekend for two . . ."

"And then I asked you if you were the same Ida Mae Clarkson that had been on *Your Ancestor's Attic*. Yes. And what
had you done with the painting?"

"And I said I sold it to this Mary Smith."

"And I said, what a coincidence." Quill turned to the rest
of the table. "I'd caught Rose Ellen in a lie. She told me
she'd picked the painting up at a flea market. Jukka Angstrom told me she made a practice of going to the show par-
ticipants and buying items as cheaply as she could."

Belter raised his voice, apparently not used to being on the
sidelines. "So then she calls me up and says, 'Belter, my boy.
You feel about crooks the way I feel about crooks. How'd
you like to help me catch a murderer?'"

Frank looked at Quill and then back at Belter. "She did?"

"I did. Your wife's an alert, capable woman, Mr. Clarkson.
I saw that when she appeared on the show. Our phone conversation confirmed it. There was a good chance she could
identify Devora as Mary Smith, if I could just get the two of
them together in the same room. And in order to do that, I
called on Belter."

Belter grinned and took a sip of his beer with a modest
flourish. "Most folks think pawnbrokers are stupid or crooked,
see. Actually they hope they're both, especially when they

have something dodgy to sell. So I call up Ms. Devora Watson, all flush with her twenty million dollars, and tell her Sarah McHale's discovered a real sixteenth-century painting under that mess your auntie had in her attic and that she's about to make a bundle on it. I tell her if she can get the painting back, I want a twenty percent commission on the deal. So Devora hauls out the old costume trunk, disguises herself as Mary Smith, and books herself into the Inn to see what she can do about it." Belter looked at his empty beer bottle, signaled Nate for two more. "What she did about it was get herself arrested for murder."

Ida Mae fanned her face with her hands. "So I'm going to have to testify at her trial?"

Quill nodded. "Probably. The police will want a statement from you, of course. The most important thing is that your identification has given the sheriff probable cause to look into Devora's activities. The chances are excellent that they will find enough hard evidence to convict her of Edmund's murder."

"My goodness," Ida Mae said. She heaved a happy sigh. "Who would have thought it? The girls at the coffee club are going to be wicked jealous!" She beamed at her husband, who beamed back.

Then he bit his lip and touched Quill's shoulder. "Just one thing, Mrs. McHale. Did we really win an all-expenses paid trip to Hemlock Falls?"

"You most certainly did, Mr. Clarkson. You most certainly did."

Turn the page for an excerpt of the
first book in the Hemlock Falls Mysteries
by Claudia Bishop . . .

A TASTE FOR MURDER

Now available in the omnibus
A PLATEFUL OF MURDER
from Berkley Prime Crime!

1

Elmer Henry, mayor of Hemlock Falls, swallowed the last spoonful of zabaglione, disposed of the crystallized mint leaf with a loud crunch, and burped in satisfaction. He whacked the Hemlock Falls Chamber of Commerce official gavel and rose to his feet. This familiar signal jerked Sarah Quilliam out of a daydream involving rum punch, Caribbean beaches, and a lifeguard. She grabbed her notebook, scrawled "HFCOC Minutes," and tried to look attentive.

Elmer looked down the length of the banquet table with a somewhat bovine expression of pleasure. Twenty of the twenty-four members of the Chamber looked placidly back. The imminence of the annual celebration of Hemlock History Days brought the members out in force. The corps of regulars— Quill, the mayor, Marge Schmidt, Tom Peterson, and Gilbert Gilmeister among them—was swelled considerably; like Easter, Hemlock History Days offered unbelievers a chance to hedge their bets.

Oblivious to the command of the gavel, Marge Schmidt and Betty Hall held a *sotto voce* conversation concerning their mutually expressed preference to die rather than consume one more bite of suspect foreign substances such as the

Italian pudding just served them. Quill rejected various witty rejoinders in defense of her sister's cooking and opted for a dignified silence.

Elmer rapped the gavel with increasingly louder thwacks until Marge and Betty shut up and settled into their seats. "This meeting is called to order," Elmer said. He nodded to Dookie Shuttleworth, minister of the Hemlock Falls Word of God Reform Church.

Dookie was thin, rather shabbily dressed, and had a gentle, bemused expression; under stress, input frequently vanished altogether from Dookie's hard drive, a circumstance wholly unrelated to his vocation and met with tolerance by his parishioners. He wiped his napkin firmly across his mouth and stood up for the invocation. "Lord, bless this gathering of our weekly session, and all its members." He paused, looked thoughtful, and suppressed a belch. "Most especially, the management of the Hemlock Falls Inn, Meg and Sarah Quilliam, for this fine repast."

Quill smiled and murmured an acknowledgment, which Dookie ignored in his earnest pursuit of the Lord's attention. "Lord, if you see fit, please send us fine weather and generous folks for the celebration of Hemlock Falls History Days next week. May these men and women seek you out, Lord, particularly in Your house here at Hemlock Falls. When the collection plate is passed, may they open their hearts and more, in Your service. As you know, Lord, the church checking account . . ."

Elmer Henry cleared his throat.

Dookie concluded hastily, "All these things we ask in Jesus' name. Amen."

"Amen," echoed the assembled members.

"Hadn't you ought to ask the good Lord for blessings on our stummicks so we don't end up in the hospital after eatin' this pudding?" Marge Schmidt demanded. A principal in the only other restaurant in town, Marge's German heritage was evident in her fair hair, ruddy complexion, and blue eyes. The protuberance of those eyes, the double chin, and the belligerence were all her own.

Quill straightened in indignation.

Marge continued blandly, "Made with raw eggs, this stuff. What d'ya call it? Zabyig-something."

"Zabaglione," said Quill. She pushed back her mass of red hair with one slim hand and said mendaciously, "It's one of Meg's eggless varieties."

"It's made with raw eggs everywheres else," said Marge. "You won't find raw eggs in good old American food. Strictly against the New York State Department of Health instructions. Din't you and your sister get that notice they sent out last week? Got one down to the diner if you need a copy."

"Salmonella," interjected Marge's companion and business partner, Betty Hall. "All of us in the restaurant business got that notice. Maybe that sister of yours can't read."

Quill reflected that nobody, including the patrons of the Hemlock Hometown Diner (Family Food! And Fast!), got along with Marge and Betty, and a response would invite acrimony. The first law of successful innkeeping was to maintain neutrality, if not outright peace. "I can't imagine anyone getting sick on Hemlock Falls cooking, Marge," she said diplomatically. "Yours *or* ours."

Marge rocked back in her chair, to the potential danger of the oak. "Me, either. No, ma'am. But that's something different from bein' in violation of the American law with weird

Italian food. Betty and me stick to pizza. And this-here pudding is a clear violation of the law. Right, Sheriff McHale?"

Myles McHale nodded expressionlessly and dropped a wink in Quill's direction. He was looking especially heroic this afternoon, and Quill made a mental note to ask him if he'd ever been a lifeguard. With that chest, it was certainly likely.

Myles said, "Why don't I just go ahead and arrest both Meg and Quill, Marge? Been wanting to do it anyhow. Locking Quill up may be the only way I'll get her to marry me. And I'd have Meg's cooking all to myself."

"Ha, ha." Marge adjusted her blue nylon bowling jacket with a sniff and subsided, muttering, "Eggless, my ass."

"Let's get to the agenda," Elmer said. "First off, Quill, will you read the minutes from the last meeting?"

"Shall I move to dispense with everything but the agenda for today?" Quill asked. She hadn't translated her scrawled shorthand and wasn't at all sure she could read last week's notes out loud.

"She can't do that," said Marge. "She's the secretary. The secretary can't move not to read the minutes."

"Then I'll so move," said Myles.

"Let's just get to the agenda for today," said Elmer. "History Days is less than seventy-two hours away, unless everyone's forgotten. What's the status as of last week, Quill?"

Quill squinted at her notes. "Booths. Four *P*'s," she read uncertainly.

There was an expectant silence.

Four *P*'s. Quill tugged at her lower lip. Four *P*'s . . . "Parade. Play. Parking . . ." She tugged harder. "Promotion!"

She smiled triumphantly. "We need a report on the status of the booths, on the parade, and on the rehearsals for the play . . ."

Elmer deciphered the remaining *P* with no trouble; Quill had been Chamber secretary for five years. Promotion was adman Harvey Bozzel's job. "So the first thing is the booths. How many we got registered, Howie?"

Howie Murchison, local attorney and justice of the peace, paged methodically through a manila folder drawn from his briefcase. "One hundred and twenty-two, as of yesterday." He peered deliberately at Quill over his wire-rimmed glasses. "I'll go slowly so you can get the information *into* the minutes. Twenty-three home-crafts. Sixteen jewelry. Fifty-eight assorted pottery and painting. Six food. Seven habadashery, that is to say, T-shirts, straw hats, and other clothing items. Eleven miscellaneous, such as used books, something referred to as 'collectibles,' and Gil's display of the new line of Buicks. Forty-three percent of the registration fees have been prepaid for a total of six hundred and fifty-nine dollars and forty-six cents."

Quill scrawled: 101. 23 ditz. 16 ? ? ? ? $659, 46 is 47%. Then, after a moment's thought: Re. NYS memo: Meg.

"And the parade report?" Elmer turned to Norm Pasquale, principal of the high school.

Norm bounced to his feet. "The varsity band's been rehearsing all week. They sound just terrific. The Four-H club has fourteen kids on horses signed up to ride. We've got eight floats, down one from last year because Chet's Hardware went out of business after the Wal-Mart moved in." He sat down.

Elmer nodded matter-of-factly. "I told Chet he'd never get

a dollar and a half a pound for roofing nails. What about the play, Esther? Rehearsals going okay there?"

Esther West owned the only dress shop (West's Best) in Hemlock Falls. She was director of the re-creation of the Hemlock Falls seventeenth-century witch trial, *The Trial of Goody Martin*, a popular feature of History Days. She frowned and adjusted the bodice of her floral print dress, then patted a stiff auburn curl into place over her ear. "I do believe that the Clarissa's sickening for flu."

A murmur of dismay greeted this statement.

"Who's playing Clarissa Martin this year?" asked Quill.

"Julie Offenbach, Craig's girl."

"Oh, my." Quill knew her. A wannabe Winona Ryder, Julie spent the summers between high-school semesters waitressing at the Inn. "She'll be crushed."

"You got that right!" hooted Gil Gilmeister. Even Quill, a relative newcomer to Hemlock Falls, knew Gil had been a star quarterback for the high school twenty years before; like Rabbit Angstrom, he'd gone into that quintessential small-town American business—car sales. Unlike his fictional counterpart, he was filled by more *Sturm* than *Angst*, with a boisterous enthusiasm for Buicks, Marge Schmidt, and town activities not unrelated to his days on the football field. "Go-o-o-o *Clarissa!*" he shouted now, thumping a ham-sized fist on the table. "Splat! Splat! Splat!"

The witch trial dramatized the real seventeenth-century Clarissa's death by pressing. Most pre-Colonial American villages burned, hanged, or drowned their witches, and Hemlockians were inordinately proud of their ancestors' unique style of execution—Hemlock Falls witches had been pressed to death. Although any large flat surface would have done,

Hemlock Falls citizens of bygone days dropped a barn door on the condemned, then piled stones on the door until the victim succumbed to hemorrhaging, suffocation, or a myocardial infarction. Julie, as Clarissa Martin, would be replaced by a hooded dummy at the critical moment, but there was a wonderful bit of histrionics as "Clarissa" was driven off to await her fate. Julie had rehearsed with enormous relish for weeks.

"Doesn't Julie have an understudy or something?" asked Betty Hall. "No?" She jerked her head at her partner. "Marge here. She could do it. She's a real quick study. Memorizes the specials at the diner every night, just like that." She snapped her fingers.

Elmer, perhaps thinking of the size of the barn door required to squash a dummy of Marge-like proportions, not to mention the creation of a new, more elephantine dummy to replace the one traditionally used for years, said sharply, "Budget," which puzzled everyone but Quill, whose thoughts had been running along the same lines but in a much less practical way.

"Marge'd be terrific," said Gil Gilmeister earnestly. Since almost everyone at the table—with the possible exception of Dookie Shuttleworth—knew that Marge and Gil had been a hot item for several years, Gil's support was discounted without any discussion. "Although," Esther whispered to Quill, "if Nadine Gilmeister could get herself out of those Syracuse malls long enough to do right by the poor man so he didn't have to spend his nights over to the diner, maybe more people would listen to him." Elmer rapped the gavel loudly, and Esther jerked to attention.

"What do you want to do then, Esther? Appoint an understudy?"

"It should be somebody stageworthy. Somebody with presence. And good-looking. The execution is the highlight of *The Trial of Goody Martin*. It's what everyone comes to see." Esther's eyes glinted behind her elaborately designed glasses. "When the actors pile the stones on the barn door, the audience should be moved to enthusiasm as Clarissa's blood spews out. Most years, as you've observed, the tourists join in."

"Well, they'll more likely laugh if fat ol' Marge is supposed to be under there," said Harland Peterson, the president of the farmer's co-op. A large, weatherbeaten man, Harland drove the sledge that carried "Clarissa Martin" from the pavilion stage to the site of the execution. "No offense, Marge," he said, in hasty response to her outraged grunt. "Now, the ducking stool—that's gonna be just fine. That ol' tractor of mine'll lift you into that pond, no problem. But we get a dummy your size under that barn door, it's gonna stick out a mile. What about Quill, there? She'd be great."

Harvey (The Ad Agency That Adds Value!) Bozzel cleared his throat. "I'd have to agree." His tanned cheeks creased in a golf-pro grin. "Try this one on, folks. 'Quill fills the bill.'"

Quill, who so far had managed to avert Harvey's advertising plans for the Inn (No Whine, Just Fine Wine When You Dine!), said feebly, "I don't really think . . ."

"I'm not sure that Julie's vomiting is going to continue through next week," said Esther thoughtfully, "but you never know. And of course, the costume is black, and just shows everything."

Myles said, "I move to nominate Sarah Quilliam as understudy for Julie Offenbach."

Quill glared at him.

"I second," said Harland Peterson.

"All in favor?" said Elmer, sweeping the assembly with a glance. "Against?" He registered Marge's, Betty's, and Gil's upraised hands without a blink. "Carried. Quill takes Julie's place as Clarissa Martin, if necessary."

Quill experienced a strong desire to bang her head against the solid edge of the banquet table. This was followed by an even stronger desire to bang Myles McHale's head against the banquet table, since he'd started the whole mess in the first place. She took a deep breath and was preparing to argue, when the Hemlock Inn's business manager, John Raintree, appeared at the door to the Banquet Room.

"Yo, John!" said Gil. "Mighty glad to see you. Sorry I missed our meeting last night. I figured you and Tom could handle any stuff that needed to be decided anyways, and I had some things come up at home."

Esther looked significantly at Quill and mouthed, "Nadine!" Then more audibly, "Poor Gil."

"No problem, Gil," said John easily, "but I won't be able to get the audit to you until next week."

"That's okay with you, innit, Mark?" Gil wiped a handkerchief over his sweaty neck. "It's not gonna hold up the loan or anything?"

Mark Anthony Jefferson, vice-president of the Hemlock Falls Savings and Loan, tightened his lips. "Why don't we discuss this later, Gil? Your partner should be present anyway, and John's on Quill's time, now."

"Oh, I don't mind," said Quill. "John's moonlighting has never interfered with our business." She looked hopefully at him. "Do you need me, John?"

"Yep."

Quill sprang out of her chair with relief. "I'll be right there. Would you all excuse me? Esther, could you take over the minutes? I'd appreciate it."

Quill made her way swiftly into the hall and closed the door behind her. "Just in the nick of time. I was about to be forced into taking Julie Offenbach's star turn. I have no desire to be dunked and squashed in front of two hundred gawking tourists." She frowned at his glum expression. "Any problems?"

John claimed three-quarters Onondaga blood, whose heritage gave him skin the color of a bronze medallion and hair as thickly black as charred toast. He had an erratic, whimsical sense of humor that Quill found very un-Indian. Not, Quill thought, that she knew all that much about Indians, John in particular. He'd been with them less than a year, and for the first time, the Inn was showing a profit. Despite the money he made between his job at the Inn and his small accounting business, John lived modestly, driving an old car, wearing carefully cleaned suits that were years out of date. He refused to touch alcohol, for reasons tacitly understood between them, and never discussed his personal life. He nodded. "Guest complaint. And one of the waitresses called in sick for the three to eleven shift. Doreen's on vacation this week; otherwise she could pinch-hit. So that means we're short two staff for the dinner trade."

"Did you try the backup list?"

John nodded Yes to the phone calls and No to the results. "Exam week for summer session," he said briefly.

"Damn." Most of the summer season help came from nearby Cornell University. "All right. I'll take the shift myself. Unless Meg's short-handed in the kitchen?"

"Not so far."

"And the guest complaint?" She swallowed nervously. "No digestive problems or anything like that? Meg had Caesar salad on the menu for lunch, and she just refuses to omit the raw egg."

"Not food poisoning, no. But we'd better comply with the raw egg ban, Quill. We're liable to a fine if we don't."

"I know." Quill bit her thumb. "*You* tell Meg, will you, John? I mean, I should take care of this guest problem."

"Tell your sister she can't use raw eggs anymore? Not me, Quill. No way. I'd walk three miles over hot coals for you, shave my head bald for you, but I will not tell your sister how to cook."

"John," said Quill, with far more decisiveness than she felt, "you can't be afraid of my sister. She's all of five feet two and a hundred pounds, dripping wet. That makes her a *third* your size, probably."

"You're half again as tall as she is, and *you're* afraid of your sister."

"Then you're fired."

"You can't fire me. I quit."

They grinned at each other.

"I'll flip you for it," said Quill.

John pulled a nickel from his pocket and sent it spinning with a quick snap of his thumb. "Call it."

"Heads."

"Tails." John caught the coin and showed her an Indian-head nickel, tail-up. "My lucky coin. Came to me from my grandfather, the Chief. I told you about the Chief before. You want to keep this in your pocket while you tell her no more raw eggs?"

"I'll take care of the guest first. Is it a him or a her?"

"Her."

"Perennial?" This was house code for the retired couples who flooded the Inn in the spring, disappeared in autumn, and reappeared with the early crocus. In general, Quill liked them. They tended to be good guests, rarely, if ever, stiffing the management, and except for a universal disinclination to tip the help more than ten percent, treated the support staff well. This was in marked contrast to traveling businessmen who left used condoms rolled under the beds—which sent Doreen, their obsessive-compulsive housekeeper, into fits—or businesswomen demanding big-city amenities like valet services, a gym, and pool boys.

"It's an older woman," said John. He paused reflectively. "Kind of mean."

"I'm good with mean." She glanced at her watch; fifteen minutes before the start of the afternoon shift. She'd just make it if John's complainer didn't have a real problem. "The wine shipment's due at four. The bill of lading is . . . um . . . somewhere on my desk."

"I'll find it. My grandfather, the Chief . . ."

"Was a tracker," Quill finished for him. "I'd like to meet your grandfather. I'd like to meet your grandmother, too, as a matter of fact—" She stopped, aware that the flippant conversation was heading into dangerous waters. John's quiet, lonely existence was his business. "Never mind. Where is she?"

"Lobby." He grinned, teeth white in his dark face. "Good luck."

Quill took the steps up to the lobby with a practiced smile firmly in place. She and Meg had bought the twenty-seven-room Inn two years before with the combined proceeds of her last art show and Meg's early and wholly unexpected widowhood. Driving through Central New York on a short vacation, Meg and Quill had come upon the Inn unexpectedly. They came back. Shouldered between the granite ridges left by glaciers, on land too thin for farming, Inn and village were fragrant in spring, lush in summer, brilliant with color in the fall. Even the winters weren't too bad, for those tolerant of heavy snowfall, and Hemlockians resigned themselves to a partial dependence on tourists in search of peak season vacations. The Inn had always attracted travelers; as a commercial property, it proved easy to sell and less easy to manage. It had passed from hand to hand over the years. New owners bought and sold with depressing regularity, most defeated by the difficulty of targeting exactly the right customer market. The relationships among longtime residents of Hemlock Falls were so labyrinthine, it was a year before Quill realized that Marge Schmidt and Tom Peterson, Gil Gilmeister's partner, had owned the Inn some years before. Marge had made a stab at modernizing. She installed wall-to-wall Astro-turf indoors ("Wears good," said Marge some months after Quill removed it. "Whattaya, stupid?") and plywood trolls in the garden.

The reception-lobby was all that remained of the original eighteenth-century Inn, and the low ceilings and leaded windows had a lot to do with Quill's final decision to buy it. Guests were in search of an authentic historical experience, as long as it was accompanied by heated towel racks, outstanding mattresses, and her sister's terrific food. If they could restore the Inn with the right degree of twentieth-century luxury, people would come in busloads.

Quill had stripped layers of paint and wallpaper from the

plaster-and-lathe walls, replaced vinyl-backed draperies with simple valances of Scottish lace, and tore up the Astro-turf carpeting. The sisters had refinished the floors and wainscoting to a honeyed pine, and landscaped the grounds.

The leaded windows in the lobby framed a view of the long sweep of lawn and gardens to the lip of Hemlock Gorge. Creamy wool rugs, overwoven in florals of peach, celadon, taupe, and sky blue, lightened the effect of the low ceiling. Two massive Japanese urns flanked the reception desk where Dina Muir checked guests in. Mike the groundskeeper filled the urns every other morning with flowers from the Inn's extensive perennial gardens. As usual this early in July, they held Queen Elizabeth roses, Oriental lilies of gold, peach, and white, and spars of purple heather.

The lobby was welcoming and peaceful. Quill smiled at Dina, the daytime receptionist, and raised an inquiring eyebrow. Dina made an expressive face, and jerked her head slightly in the direction of the fireplace.

An elderly woman with a fierce frown sat on the pale leather couch in front of the cobblestone hearth. A woman at least thirty years her junior stood behind the chair. The younger one had a submissive, tentative air for all the world like that anachronism, the companion. Quill's painter's eye registered almost automatically the lush figure behind the modestly buttoned shirtwaist. She could have used a little makeup, Quill thought, besides the slash of red lipstick she allowed herself. Something in the attitude of the two women made her revise that thought; the elder one clearly dominated her attendant and just as clearly disapproved of excess.

"I'm Sarah Quilliam," she said, her hand extended in welcome.

"I'm Mavis Collinwood?" said the younger woman in a Southern drawl that seemed to question it. Her brown hair was lacquered like a Chinese table and back-combed into a tightly restrained knot. "Mrs. Hallenbeck doesn't shake hands," Mavis said, in a voice both assured and respectful. "Her arthritis is a little painful this time of year."

Only the glaucous clouding of Mrs. Hallenbeck's blue eyes and the gnarled hands told Quill that she must be over eighty. Her skin was smooth, shadowed by a fine net of wrinkles at eye and mouth. She sat rigidly upright, chin high to avoid the sagging of throat and jowl. Her figure was slim rather than gaunt, and Quill took in the expensive watch and the elegant Chanel suit.

Mrs. Hallenbeck fixed Quill with a basilisk glare. "I wish to speak to the owner."

"You are," said Quill cheerfully. "What can I do for you?"

"Our reservations were not in order." The old lady was clearly displeased.

"I'm very sorry," said Quill, going to the ledger. "You weren't recorded in the book? I'll arrange a room for you immediately."

"We were in the book. I had requested the third-floor suite. The one overlooking the gorge, with that marvelous balcony that makes you feel as though you were flying." She paused, and the clouded blue eyes teared up a little. "My husband and I stayed here, years ago. I am retracing our days together."

Quill's look expressed sympathy.

"That girl of yours. She put us into two rooms on the second floor. It overlooks the back lawn. It is not a suite. It is not what I require. I demanded to see the owner, and John Raintree said that these arrangements had been made and could not be changed."

"Let me see what we can do." Quill checked the booking: *Hallenbeck, Amelia, and Collinwood, Mavis.* The reservation had been made three months ago, by one of the gilt-edged travel agencies in South Carolina. Paid for in advance with an American Express Gold card. There it was: *Requested Suite* 312–314. And just as clearly marked in John's handwriting were their current rooms: *Confirmed 101 and 104.* "Did Mr. Raintree say anything at all about why the rooms were booked this way? He's a wonderful help to us, Mrs. Hallenbeck, and rarely makes mistakes. It's not like him to make a change like this without a reason."

"He did not say one word." The tones were decisive. If she'd had a whip, she would have cracked it.

Quill suppressed a grin. "I'm certain that no one's in three-fourteen. Shall we go up and see if it's suitable for you?"

Mrs. Hallenbeck nodded regally. The three of them went up the stairs. Any notion that John may have booked them into first-floor rooms due to Mrs. Hallenbeck's arthritis was quickly dispelled; she took the steps with a lot less effort than Mavis Collinwood, who began to breathe heavily at the second-floor landing. Quill unlocked the door to the suite and stepped aside to let them enter.

Quill loved all twenty-seven rooms at the Inn, but 314 was one of her favorites. A white Adams-style fireplace dominated the wall opposite the balcony. The carpeting was crisp navy blue. The couch and occasional chairs were covered in blue-and-yellow chintz, the colors of Provence. French doors opened out onto a white-painted iron balcony cantilevered over the lip of Hemlock Gorge, giving 314 a panoramic view of the Falls.

Quill stepped out and watched the cascade of water over granite. Bird calls came from the pines and joined the water's rush. Sweet smells from the gardens and the hemlock groves mingled with the daffodil-scent of fresh water. Mrs. Hallenbeck followed Quill onto the balcony, her chin jutting imperiously. She inhaled. "Dogwood," she stated precisely, "and one of the scented roses."

"Scented Cloud," said Quill. "It's a lovely rose, too. We grow it out back."

"This," Mrs. Hallenbeck said, "is what I asked for. I will walk in the hemlock glade after dinner."

"I'm sorry about the confusion, Mrs. Hallenbeck." Quill drew her inside the suite. "I'll see that your luggage is brought up here. Would you like some tea? I can have it brought to you, or you can have it in the dining room."

"An English tea? I believe your brochure described an English tea."

"Yes. A traditional high tea, with scones, Devonshire cream, and watercress sandwiches."

"Perhaps there will be no charge for that, since I have been seriously inconvenienced."

Quill, slightly taken aback, swallowed a laugh. "I'll be sure that there isn't."

"Then we shall be down after Mavis unpacks us." She nodded dismissal. Quill meekly took the hint, and went back to the Chamber meeting. She took the stairs slowly, not, she told herself, because she wasn't anxious to get back to the meeting, but because it was a beautiful July day, the Inn was booked solid for the week of History Days, and a relaxed country environment was one of the many reasons she'd left her career as an artist to move to Central New York.

"There you are," said Esther West, as Quill stepped into the lobby. "We're taking a bit of a break before we go back and vote."

"Somebody else volunteered to take Julie Offenbach's place?" Quill said with hope. "I've got a couple of ideas for you, Esther. What about Miriam Doncaster? You know, the librarian. She's a heck of a swimmer. I couldn't swim to the side of the pond as gracefully as she could after being dunked in the ducking stool."

"No. Everyone agrees you'd be the best Clarissa. Marge wants us to vote on whether or not the monthly Chamber meetings should be held at the Hemlock Home Diner instead of here."

"Oh," said Quill.

"But we all decided to take a bio break before we voted, and anyhow, Myles and Howie both thought that you'd probably want to be there for the discussion part."

"You bet I would," said Quill. "That monthly Chamber lunch is a good piece of business. John'll have my guts for garters if I lose it. Maybe I'd better have him sit in." An increasingly noisy argument from the lobby succeeded in drawing her attention. "Excuse me a second, Esther. Dina seems to need help."

Dina, one of the Cornell Hotel School graduate students on whom the Inn depended for much of its staff, was scowling ferociously at a middle-aged man at the counter. An elegantly dressed man in his thirties stood behind him, watching with interest.

"Can I give you a hand here, Dina?"

"I've been trying to tell this guy that we're booked for the week. He said the Marriott called and made reservations for him this morning." She scowled even harder. "Then he said well maybe the Marriott forgot to call, but that places 'like this' always hold back a room in case of emergencies, and he wants it."

"Keith Baumer," said the middle-aged man. He extended his hand. Quill took it. He grinned and wiggled his fingers suggestively in her palm. "You the manager, or what?"

Quill freed herself. "I'm really sorry, Mr. Baumer, but Dina's right, of course. We're booked for the week."

"Come on, kiddo, I need some help here. I've got a sales convention at the Marriott, and the bastards overbooked. I hear this is the only decent place to get a room. I know you guys; you're always holding something in reserve. Whyn't you check the reservations book yourself? I'm here for the week. I don't mind paying top dollar." He grinned and edged closer to her.

Quill took two steps back, hit the counter, and repeated, "I'm sorry, Mr. Baumer. We simply don't have a room available." The phone shrilled twice, and Dina picked it up as Quill continued, "We'll be happy to call a few nearby places for you—"

"Quill?" said Dina.

"—but I'm afraid you're going to have a rough time if you want to stay close to your sales meeting. This is the height of the tourist season . . ."

"Quill!" Dina tugged at her sleeve. "We just got a cancellation. Couple that was booked for the week for their honeymoon, Mr. and Mrs. Sands. Only it's Mrs. Sands that just called, and she said they had a fight at the wedding and the whole thing's *off*! Isn't that sad?"

"There," said Baumer. "Not that I believe that phony phone call for one little minute. What? Ya got a button down there?"

Quill counted to ten. "Would you check him in please, Dina? Enjoy your stay with us, Mr. Baumer."

He cocked his head, swept a look from her ankles to her chin, gave her a thumbs-up sign of approval, then leered at Dina. "Okay, dolly. You take American Express Traveler's Cheques?"

Quill looked longingly at the Japanese urn nearest Baumer's thick neck.

"Too heavy," said the man who'd been waiting behind Baumer. "Now, that replica of the Han funeral horse on the coffee table? Just the right size for a good whack."

Quill choked back a laugh. "Are you here to check in? Let me help you over here." He was, thought Quill, one of the best-looking men she'd ever seen, with thick black hair attractively sprinkled with gray. He wore a beautifully tailored sports coat.

"Quill," Esther called, "we're going back to vote now."

"I don't mind waiting for young Dina, there," he said. "I'm Edward Lancashire, by the way."

"We're looking forward to having you at the Inn, Mr. Lancashire."

"You go ahead to your vote. I'll be just fine."

Quill went back to the conference room and sat down, a little breathless.

"Who was *that*?" hissed Esther. "The second one, I mean. The first one sounded horrible."

"The first one *was* horrible. Speaking of horrible, where's Marge?"

"In the kitchen." Quill froze. Esther looked at her watch. "This darn meeting's got to get over soon; I've got way too much to do on the costumes."

"The kitchen? Marge is in Meg's kitchen?"

"She was headed that way."

"Oh, God," said Quill. "I'll be right back."

Quill pushed open the kitchen door to silence, which meant one of two things: either Meg had discovered Marge among her recipe books and had killed her, or nobody was there.

The flagstone floor was clean and polished. The cobblestone fireplace in the corner, where Meg had a Maine grill to do her lobsters, crackled quietly behind the Thermo Glass doors that kept the heat from the rest of the kitchen. Meg's precious copper bowls and pans hung undisturbed in shiny rows from the pot hanger. No sign of either Marge or, for that matter, her sister. Quill pulled at her lower lip, went to Meg's recipe cabinet, pulled out the lowest drawer, and flipped through the *Z*'s. *Zuppa d'Inglese*, zucchini, zarda, zabaglione. She edged the zabaglione card carefully out of the file. Was that a greasy thumbprint? It was. But was it Marge's or Meg's? And if it were Marge's, did that mean she was going to place a phone call to the Board of Health? She read the recipe gloomily. There it was in Meg's elegant script: four raw eggs per serving. She closed the file drawer and marched determinedly back to the conference room.

It was empty, except for Myles.

"Where'd they all go?" Quill demanded. "Did they vote on whether or not to move the meetings to Marge's diner?"

"Since neither you nor Marge were here, Howie voted to table. Esther asked for an adjournment because she's still sewing costumes. I waited for you to see what you wanted to do tonight. Would you like to go to supper? Can you get away about eight thirty?"

"Myles, can you take a fingerprint from a recipe card?"

"Yes, Quill," Myles said patiently. "Do you want to go to supper? I thought I'd make a stir-fry at my place."

"Where was Marge, when I wasn't here?"

"I don't know. She came back in here grinning and said she had to make a phone call. Why?"

Quill gazed at him thoughtfully. Myles had strong views on law and order. He had an annoying tendency to spout phrases like "due process" and "probable cause." Those gray eyes would get even icier if she asked him to arrest Marge for snooping. That strong jaw would set like an antilock brake at the merest suggestion of a phone tap on the Hemlock Home Diner. There was no way he'd test a recipe card for fingerprints without uncomfortable questions regarding the existence of an eggless zabaglione.

She decided to answer his first question, and solve the Marge problem herself. "Why don't you come by the kitchen for dinner about eleven, after we close? You made dinner last night. It's my turn."

"Fine." He kissed her on the temple. Quill wasn't fooled for a minute. This was a man who'd lock her in stir the instant she whacked Marge up the side of the head with Meg's skillet.

Halfway out the door, Myles turned to look at her. "You sure nothing's wrong? You're not coming down with anything, are you?" His eyes narrowed. "Wait. I know that look. You're fulminating."

"No," said Quill absently. "One of the waitresses is, though." She gasped and glanced at her watch. "The second shift! It's after three o'clock! Damn!" She sprinted past him and ran down the hall.

ELLERY ADAMS

❧

Wordplay becomes foul play . . .

A Deadly Cliché

A BOOKS BY THE BAY MYSTERY

While walking her poodle, Olivia Limoges discovers a dead body buried in the sand. Could it be connected to the bizarre burglaries plaguing Oyster Bay, North Carolina? The Bayside Book Writers prick up their ears and pick up their pens to get the story . . .

The thieves have a distinct MO. At every crime scene, they set up odd tableaus: a stick of butter with a knife through it, dolls with silver spoons in their mouths, a deck of cards with a missing queen. Olivia realizes each setup represents a cliché.

Who better to decode the cliché clues than the Bayside Book Writers group, especially since their newest member is Police Chief Rawlings? As the investigation proceeds, Olivia is surprised to find herself falling for the widowed policeman. But an even greater surprise is in store. Her father—lost at sea thirty years ago—may still be alive . . .

penguin.com